The Books and Bakes Shop

Elaine Walsh

Copyright © Elaine Walsh 2021

All rights reserved.

Cover design and illustration © Emily Stalley Design &
Illustration 2021

This is a work of fiction. Names, characters, businesses,
places, events, and incidents are either the products of the
author's imagination or used in a fictitious manner. Any
resemblance to actual persons, living or dead, or actual
events is purely coincidental.

ISBN-13: 979-870763418

Acknowledgments

I would like to thank, my test readers and supporters. You know who you are.

Mostly, I thank Debbie Hooker who has encouraged my writing from the start. The idea of The Books and Bakes Shop was first discussed over cake and coffee in the Crypt Café at St Martins in-the-Fields, on a dark winter day four years ago. She is my editor and honest critic. Thank you, Madge.

Thank you also to my creative director and husband, David Calvert, for his visual direction, website and great cups of tea.

Finally, thank you to Emily for the fabulous book cover. What a great interpretation of a brief!

Chapter One

Katie grimaced as she struggled to push open the pub door. Cold rain lashed down on top of her and she couldn't keep her umbrella open over her head and shove the door with her shoulder at the same time. With one final thrust, she was in. She shut down her umbrella and put it in her handbag trying not to drip too much on the floor as she made her way over to the bar. Once there, she ordered two glasses of red wine. Just the thing to warm her and her friend on such a miserable wet evening. She was meeting up with her best friend, Caroline. They hadn't had a decent catch up for ages. She was really looking forward to it. She gathered up the glasses and took them over to a table by the window and sat down. She gazed out of the window onto the street and could see her reflection in the glass. Her curly auburn hair rested on her shoulders and her green eyes stared back at her. She frowned as she looked at the freckles on her nose. She had never liked them. She sighed. She was twenty-nine years old, not bad looking but stuck in a rut.

She turned around to see Caroline battling to get through the door as well. Katie watched as she flicked the rain out of her long brown hair and saw her face break into a beaming smile as soon as she saw Katie. Katie got up and gave her a big hug.

'Hi, Caro, so good to see you.'

'Likewise, it's been way too long. Glad to see you have got us organised for a decent natter' said Caroline pointing to the wine. 'So, how have you been?'

'I'm okay. Still stuck in that pokey little flat though, but it's all I can afford since I split up with Gary.'

'How are you feeling about that these days?' asked Caroline.

'Oh, you know, fine and not fine.'

'What does that mean?'

'Well, it's not that I want to get back with him or anything like that, it's just thinking about him makes me cross for all sorts of reasons. When I met him, it was just after I had joined Snap, the publisher where we met.'

'Crumbs, I can't believe that was about eight years ago now.'

'I know. Anyway, back then he seemed just what I needed, and we had a lot of fun together working and playing hard. It seemed the right thing to do to move in with him. We certainly made the most of being young in the City.'

'I remember that too,' said Caroline laughing.

'Okay, okay,' said Katie nodding in agreement. 'But as you know, I had always thought we would move forward with our lives and settle down and have children. Goodness knows how much I long to have a baby of my own.'

'Yes, yes I do,' said Caroline seriously.

'Anyway, you remember how Gary kept fobbing me off with excuses like "We're still so young" and "Let's make the most of the fun we're having" which I naively thought meant we would have kids one day. Well, it all ended in tears when he dumped me for Tara.'

'Ah yes, Tara with a lisp,' said Caroline.

'The annoying thing is that Tara's actually quite nice. But the kick in the stomach for me was that not only did he leave me for the young blonde office apprentice, but Gary got her pregnant with twins!'

'She must have had them by now,' said Caroline.

'Yeah, it's over a year ago. Gary still comes into the office occasionally, but I manage to avoid him. He is now head of regional sales. Guess he needs the money to look after his new family,' said Katie.

'He was always after a quick buck, as I remember,' said Caroline as she picked up her glass and took a sip of wine.

'I'm sorry Caroline,' said Katie. 'We haven't met for ages and all I've done is moan about my own misery. I am either spitting about Gary or banging on about wanting a baby.'

'Don't worry,' replied Caroline. 'It makes me feel so much better about my life!'

Katie felt bad. There she was getting tied up in her own dramas. She had forgotten that Caroline had been going through a bit of a sticky patch with her boyfriend, Andy. He tended to be a bit clingy according to Caroline but Katie had always thought that is because he cared so much about her.

'So, tell me. How are things with you? The last time we spoke you were seriously thinking about splitting up with Andy.'

'Yeah. You remember how I was finding him a bit claustrophobic. He always wanted to know where I was and what I was doing. Having my wings clipped doesn't sit well with me, as you can imagine,' said Caroline laughing.

'Yes, I certainly can,' replied Katie laughing too.

'Anyway, we had a bit of a heart to heart and all his silly insecurities came out. So, I began to understand why he was behaving that way. It's because he loves me so much, apparently.'

'Can you see the "I told you so sign" on the top of my head?'

'It couldn't be more obvious,' said Caroline grinning. 'So, we are good, and my news is that Andy has asked me to think about moving in with him.'

'Oh my god!' exclaimed Katie. 'That's a bit of a shift from where you were the last time I saw you.'

'I know,' said Caroline quietly.

'So how to you feel about that?'

'I am thinking about it. You know me well enough by now. I am not one to jump into things. But things with him feel good. So, watch this space!'

'What about the new job?'

'Good news there as well. I've been promoted to editorial manager.'

'Oh well done. You were always more ambitious than me. You deserve it.'

'Thanks. But what about your job? Still drifting? I can't believe you are still at Snap after all this time.'

'Yeah. I probably should have left by now but I don't really know what to do next. I keep my head down at the office and don't socialise much. I think people have been unsure about how to treat me since I split up with Gary. It was easy for everyone when we were a couple. I guess I should push myself into taking on more responsibility in the editorial team, but I haven't pushed myself forward and am stuck where I am as an assistant. I am just so grateful to be working with books particularly as I have always been so passionate about reading and messed up going to university to read English,' said Kate sighing wistfully.

'But you didn't go, so there's not much point on dwelling on that.'

'You're right. I always blame that decision on my Dad dying so suddenly and me not coping very well. But if I'm honest it had a lot to do with me being immature and somehow feeling guilty. Like I shouldn't be allowed to be happy when my Dad was dead.'

'I guess you were entitled to feel a bit messed up. You just have to focus on what you are doing now.'

'Right again Caro, easier said than done though. The thing is I have had some bad news this week which has brought back the memories of that time. My Uncle Simon died.'

'Oh no, not that lovely uncle you spent summer holidays with as a kid?'

'Yes, that's the one. I spent the summer staying with him after my Dad died. It was a long, hot summer and I spent my days walking along the coast path and helping in my uncle's shop. He owned a bookshop on the high street. I used to curl up on the corner and read his stock!'

'That doesn't sound very helpful,' said Caroline chuckling.

'No. I suppose not,' replied Katie smiling.

'How did he die?' asked Caroline.

'A heart attack, it was all very sudden. He collapsed and went to hospital, but they couldn't revive him. It turns out my mum is recorded as his next of kin, so she was notified. I am feeling a bit sad and guilty for not seeing much of him over the last few years. I always seemed too wrapped up in Gary and made excuses not to keep in touch.'

'Well, there's nothing you can do about it now' said Caroline in her direct and straight to the point way. 'Can you go to his funeral?'

'I hope so, I've arranged to speak to my mum when I get back this evening. She was trying to sort out arrangements today. I know I can't do anything about my uncle, but I can up my game and make more of an effort to see my mum. I have neglected her a bit too.'

'Yeah, these things make you think, don't they? Do you need to head off to speak to Susan, I mean your mum? We can always fix another time to meet up?'

'Thanks Caro, yes I had better get back. I'll let you know what's going on and we can work something out.'

5

'Sounds good to me,' said Caroline as she finished her wine and stood up to leave. Katie did the same and drew Caroline into a big hug.

'Thanks for listening and I'm sorry we cut the evening short in the end.'

'Don't be silly. We'll speak soon.'

They left the pub. Katie headed off to catch the bus back home. As she sat on the bus, she gazed out of the window. It was a filthy night. The rain just kept on pouring down. She couldn't help but dwell on that summer when her Dad had suddenly died. She could feel her eyes misting up with tears as she remembered. She was only eighteen. She had been all set to go to Warwick University in the autumn. Before she left for university, she had gone with her mum and dad on holiday to Spain. She smiled to herself as she remembered how her dad had splashed out a bit and had rented a lovely villa with views stretching out towards the sea. He always got up first to put coffee on and make fresh orange juice. She still didn't really know what happened, but she remembers waking up to a loud crash and hearing her mum screaming out to her to call an ambulance. There was nothing anyone could do. He had slipped or tripped on the narrow stairs going down to the kitchen. When he fell, he must have hit his head and the impact of that was fatal and he died instantly.

She remembered where her uncle had lived. It was a lovely town on the Suffolk coast called Broxburgh. He lived in a handsome Edwardian house on a road that sat uphill behind the high street. She stayed in a room at the top which had a huge sash window. She could still conjure up the view of the sea over the rooftops. By the end of the summer, she had been able to start to come to terms with her grief and realised it wasn't all about her. She found the maturity to go home and support her mum.

She got back to her flat at about eight o'clock. She opened the door and switched on the light. Katie looked around her. It was gloomy. It wasn't really a flat just a one room studio with a small boxroom with just enough space to fit in a single bed. She pulled herself together, determined to stop feeling sorry for herself. The sudden death of her uncle had made her think. She needed to stop dwelling on her old life and start thinking more positively about her future.

She had a bottle of red wine open left over from the weekend. So, she poured herself a glass and took it over to sit at a small table by the window. She looked out. It wasn't exactly a picturesque view. It faced the back of the block of flats. All she could see were the bins, never mind. She picked up her mobile and called her mum.

'Hi sweetheart, have you just got in?' Susan answered.

'Yes, is now okay to talk?'

'Yes, of course. How have you been today?'

'Ok. I have just had a drink with Caroline. She always cheers me up,' replied Katie.

'That sounds nice. Now, things have moved quite quickly today. As Simon died in hospital there is no need for a post-mortem investigation, thank goodness. So, it looks like the funeral will be next week, possibly Friday. Do you think you might be able to make that?'

'I should think so. I haven't taken any holiday yet this year so that should be fine.'

'Oh good,' said Susan. 'Now just something to think about, but as the funeral will be at the crematorium in Woodbridge, I don't know how you would feel about staying over somewhere and having a visit to Broxburgh, a bit nostalgic maybe but it might be nice.'

'Do you know, I think that sounds like a lovely idea. It would be good to spend a bit of time with you.'

7

'Wouldn't it,' said Susan enthusiastically. 'Get things sorted out at work and let me know. Then we can sort out arrangements.'

'Ok. Speak soon. Bye.'

Once she had finished the call, she felt drained and didn't fancy the wine anymore. So, she went over to the kitchen area, poured the wine away and made herself a large mug of peppermint tea. She was exhausted so she took herself and her tea off to bed. She barely managed to finish drinking it before she switched off the light next to her bed and fell asleep.

Chapter Two

It was the day of Uncle Simon's funeral in Suffolk. Katie was staring out of the window of the train as it passed through a series of commuter towns before finally breaking out into the greenness of the countryside. As she gazed out, she reflected on the days since she had found out her uncle had died. It had been up and down. All sorts of emotions had been swirling around. She had been thinking a lot about the times she had spent in Broxburgh. Not just that time after her father died but, when she had spent summer holidays there as a child with her mum and dad. It was such a special town. They had stayed in various cottages and she remembered happy times picking up pebbles from the beach and feasting on chips swinging her legs as she sat on the wall facing out to the beach. At the moment, she felt she was just drifting in her life. Maybe a bracing walk by the North Sea and some local fish and chips would make her see clearly again.

She reached Woodbridge station. As expected, her mum was waiting to meet her. She hadn't seen her for a few months. Katie noticed how nice she looked, even though she was dressed for a funeral. She was wearing a tailored black trouser suit with a baby blue blouse. She had coloured her hair, so she had auburn highlights. It was cut to a different style too, short with feathered layers. It suited her. Katie was now glad she had made an effort too. She was wearing a black jersey dress which draped gracefully over her body. She glanced at her reflection in one of the station windows. She had lost weight since she had been on her own, but she still had generous feminine curves. Susan walked towards her and they embraced warmly.

'Hi Mum,' said Katie. 'You look great.'

'Thank you. I decided I was long overdue for a makeover. I thought I would try and make an effort in memory of your dad's brother. You look lovely too. You look much brighter since I last saw you. How are you really?' she asked.

'I am okay, I promise,' replied Katie. 'I just feel as though I am drifting along and heading nowhere at the moment.'

Susan frowned at her, looking concerned.

'Don't worry Mum, I am nowhere near like I was after Dad died. I'm still licking my wounds a bit after Gary, but I will be fine.'

'Mmm… let's get going before we are late for the funeral and we can have a proper catch up later.'

Katie and Susan got into her black Renault Clio and drove off to the crematorium. Once they arrived, they parked up and headed over to the main building. There was no one else around so it looked like they were the first to arrive. The crematorium was peaceful in a lovely setting, surrounded by trees. Their leaves were whispering in the wind adding to the peaceful atmosphere. There were attractive seating areas dotted around but it was February, and they could feel the bite of the north east wind. So, they went into the reception area and waited for others to arrive.

'I guess we are the only relatives Uncle Simon had left,' said Katie.

'Yes, we are. When I was called to the hospital when Simon was dying, there was someone else there, James, a friend of Simon's from Broxburgh. He was able to give me details of his friends in Broxburgh and ideas about what he would have wanted at his funeral. I tried to let as many people know about his death as I could. I even put an advert in the local paper just in case.'

A few people started to arrive. Susan greeted them introducing herself. Most of the guests were friends of her uncle as well as those in Broxburgh who had known him and came to pay their respects.

The funeral was short. Susan read a poem and managed to say a few words about Uncle Simon as did a couple of his friends. At the end of the service, they said their goodbyes to the guests and headed back towards the car.

'Is there a wake or something?' Katie asked her mum.

'No. One of Simon's close friends contacted me after I had put the ad in the paper. He was one of the people who spoke about him today. Apparently, he knew Simon quite well. He suggested that a quiet service of remembrance would be enough and that is what Simon would have wanted. So, that's what I've done.'

Katie sighed. 'He was a lovely man and all his friends who we met today seemed to care about him a lot. Let's get to Broxburgh. We can sort out saying a proper goodbye to him there. I am sure he would have appreciated us toasting him over a glass of wine or two.'

'Definitely,' said Susan. 'Come on, I can't wait to smell the sea air.'

They didn't speak much for the rest of the journey. The radio was playing, and Katie mostly stared out of the window thinking how lovely the Suffolk countryside was even in the middle of February. The clouds which had started the day had cleared and the sun was out now. The flat landscape was stretched out towards the sea. It was beautiful.

She stole a sideways look at her mum. That haircut really suited her. She seemed different somehow, more confident and light-hearted. Maybe her mum had met someone? As far as she knew she hadn't had a boyfriend since her dad had died. But that was over ten years ago now. She wanted her mum to be happy so, if there was someone, as long as he was right for her, she was cool about it.

They arrived in Broxburgh late in the afternoon. Katie had booked a couple of rooms at a hotel which looked out over the sea. After they had checked in, Katie said 'It's looking a bit dark out there now, so I don't really fancy a stroll by the sea. I guess we can leave that until tomorrow morning. Why don't we chill for an hour or so and then meet later for a drink?'

'Sounds good to me,' replied Susan.

Katie was down first. She found a table by the window and waited for her mum. Only a few minutes later, she spotted her and waved her over to the table.

'Hi sweetheart,' said Susan. 'What would you like to drink?'

'A large glass of white wine would be lovely,' Katie replied.

She watched her Mum coming back with a bottle.

'Crumbs Mum, that looks serious!' exclaimed Katie.

'Not really, I just thought we are bound to have more than one glass and so a bottle is better value.'

'Yeah right,' said Katie smiling.

'So, love,' said Susan as she poured the wine. 'How are you really?'

Katie knew what her mum meant. She had seen her through her breakdown after her dad had died and her humiliating break up with Gary. However, Katie realised as she looked across the table at her mum that she didn't want to carry on being an emotional drain on her. She was okay. She just needed to take more control of her life. She loved her mum and couldn't imagine her life without her support, but Katie felt she was ready to move on to wherever that might be.

'Honestly Mum, I am fine. In a way, Uncle Simon dying has made me think a bit. I was really upset when Gary dumped me. I know now it was the right thing as our relationship wasn't going anywhere. We had been great together when we went out on the razz, but things changed. You know how much I want a baby, but Gary said he didn't and so us splitting up was inevitable. The thing that really gets me is that he goes off with Tara and she had twins. It makes me feel like he used to say he didn't want a baby as an excuse to get rid of me.'

'I am sorry love. I know how much you want a baby. It sounds a bit of a cliché, but you are still young, and you never know what's around the corner. You know I never really took to Gary. He always seems a bit self-centred and greedy to me. I felt he didn't really value you as you are. So, in a way I am glad he's gone.'

'I know Mum, but I feel I have wasted so much time. There is not much prospect of me meeting anyone now. Internet dating is so not my thing. My life feels like it is on hold. Anyway, enough of me, what's going on with you?'

'Actually, there is something I want to talk to you about. I am not sure how to say this so I will just spit it out. I have met someone. I met him at work. He joined about six months ago and we just hit it off. I was a bit reluctant to go out with him at first as there hasn't really been anyone since your dad. But he was persistent and won me over in the end,' said Susan. Katie saw from her mum's face how anxious she was about what her reaction would be to this news.

'Funnily enough, I thought there was something different about you. You seem brighter. I love what you have done with your hair. Tell me more about him,' said Katie softly.

'His name is John. He is a couple of years older than me. His wife died about ten years ago from breast cancer. He doesn't have any children. It's still early days but I would love you to meet him. He is kind and thoughtful and makes me feel special. It is a long time since I felt that way.'

Katie could see her mum was eager for her approval. Katie didn't feel resentful that her mum had found someone. To her surprise, she was envious her mum had found someone full stop. Here she was at twenty-nine on her own with a dead-end job. There seemed little prospect of her meeting someone any time soon, let alone getting the chance that things might work out such that she could have that longed for child. But she was not going to share any of that. She had to stop feeling so sorry for herself. She felt a change in herself over the last few days when she had been thinking about her dad and Uncle Simon. Both in their own way had loved and encouraged her. Only she could change her life so she decided that she would enjoy her time with her mum and once she got back to London, she would have a real think about how she could do that.

'Mum I am really pleased for you. I just want you to be happy and yes, of course, I will meet him. Shall we order something to eat while we finish off this wine?' suggested Katie.

'Yes let's,' said Susan looking relieved. She picked up the menu. 'What do you fancy?'

They ordered some bits and pieces to eat and enjoyed chatting while they ate. When they had finished Susan said. 'You look shattered love. Why don't we call it a night and then we'll be up for a wander round Broxburgh tomorrow?'

'You're right,' replied Katie 'I am tired, and you must be too.'

They left the bar and headed off to their rooms.

'Night Mum,' said Katie giving her a hug.

'Sleep well sweetheart,' replied Susan. 'See you in the morning.'

Katie woke up feeling fresh after a good night's sleep. She quickly showered, dressed and went down to meet her mum for breakfast.

'Morning, sleep well?' said Susan breezily.

'Oh yes thanks much better than I thought. What shall we do after breakfast?'

'Well, it looks like a lovely day outside albeit a bit cold, so I thought we could go for a walk around the town and along the sea front. We could finish off with a bag of chips on the beach before we have to think about heading home.'

'That sounds like a great plan,' replied Katie.

They had their breakfast, checked out of the hotel, put their bags in the car and set off down towards the town all wrapped up for the cold. Mum was right, thought Katie. It was a lovely day. She could smell the salt from the sea. The clear blue sky and sharp sunshine made the pastel painted shop fronts look so inviting. As they walked down the high street memories came flooding back to Katie.

'Let's go and look at Uncle Simon's bookshop,' she said.

'Okay,' said Susan. 'If my memory is correct, I think it's just down there on the right, isn't it?'

Katie remembered it so well. She quickened her pace as they got nearer. As they stood outside of the shop, she said 'Oh no Mum, look at the state of it.'

She remembered the shop window had always had a tasteful display of the new books and the lattice frame windows had always been kept spotlessly clean. The rest of the shop front had been painted white. Now the shop was closed and dilapidated. She moved in close to the window. She could just see into the shop through a gap in the blinds. The inside was dusty and in disarray with boxes of books strewn across the floor. It looked dark and abandoned.

'Oh,' said Susan. 'What a shame. It used to be such a lovely shop. I wonder how it has got so run down. I didn't know if he had been unwell for any length of time. His heart attack had been so sudden.'

'Yes, it was,' replied Katie. 'I spent so much time reading in there and helping customers find books they wanted that summer I spent here. I guess it couldn't always stay the same, but in my mind it had.'

'I don't think it would be a good idea to walk up to his house just in case it is in the same state,' said Susan. 'I don't know what will happen to it all now, but I think we should concentrate on our good memories. Let's see if we can spot some of the lovely cottages we stayed in when we had those holidays when you were little.'

'Yeah, I guess you're right,' replied Katie as she shrugged her shoulders.

They moved on down the high street. Most of the other shops were still there. The butcher, traditional chemist and newsagent all seemed to be thriving. Her mum gently chatted as she pointed out the cottages where they had stayed. Katie suddenly felt her eyes fill with tears. She didn't want to break down in front of her mum. What was wrong with her? Why did she feel like crying now when she was having such a nice time?

They turned down an alleyway from the high street towards the sea. Ahead of her, Katie saw a covered seating area with wooden benches. She drew a sharp intake of breath. The memory of a boy, Joe who had stolen her heart that summer she spent here ten years ago, jumped into her head. She wondered what had happened to him.

'You okay love? You look a bit far away,' said Susan.

'Yes, yes, I'm fine. A few memories just popped into my head which made me think a bit. Do you mind if I sit here for a while and stare at the sea?' asked Katie.

'No of course not. I'll leave you here. It will give me the chance to go into that rather lovely boutique we passed in the high street. Why don't I meet you at the chip shop in say thirty minutes?'

16

'Perfect,' replied Katie. 'I'll see you there.'

Katie sat down on the bench facing out to the sea. As she stared at the blue water reflecting the sky and twinkling in the sunshine, she allowed her memories to march back into her head. How had she met Joe? That was it. He had been part of Uncle Simon's mission to make her get out and about a bit that summer. One of his friends had a daughter who was about her age. He had asked his friend if she would see if Sally would be prepared to meet up for a coffee or something. It was all rather embarrassing as she recalled and made her look like a real loser. She couldn't really say no, so she met up with Sally late afternoon one Saturday in a tea shop on the sea front. It all seemed a bit lame now. However, as it turned out she and Sally hit it off and chatted easily about themselves. Katie remembered finding it easy to open up to her about her Dad and her failure to deal with her grief. She recalled Sally listening and being sympathetic without being patronising. After that they met up a few times and Sally suggested she joined her and a few of her mates at the pub one Saturday evening.

She remembered that evening clearly now. She hadn't bothered much about how she looked as she had no reason to. As she sat in the pub, she found Sally's crowd easy to be with and soon became caught up chatting to them. She can still remember the moment she looked up and saw Joe. He wasn't overly tall, about five feet eleven. He was lightly tanned from the sun and salty sea air. She remembered he was lean and toned suggesting he had a physical job or did lots of exercise. He had dark brown hair which was thick but not well cut. His eyes were a very dark brown and she could remember how she felt as he turned those eyes on to her. In that moment, she had wished she had bothered to make an effort with her appearance. She had quickly cast her eyes away from his stare and looked down at her glass. He came over to the table and she remembered Sally introducing him as her brother.

Katie sighed as she thought about him. By the end of that evening he had managed to manoeuvre himself, so he was sitting next to her and they were chatting. He had suggested he showed her a bit more of what Broxburgh had to offer so she had ended up agreeing to meet him the following day. After that they spent as much time together as they could. He was an apprentice joiner and worked for a local firm. She smiled as she remembered his arms made lean from the physical labour of working with wood and his strong hands.

It all seemed a bit innocent and naive now. What would Caroline say if she shared her memories of Joe with her? She would probably just dismiss it in her practical way as just a "holiday romance". It was in a way, but he had been special to her. Her stomach flipped at the memory as she pictured him smiling at her as they messed about on the beach skimming pebbles into the sea.

The summer had come to an end and she had gone back home to her mum. She couldn't quite remember why they had not kept in touch. She remembers being hurt that he had not bothered to try and contact her, but they were young.

She felt a bit chilly as the wind was starting to pick up. She looked at her watch. Crikey, she would be late for her chips. She gathered herself up and started to walk along the path towards the chip shop. She turned and looked towards the pub where she had first met Joe. Beyond the pub she saw a tiled roofed shelter with pew style seats looking out to the sea. Then she gasped as a memory grabbed her. It was there, on a seat in that shelter, where Joe had first kissed her all those years ago. She could still remember him gently pulling her towards him and feeling his lips soft and firm drawing her into his kiss. She could even remember the thrill of it.

She started walking more quickly, chastising herself for being so soppy. It was a long time ago now and she had been barely out of her teens. So much had happened since then, she was a different woman now. She banished her indulgent reminiscing and picked up her pace as she went to find her mum and her chips.

Katie caught up with her mum at the chip shop. They took their chips back to the car. The wind made it too chilly to sit outside on the beach, but they still had a lovely view of the sea from the car. Once they had finished, they said their "goodbyes" to the sea and set off. They drove out of Broxburgh and towards Woodbridge so her mum could drop her off at the station. The Suffolk countryside still looked just as lovely. Katie felt glum that she was going back to London and her dull life there. They reached the station mid-afternoon. Susan got out of the car so she could give Katie a proper hug.

'You take care of yourself, my darling,' she said. 'Try not to be too down about things and keep in touch. You know I am always there for you if you need someone to talk to.'

'I know Mum, thank you. I will be fine. As I said last night, I feel much better than I have done for a long time. I really think I am over the Gary debacle and ready to move on. The question is where?' Katie replied laughing. 'I will text you when I get home and I would love to meet John. So, give me a call in the next day or so and we can sort out a meet up.'

Susan beamed at her, obviously relieved with Katie's attitude. 'Will do sweetheart, take care.'

She gave Katie another big hug and Katie turned into the station to catch her train.

Fortunately, the train was on time and she was back in London by early evening. She pinged Caroline a quick text to see if she was around for a drink.

'*Sorry. No can do. Andy and I on date night! Later in the week*?' Caroline texted back.

'*Yeah, fine. Have fun.*'

'*You ok?*' replied Caroline.

'*Yup. Don't fret. Will catch up when we meet xx.*'

'*Ok*' Caroline replied.

Katie hopped on the tube and managed to easily get her bus connection back to her flat.

She dumped her bag on the floor and made an omelette with some eggs she had left in the fridge. There was also a bottle of white wine beckoning her. Sod it, she would have a glass. She sat down at the small table facing the window and gazed at the dismal view and stared at her reflection in the window. This time she felt more upbeat about what she saw. Still the same auburn hair and freckles but her eyes seemed to have more of sparkle. Yup, she was on the way up. She just had to work out where to climb to. She was tired after the journey and the wine, so she had a shower and went to bed trying not to think about work the next day.

Chapter Three

The next few days passed pretty much the same as they always did. She went to work and came back to the flat to eat and sleep before getting up and starting all over again. As promised, her mum had been in touch about meeting John, and she was going for lunch on Sunday. For some reason she was a bit anxious about meeting him. It was difficult to imagine her mum with someone else other than her dad, although Katie understood that her mum had been on her own for too long now. Anyway, she was having that catch up drink with Caroline this evening so she could bend her ear about it.

They met at the same pub. Katie was first again, so she decided to follow her mum's example and just go for it and buy a bottle. She found a table by the window and waited for Caroline. She turned up only a few minutes later.

'Hi,' said Caroline. 'Oh, I can see we're in for the long haul!' she exclaimed when she saw the bottle.

'I blame my mum,' replied Katie. 'That was her trick when we were in Broxburgh. She justified buying a bottle on the basis it would work out cheaper than buying glasses!'

'Mmm…,' said Caroline. 'A flimsy argument I think but I am happy to go with it. Get pouring and we can settle down for a chat.'

Katie poured the wine and toasted Caroline with her glass.

'Well,' said Caroline. 'You seemed to have brightened up since we last met. It's great to see you again as well. I see nothing of you for weeks and then twice in a fortnight.'

'You're right,' said Katie. 'I am feeling much better since we last met. It's funny but since Uncle Simon died, I have spent a lot of time reflecting on things. I am not pissed off with Gary anymore. If anything, I can see that it would never have worked long term and that he was not right for me. As I said to my mum, I think I probably only hung on for so long because I forlornly hoped he would give in and say he wanted a baby. As it turns out he obviously did but not with me!'

'I am pleased you said that. It was hard as a friend to say what I thought but, you know, I never liked Gary. I thought he was only ever out for what he wanted. He shafted you on the split up and you ended up in that glorified bedsit while he kept that lovely flat using the excuse of needing it for his kids. I mean really, the nerve!' said Caroline quite agitated.

'Wow don't hold back now Caro,' replied Katie. Caroline looked concerned. 'Don't look like that,' said Katie. 'I am only teasing. You're right. I have been a bit of a doormat and I need to stop that. I want to move forward. I don't seem to have the imagination to think of anything, I am sure I will at some point.'

'How was the funeral and your little trip to the seaside?' Caroline asked.

'Good thank you. I mean the funeral was gloomy as you would expect. Some of Uncle Simon's friends came and they seemed nice. Broxburgh was as lovely as I remembered but it brought all sorts of memories back,' said Katie.

'In what way?' asked Caroline.

'Oh, a bit silly really, I remembered a holiday romance I had when I spent the summer there after my dad died. I don't know why but it stirred things up in me. I want something to change,' said Katie.

'That sounds interesting,' said Caroline. 'Tell me about the romance.'

'He was called Joe. I met him because I had become friends with his sister, Sally. He bewitched me. I know things were much more intense when we were younger, but I remember how he made me feel. He was sexy, obviously, with deep dark brown eyes and young fit body but there was more to it than that. Well, so I thought at the time. Anyway, the romance ended when I went back home when the summer ended. I'm just being a bit nostalgic.'

'Or daydreaming perhaps?' said Caroline.

'You're right. I am. The other news is that my mum has a boyfriend.'

'Gosh,' exclaimed Caroline. 'Now that is news. What's he like?'

'I don't know,' said Katie. 'I am going to meet him on Sunday and I'm a bit nervous about it.'

'Why's that?' asked Caroline. 'I would have thought you would want her to be happy.'

'Oh, I do, absolutely' Kate said. 'I'm being selfish again.'

'Are you jealous?' asked Caroline, characteristically straight to the point.

'No. Well maybe, I am envious certainly. Crumbs, what a cow I am being. I am feeling sorry for myself and so am being mean about my mum. I am sure it will be fine. It just feels a bit weird me feeling protective about her when she has always been there for me even when I didn't deserve it. You know "blah, blah, blah" about me is getting a bit dull. Tell me about you and Andy. How are things going?'

'Good. Andy is much less clingy now he feels more secure with me. Crikey, maybe men are a bit more sensitive than we thought!' said Caroline laughing.

'Steady, don't rock my world,' said Katie laughing back.

'And I have made a decision. Like you, since we last met, I have been doing some thinking. I have been pushing back against how I really feel about Andy to protect myself. But I understand now why Andy wants to be with me so much. It's because he loves me. And I love him too. So, I'm going to move in with him,' said Caroline softly.

'Oh, Caro, that really is great news. It is so obvious how Andy feels about you and he is lovely. I am so pleased for you, honestly. And, no, before you say anything, I'm not jealous. Well, maybe just a teeny bit!' said Katie grinning.

They carried on chatting until it was time to make a move.

'Thanks Caroline,' said Katie. 'You are a star to listen to me going on as I do.'

'No problem,' replied Caroline. 'You would do the same for me. Let me know how things go on Sunday.'

'I will,' replied Katie. 'And I am genuinely thrilled for you about Andy.'

They hugged and went their separate ways home.

Chapter Four

It was Sunday already and Katie was on her way to meet her mum's new boyfriend. She was keen to meet him now and see what he was like.

She arrived at about midday. Her mum still lived in the same house Katie grew up in. It was an unremarkable nineteen thirties semi-detached house in a typical suburban street in the town of Sudbourne in Hertfordshire. Once she had left and moved to London, she hadn't come back to visit very much. She realised now how much Gary had dominated and controlled her life. They always seem to have something else to do at weekends, usually involving Gary's friends. She had always found excuses not to visit to keep Gary happy. She walked up the path to the front door. Her Mum had obviously been looking out for her as the door suddenly opened.

'Hi darling,' said Susan. 'Lovely to see you. Come in.'

Katie went inside into the hall and carried on into the lounge. John was there and immediately stood up and stretched out his arm to shake her hand which Katie readily took.

'Hello,' said Katie. 'You must be John.'

'Yes, I'm so pleased to meet you Katie,' he said.

She could see her mum nervously hovering next to him. Katie wanted to put her at her ease.

'Mum, why don't you make me a cup of tea and then we can sit down and have a chat?' said Katie.

Katie followed Susan into the kitchen.

'Relax, the first impression is good. It will be fine.'

'I do hope you like him, love. It is going really well, and I am happier that I have been for a long time.'

'I can see that. I'm pleased for you. We just have to get me sorted out now!' replied Katie.

'You will find your way, Katie. I have no doubt' said Susan gently patting her on her arm.

After that they took their tea into the lounge and Katie found John easy to talk to. He seemed like a thoroughly nice man. Susan went off and prepared lunch and left her to continue her conversation with John.

'So,' said John. 'This is a bit difficult for me. I don't know what to say other than I really care about Susan and don't intend to mess her about.'

'I like the honest approach,' said Katie. 'But I don't really have the right to object, given I have been a bit neglectful over the past few years and taken up with myself. So long as you make her happy and treat her well, I am delighted for you.'

Lunch went well with easy chatter over homemade quiche and salad. John cleared things away and said he would pop the kettle on. Susan went over to the sideboard and picked up a letter.

'This came for you,' she said.

Katie took the letter and opened it. It was from solicitors. A firm called Brook & Blankfield.

'Mmm…,' said Katie. 'This is odd.'

She started reading. It was quite a surprise. The first part of the letter explained that the firm acted on behalf of the estate of her uncle and it was in the process of contacting the beneficiaries under his will. Katie read on but at first didn't really register what the letter was saying. Most of his estate had been left to a dog trust charity. Then she came to the part of the letter which affected her. She read the words and was gob smacked.

'Mum' she said. 'Listen to this.'

"To my niece Katie Lewis the daughter of my brother Harry and his wife Susan, I bequeath absolutely without tax the commercial property known as the "Bookshop" on the

high street at Broxburgh. In addition, I bequeath £20,000 to allow my niece to restore that bookshop into a viable business."

'Crumbs,' said Katie. 'What has he done?'

'It's no surprise to me,' said Susan. 'He cared very much about you. We found it difficult to keep in touch after your Dad died, but he spoke to me after you spent that summer with him. He understood your passion for literature but also that you were unable at that time to embrace it, but I had no idea he had this in mind. You might want to speak to the solicitors. Find out if you don't take up the option to try and turn it back into a business whether you can sell it and buy yourself a flat or something.'

John came back with mugs of tea.

'What's up?' he said. 'You both look a bit shocked. Is everything okay?'

'Yes, fine,' said Katie. 'But you're right. I have had a bit of a shock. My uncle has left me his bookshop. I never expected anything like that. I don't know what to think. I need that tea though!'

John passed her a mug. Katie took the tea and said, 'well this gives me something to think about.'

'It certainly does,' said Susan. 'Do you want to talk about it?'

'No, I don't think so,' replied Katie. 'I need to go away and think about what this means. On that note, I should head back to London.'

'Would you like a lift to the station Katie?' asked John.

'Yes please,' replied Katie. 'That would be great.'

Katie got ready to leave. She was in a bit of a daze. She couldn't quite believe what she had read. The owner of a bookshop. That took some getting used to.

'Thanks for coming love. Let me know when you get back. I don't know what to say to you about your Uncle

27

Simon's gift, but what I do know is that you will work out what's best for you.'

'I know that, and don't fret. I like John and he seems like he really wants to be with you. So, I'll leave you to it and I'll let you know what I decide to do about the bookshop. I need to get my head around all of it. Take care and thanks for lunch.'

Katie gave her mum a big hug and walked off to get her lift to the station

She got back to her flat early in the evening. She texted her mum, poured a glass of wine and sat herself down at her usual spot ready to stare at the window again and see if she could make any sense of what had happened. It felt like her Uncle Simon had known and cared about her more than she realised. That gave her a warm fuzzy feeling in her stomach but also made her a bit sad that she hadn't bothered to see him more over the last few years. Well, there was nothing she could do about that now. But what she could do was seriously think about whether she could take on the bookshop. She remembered how neglected it had looked with the dilapidated windows and abandoned books. There was of course the £20,000 he had also gifted to her. But how long would that last? And obviously the shop needed some money spent on it for repairs. However, she would only have basic overheads to pay. She felt a fizz of excitement. Could she do it? Did she have the courage to up sticks and move to Broxburgh and take this on?

Her phoned pinged. It was a text from Caroline. '*What was John like?*'

'*Really nice*' replied Katie. '*Need to talk to you about something else.*'

'*What's happened now?*'

'*Uncle Simon has left me the bookshop.*'

Then her phone rang.

'Hi Caro. You okay?'

'Yes, I'm fine but what on earth is going on with you?' asked Caroline.

'Crumbs,' said Katie, 'All sorts of things. You know I went to see Mum today to meet John and yes as I said he is okay. It's just a bit weird seeing her with a live-in man. And yes, before you ask, it is obvious they are living together; slippers under the table and all that. I'm fine with that I promise. The big shock was Uncle Simon leaving me his bookshop. It is a bit more than that. He has also left me some money, about £20,000 apparently, to give me the chance to set up the bookshop as a business again.'

'Wow,' said Caroline. 'How do you feel about that?'

'Excited, scared, anxious and I just don't know what to do.'

'I get that,' said Caroline. 'But really what is there to think about? You go on and on about how hard done by you are and how your life is rubbish and going nowhere so why not grab this opportunity?'

'I know but it seems such a big step. I haven't really got my head round it yet. I am going to speak to the solicitor and find out if I can sell the shop anyway and keep the money. That might give me some options.'

'Well, that sounds like a sensible plan, but do you really need to do that? It sounds like an opportunity not to miss. Look, a word of advice, don't mention any of this to anyone at work in case it gets back to Gary. You know what a greedy sod he is, and he might just try and make some misplaced claim on all of this.'

'Yes, I've already thought of that,' said Katie.

'Good. Look sleep on all of this and give me a call or something tomorrow. I can't wait to hear what you are going to do.'

'Will do and thank you for listening.'

Katie sat at the table and stared at the window. She could find all sorts of excuses for dithering but as soon as she had hung up from her conversation with Caroline, she knew what she was going to do.

She arrived at work the following day before anyone else as usual. She sat down at her desk with a mug of tea and logged on to her computer to compose an email to her boss. It was short and to the point. She was handing in her notice. She only had to give one month but knew she had some leave carried over from last year, so her leaving date would be three weeks from today. Katie stared at the email and summoned up the courage to press the send button. Then it was done. She felt sick.

All she could do was get on with her work, keeping in mind what she needed to complete before she left and what she would need to hand over. She would have to give notice on her flat. She thought her notice period was only a month as well, but she dug out the managing agents' contact details and sent them an email to ask. She then panicked about where she would live in Broxburgh. She remembered there was a flat above the shop, but her uncle never used it to live in. As far as she could remember it was used for storage. Crikey, what had she done? Perhaps she should have thought about things a bit more carefully before she had handed in her notice. She had the letter from the solicitor with her so she could call at lunchtime and see if she could find out what her options were. A reply from her boss dropped into her inbox.

'*Morning Katie, I have received your email regarding your notice. Can you come and see me now to discuss?*'

'*Yes, no problem. I am on my way.*' Katie replied and got up to make her way to her boss's office.

Her boss, Janet, had a room on the other side of the office behind a glass wall. Katie knocked at the office door and Janet beckoned her to come in.

'Hi Katie, please sit down,' said Janet.

'Thank you.'

'So, what's this all about?' asked Janet, I thought you were happy here. You know from your last appraisal that your work is appreciated, and I thought you were keen to stay and progress, I know you have had some personal difficulties but to your credit you have not let that affect your work.'

Katie explained what her uncle had done and that, crazy as it might seem, Katie was serious about giving it a go.

'I see,' said Janet. 'I don't really know what to say. That seems quite a project. I wish you well Katie. I always felt you never quite fulfilled your potential here. Maybe this opportunity is what you have been waiting for. I will book a time in the diary this week to go through with you what needs to be done before you go.'

'Thank you, Janet,' said Katie. 'Just one thing, would you mind keeping this confidential between us? I have my reasons and want to leave quietly without this becoming public knowledge to everyone in the company.'

'Of course, I am under no obligation to share your reasons for leaving. I promise I will keep it confidential,' Janet reassured her.

When Katie got back to her desk there was a reply from the managing agents. Her notice period was one month, and they asked if she wanted them to treat her email as notice. She confirmed she did. So, she would vacate the flat at the end of the month. Things were moving fast but now she had started she should carry on before she lost her nerve. If she did change her mind, she was pretty sure she could turn things back again.

At lunchtime, Katie took herself off to a quiet room in the office and called the solicitors.

'Good afternoon, Brook and Blankfield solicitors, how can we help?' was the reply.

'May I speak with your reference "PB" if possible, please?' said Katie.

'That's Peter Blankfield. I'll see if he is available. Who may I say is calling?'

'Katie, Katie Lewis.'

'Peter Blankfied speaking. How can I help?' he answered.

'Hello' said Katie. 'My name is Katie Lewis. You sent a letter to my mother's address about the will of Simon Lewis, my uncle.'

'Ah yes,' was the reply. 'I remember. Let me just dig out the file. Okay got it. What did you need help with?'

'Your letter says that my uncle left me the bookshop and a lump sum to get the business going again,' said Katie.

'That's right,' Peter confirmed.

'I wanted to know what would happen if I decided not to take on the bookshop and try and get it going as a business again?' Katie asked. 'Would I still get the property which I could sell and keep the money as well?'

'In short, yes you would,' Peter replied. 'I knew your uncle. We have rubbed along together in Broxburgh for many a year. He spoke to me about you. He was very fond of you. But you must know that. He understood your passion for literature and books and felt life hadn't been great in the opportunities it had given you so far, coupled with a few bad choices you managed to make all by yourself. Anyway, he didn't want to tie you down but just to make you think. If it is not what you want, let me know and I can help with the sale and related matters.'

'He's certainly made me think. I have pretty much made up my mind though. I am going to go for it, so I guess I need to know what I need to do to get keys and deal with any other formalities,' said Katie.

'Well, I will need to go through the legal documents with you and get your signature. Then I can sort out the legal transfer of the bookshop into your name. I will also need your formal authority to transfer the £20,000 into your bank account.'

'Oh,' said Katie. 'Does that mean I need to come to Suffolk to see you?'

'Not necessarily, where are you based? London?'

'Yes, yes I am.'

'Well, I happen to be in London on Tuesday next week. If we can sort out a convenient time and somewhere to meet, I can bring the papers with me.'

'I'm sure I can sort something out. Any chance we could meet at lunchtime as I am still working but could get away then?'

'No problem. Give me your email address so that I can propose a time and place to meet.'

When she came off the phone she was shaking. Was she really doing this? She was. Crumbs. By now it was the end of the day. Time to head home.

Back at her depressing little flat, she poured herself a glass of wine and picked up her phone. First on the list was her mum.

'Hi, Mum,' said Katie.

'Hello sweetheart. How lovely to hear from you. Thanks again for coming to see us on Sunday,' she replied.

'No problem. It was good to meet John. I approve!' chuckle Katie. 'Anyway, the reason I'm calling is to tell you that I have decided to go for it and take on Uncle Simon's bookshop. I know it sounds a bit mad.'

'Wow,' Susan gasped. 'I'm not sure what to say. You're right it does sound a bit mad, but you sound very definite about it.'

'I am,' said Katie. 'Caroline helped. She pointed out that I have spent a long time licking my wounds and wanting to change my life and here is an opportunity on a plate so I couldn't really argue, even against myself.'

'Well,' replied Susan with a quiver in her voice. 'Let me know if John and I can help. I am sure he would be willing to help with the move.'

'I hadn't got as far as thinking about that,' replied Katie 'but thank you I will probably take you up the offer. I had better go. I need to have some supper and start making some plans. Oh, I also spoke to the solicitor who was extremely helpful and knew Uncle Simon. He is meeting me in town next week to sort out the formalities and give me the keys.'

'Okay love,' said Susan. 'And Katie, I'm so proud of you,' she added as she hung up.

She texted Caroline. '*Handed notice in today. Am going for it. Ta for the nudge.*'

'*Crikey. Didn't expect you to decide so fast. I can't speak now am out with Andy.*'

'*No probs. Just wanted to let you know. Will be in touch xx.*'

Katie was too wound up to think much about food. She made a sandwich, grabbed another glass of wine and sat herself down at the table again and started talking to the window.

'Well Window,' she said. 'Looks like I've only got you to talk to. Guess what? I've inherited a bookshop and I am daft enough to leave my London life and head off to the Suffolk coast to take on. I'm a bit scared about that, obviously. But I'm also really excited as well.'

Was she going completely mad? Perhaps it was the effect of a second glass of wine. She stopped talking to the window and reflected on Uncle Simon. Instead of feeling guilty about not seeing as much of him as she should have, she felt warm and cared for, as he had so obviously continued to care for her after her summer with him. She would not let him down. She would make him proud and bring his bookshop back to life.

Chapter Five

It had been over a week since Katie had handed in her notice. Sorting things out at work had not turned out to be as manic as she had expected. She wasn't quite sure how to take it, but her colleagues had been surprisingly helpful in coming forward to help with the handover of her work. She couldn't work out if they were doing it to impress Janet or whether they were just relieved she was leaving. The atmosphere in the office was still a bit awkward because of her split up with Gary. Once she had left, her colleagues wouldn't have to worry about that anymore. Either way, she didn't really care. She was grateful, as it meant she had more time to plan her move. She was so excited.

She looked up from her desk as she heard a bit of a commotion in the reception area. Then she heard a familiar voice.

'Hi gals,' it said. 'Your day has just got better as I am here to deliver the great news of my sales figures and give you names of all the new leads; I have managed to collect this week.'

Katie immediately recognised that puffed up self-important tone. It was Gary. She had checked the office group diary that morning and hadn't noticed he was booked in for a meeting with Janet. If she had, she would have made sure to make some excuse to be out of the office. But then Gary always overrated his importance and so it wouldn't have occurred to him to check and see if Janet was available. It was infuriating that Katie knew that Janet was free this afternoon, so would have no reason to send him away. That meant he was going to come into the main office. She so didn't want to bump into him. Not just because she had managed to avoid him whenever he had come into the office over the last eighteen months, but also because he would find out from the "gals" that she was leaving. He would seek her out and manage to wheedle out of her what had happened and where she was going. Katie knew that despite the fact they had split up for some time now, she still felt vulnerable to his control over her. It was stupid but these things took time to really go away. Even if the 'gals" didn't tell him, he would know from her expression that something had changed, and she knew she would flounder and tell him what was going on. Moving away from London and her former life with Gary was absolutely the right thing to do. She wasn't going to jeopardise that. So, she did the daftest thing she had done in a while and slid off her chair and hid under her desk. Katie was mortified to notice that in her haste to hide, she had knocked her handbag off her desk, and it was now sitting on the office floor in front of her.

Janet walked past and couldn't help but notice the bag on the floor. She peered under the desk and raised an eyebrow as she saw Katie hiding. Katie put on a pleading expression and looked straight at Janet. Janet responded by putting a finger over her mouth signing that she wouldn't say anything. She turned round to face Gary who was walking towards her and used her foot to push Katie's handbag under the desk.

Katie watched Janet as she went to greet Gary.

'Good morning Gary,' she heard her say. 'Why don't you come into my office and I can organise some coffee.'

Katie waited a few minutes before peeping out from under the desk. She reckoned it was safe to come out now. Gary wouldn't be able to see her from Janet's office. Katie was grateful to Janet. She understood the awkwardness about Gary. It had been good of her to steer Gary away. Once out from under the desk, she grabbed her bag. Time for an early lunch break. By the time she got back, Gary should be gone.

Katie headed for the shops. Recently, she had been spending most of her lunch breaks hanging out in Waterstones browsing the books. She kept daydreaming about her Uncle's shop. She was so looking forward to the move. But today her excitement was damped by the arrival of Gary at the office. She was cross with herself for reacting so pathetically. Her new life couldn't come quick enough. She made her way back to the office and was relieved to find that Gary had indeed gone so she could get her head down and get on with the work she had to do.

Back at her flat in the evening, she sat on the floor surrounded by empty boxes. On the day she had given notice on her job and flat, it seemed like she had loads of time to get organised for her move. But here she was, with less than two weeks, and she still hadn't packed any boxes. The move to Broxburgh still seemed like a dream and she couldn't focus on the reality of it. Now she only had about ten days left before the move. She had thought she would have been able to have visited Broxburgh one weekend, even if it had just been for a day. Then she could have had a look at the flat above the shop and work out if it was habitable. The only thing she had managed to do was order a new bed. She had left some keys with Peter Blankfield, the solicitor. He had kindly agreed to sort out the delivery for her. She was now getting a bit panicky about getting everything done in time. It was not like her. She was such a planner and organiser. She would start tonight and finish off at the weekend.

The weekend arrived and she still hadn't finished packing. It was Saturday and she had a load of stuff to get rid of. Her phone rang. It was Caroline.

'Hi Caroline,' said Katie. 'I wasn't expecting to hear from you this weekend. Everything okay?'

'Yes fine. I was just wondering how you are getting on and, to be honest, feeling a bit of a rubbish friend because I can't help you this weekend.'

'Don't be daft Caro. I admit I am a bit behind but that's my fault. Actually, I'm quite happy sorting on my own. After all, it is all my stuff and I need to decide what stays and what goes. Only I can make those decisions. Today I will take a load of stuff to the secondhand shop and tomorrow I can concentrate on packing. It's all quite liberating and making me realise this is really happening. Up to now, it's all felt a bit unreal.'

'You're right,' said Caroline. 'I will keep my contribution to buying the drinks next Thursday if you're still on for that?'

'Absolutely, sounds good to me' replied Katie. 'Have a fab weekend I'll see you next week.'

'Okay, Bye.'

Katie's weekend passed as she had planned. She exhausted herself with trips to the secondhand shop and the tip. By Sunday evening, she was sorted. She poured herself a glass of wine and sat cross legged in the middle of the room surrounded by boxes. It was really happening now. All she had to do was get through the last few days at work and then she would be off. She didn't expect Gary to make another appearance at the office. So, she would never have to see him again and she determined to banish him from her thoughts.

By Thursday, Katie was back in the pub having a drink with Caroline.

'So, your last day at work today and the only person attending your leaving drinks is me who doesn't work with you anymore,' teased Caroline.

'Oh, stop it,' said Katie. 'You know how anti-social I was at work. It was never the same after Gary and I split up. I was quite clear I didn't want a leaving bash. In the end, everyone at the office has been really nice. They got it that I just wanted to leave quietly but still got me a card and a very generous whip round. It feels good to leave on such friendly terms after all the years I have worked there. Janet was especially complimentary and said I shouldn't hesitate to contact her if things didn't work out.'

'Well, that's not going to happen,' said Caroline raising her glass in a toast to Katie.

'No, it's not,' said Katie firmly. 'Even if they don't, I wouldn't go back to Snap. So, I guess this is our last drink in this pub before I move off to Broxburgh.'

'That's this Saturday, isn't it?' said Caroline.

'Yes. Mum and John are coming to collect me first thing. I have nearly finished packing and sorting everything out. I don't seem to have too much stuff which says a lot about my dismal life in London.'

'Now, stop that self-pitying talk,' cautioned Caroline. 'Let's call it a night and you can go home and finish packing. I'll see you soon, I'm sure.'

'Thanks Caroline,' said Katie as she felt tears welling up in her eyes.

'Hey, none of that,' said Caroline 'you'll start me off. There's nothing to get soppy about. You're off on a new adventure and I will have the benefit of lots of lovely weekends by the sea.'

'I know,' replied Katie. 'It's just that suddenly I find it all a bit overwhelming but really exciting at the same time.' They shared a big hug and headed off home.

Chapter Six

Saturday came around quickly. She was having a cup of tea waiting for her mum and John to arrive. She had a swirling feeling in her stomach. The day she was going to move to Broxburgh and take over the bookshop. She took her tea over to the table.

'Goodbye Window,' she said. 'I'm sure you won't miss me! No offence but I won't miss you.' She was going a bit crazy in her excitement. She heard the doorbell. Her Mum and John were here. She rushed down to let them in.

'Gosh,' said John as he stood in the middle of the tiny lounge. 'You have been busy.'

She could see what he meant as she cast eyes around. They were surrounded by boxes all carefully labelled with what was in them. She had little idea what to expect once she got to the bookshop so she had made sure she would be able to find what she needed quickly.

'Fancy a cuppa before I pack the kettle?' asked Katie.

'No thanks love. We had a coffee before we set of. That should do us until we get to Broxburgh. Why don't we get going? We need to get the van back today.'

'Fine with me,' said Katie.

They began to take down the boxes and load up the van which they had hired for the day. It took them about an hour to load up. Katie chose not to turn around and take a last look. She wanted to move forward, so she climbed in the passenger seat between John and her Mum. They were off. Now she felt excited. Susan gave her a reassuring pat on her knee.

They were lucky with the traffic and got to Broxburgh at about midday. Conveniently, they were able to park up outside the bookshop.

'What luck,' said Katie. 'A good sign surely?'

'John,' said Susan. 'Why don't you pop to that nice deli across the road and get us some sandwiches. Katie and I can open up and we can have a cuppa and something to eat before we unpack.'

'Okay,' said John. 'See you in a bit.'

Katie knew what her mum was up to, she wanted to be with her when she opened the door just in case the inside was a bit of a shock. They went in. It was not great but what Katie saw she had expected. She remembered from her visit a month or so ago the boxes of books strewn all over the floor. They slowly picked their way to the back of the shop.

'If I remember correctly, there are some stairs up to the flat on the right.' said Katie. 'Yup, here we go.'

Katie slowly climbed up the stairs and opened the door into the flat with trepidation. What greeted her was a surprise. It wasn't the storage room she remembered. She stepped into a light airy space and walked across the room to look out of the window. She could see out onto the high street and spotted John coming back with the sandwiches.

'Mum, can you pop down and let John in?' asked Katie. 'I'm going to carry on looking round.'

'Okay sweetheart,' replied Susan.

Katie turned around and looked at the room. Peter, the solicitor had said the flat was furnished to a basic standard. She put her head round the bedroom door. Phew, the bed had arrived.

She checked out the bathroom. It just had a basic shower but that would do. There was a small kitchen but she wasn't a great cook so that would be fine too. She went back into the lounge and found her mum and John.

'Well,' said Susan. 'The downstairs is a bit of a mess but up here it's not so bad.'

'No, it's okay,' replied Katie. 'It all needs a good clean but that's easily sorted. I can look around the secondhand shops for some bits and pieces. Some new curtains and a throw for the sofa with some brightly coloured cushions will brighten things up. I am not too fussed about the flat, it's the shop I really want to concentrate on.'

'I know you labelled everything carefully, so let's find that cleaning box and get cracking,' suggested Susan.

'Slow down Mum,' said Katie. 'You and John have to get back in time to return the van. I am so grateful for your help today, but I feel I want to do this myself if you don't mind.'

'Oh' Susan replied looking at John who quietly nodded back at her, 'yes I suppose I can understand that. Why don't we eat the sandwiches and find the kettle and make a fresh cup of tea? We can then unload the boxes from the van and leave you to it.'

'Sounds like a plan Mum, thank you,' said Katie.

'Okay, leave it with me,' said John, 'I'll go and find the kettle box.'

He found it in no time, due to Katie's fabulously organised labelling. Katie and her mum sat on the small sofa with John perching on the end while they ate their sandwiches and drank tea. Katie gathered up the mugs and rubbish and dumped them in the kitchen.

'Okay,' said Katie. 'Let's get cracking with unloading the van.'

It took them less than an hour to unload the van. The lounge floor was now covered in boxes.

'I think that's the lot Katie,' said John. 'I guess we should think about getting back.'

'Thank you so much for all your help today,' said Katie.

'No problem,' he replied. 'I was happy to help.'

'John love,' said Susan. 'Could you fetch that last mystery box I put under the seat?'

John looked a bit puzzled but then smiled. 'Oh, right, that one, back in a minute.'

Katie turned to her mum and gathered her into a fierce hug. She looked at her face and could see tears in eyes.

'Hey,' said Katie. 'I'll be fine, really. I kind of feel at home already. It feels right to be here. Text me or give me a call when you get back. Once I've got things a bit more sorted you can come and visit and see how I'm doing.'

John returned carrying what looked like a wooden crate. Susan took it from him and handed it to her.

'Wow what's this?' Katie asked. She peered into the box. The first thing that caught her eye was a bottle of her favourite Sauvignon Blanc. 'That can go straight in the fridge,' she exclaimed. 'I think I turned it on.'

'You didn't,' said Susan 'but I did!'

Katie continued to look in the box. There was a homemade quiche and coleslaw as well as bread and all the bits needed to make breakfast next morning.

'Oh Mum,' said Katie. 'You didn't have to do this.'

'I know,' replied Susan. 'And I know you could have found some bits and pieces from the high street, but I just wanted to make sure you had something and didn't have to bother on your first night here.'

'It's great. Thank you. I can get on and get things organised and look forward to this with a glass of wine to toast my new home later,' said Katie. 'Now get going. You need to be on your way.'

Katie went down with them and waved them off with another hug for her mum and for John too. She turned back into the shop and closed the door behind her. She locked the door as she would not be going anywhere for the rest of the day.

As she walked through the shop, she spotted a small table with a couple of wooden chairs stacked up against it. That would be handy upstairs in the flat. She took the chairs up first and came back for the table.

44

By now she realised the day was fast disappearing. She needed to get on and clean the flat and make up her bed. Well done, Mum, she thought as she noticed the boiler was on. She must have done that when she turned on the fridge. That reminded her. She picked up the bottle of wine and put it in the fridge. She found her clearly labelled cleaning stuff box. Primed with a bucket of hot water she set to work. It took about three hours to pretty much clean the flat from top to bottom. She made up the bed, unpacked 'bathroom' box and looked round the flat, rather pleased with herself.

Her phone pinged. It was a text from her mum. '*Back home now. Van returned in one piece! All ok with you*?'

'*Yes. Just finished cleaning. Might be time to break open that bottle soon*' replied Katie.

'*Well, you enjoy it love. Keep in touch x*'

'*Will do. Thanks again xxx*'

Katie went into the kitchen. It was more of a kitchenette really. She didn't mind, it was big enough for her. She found her 'kitchen essentials' box and unpacked a wine glass, some plates and cutlery. She turned around and could see across the lounge to the window beyond. It was starting to get dark. The "sun is over the yard arm" she whispered to herself as she opened the fridge and got out the chilled wine and poured herself a large glass.

She took it over to the table she had rescued from downstairs. She had placed the table in front of the window. She sat down and stared in front of her. What a change to her life in just twenty-four hours, she reflected. Last night she had sat at the table in her old flat saying goodbye to a window. Here she was she in front of another one but what a difference. Okay this window also had cracked paint but as she looked out of the window what she saw could not have been more of a contrast. No more bins, she now had a view of Broxburgh high street. She lifted the sash window to let in some air. It was cold but so refreshing. She could smell the salt from the sea mixing with the irresistible smell of chips and battered fish frying. She would resist the temptation to queue for a portion. She had her mum's quiche and there would be plenty of other occasions she thought. She could hear the gentle buzz of voices rising from the street as people chatted and called out on the way to queue for chips or making their way to one of Broxburgh's variety of restaurants, or perhaps just to the pub. The Italian restaurant opposite looked welcoming as the low lights and candles twinkled on the tables.

She got up and picked up her phone which she had left on the sofa. She took a photo of the window. It looked a bit blurred, but it gave the right impression. She messaged it to Caroline with the caption.

'*I'm here! What a difference x*'

Caroline didn't reply. Katie didn't think anything of it. It was Saturday night and Caroline was probably out with Andy or with him at home and didn't want to be disturbed. She was pleased things seemed to be going well for her. Caroline and Andy were good together. Caroline needed to stop being so independent and let him in more rather than always fighting against his kindness. She of course was an expert on relationships. Look what a mess she had made of hers. She gave herself a mental slap. The days of feeling sorry for herself in that department and mooning over what might have been were over. She had a new challenge to get on with now. She still had to pinch herself to check that all that had happened recently to change her life was true. Her mum was right. She was still young. Her life had turned round once already and might do so again. It was time to eat some supper and get some rest. She would need her strength for tomorrow. There was lots of work to be done.

Chapter Seven

Katie woke up with a start and was anxious for a moment as she didn't recognise where she was. It only took a second to remember. She was in her new home. The memories of the previous day came flooding back. She checked the time. It was already eight o' clock in the morning. She couldn't believe how well she had slept. She was surprised as she had drunk a couple of glasses of wine. There was no time to lose. She jumped out of bed and went to shower and dress ready for the day ahead. She made some tea and toast and readied herself to face the bookshop downstairs.

She stood in the middle of the shop. In all the excitement of arriving yesterday, she hadn't quite appreciated what a mess the place was in. The blinds in the shop window were drawn down. She opened one to let some light in. She could see things a bit more clearly. She remembered how the place had looked when she had stared through the window the day after Uncle Simon's funeral. She recalled the boxes of books strewn over the floor, but she had not appreciated the state of the shelves. She rolled back her shoulders. She would have to look at this methodically, so she could properly assess what needed to be done.

She started with the window at the front of the shop. She drew up the rest of the blinds to let the light flood in. There was a platform fixed against the window which used to support the window displays Katie remembered. It had always looked so vibrant and inviting with new books. The shelf had started to come away from the wall beneath the window. She turned to her right to survey the shelves fixed to the wall. She remembered that used to be the fiction section. There were a few books left on the shelves, but they looked dusty and abandoned. What had happened to her uncle? Peter the solicitor said he would be in touch once she had settled in. Perhaps she could ask him? She turned around to look at the other wall of shelves. That was where the non-fiction and reference sections used to be. They were not in any better state. A few random dusty books remained. What a shame.

Her phone rang. It was Caroline.

'Hi Caro,' answered Katie.

'Hey Katie, sorry I didn't pick up your call last night, I was busy with Andy,' said Caroline.

'Stop there,' said Katie. 'Too much information!'

'Sorry but things are going great between us.'

'Pleased to hear it,' said Katie.

'So, what's happening?' asked Caroline.

'Gosh, where to begin,' replied Katie.' I am standing in the shop. It's awful Caro; like it's been abandoned. There are a few books on the shelves, but they are dusty and neglected. There are boxes of unpacked books on the floor. I haven't even ventured into the back yet.'

'You knew it was like that though, didn't you?' said Caroline.

'Yes, but it is a bit more real when I actually see it. I was so upbeat and excited yesterday and now I can appreciate what I am up against,' said Katie.

'You can't sort it out in one day, so chill a bit and enjoy your new surroundings' advised Caroline.

'Yeah ok,' said Katie. 'I do feel a bit under pressure to make things work.'

'I get that,' said Caroline. 'But that doesn't mean you have to trap yourself in the shop and not go out. Take a break and enjoy that fresh air. I'm jealous stuck here in stuffy London.'

'You're right. I will. What's happening with you?' asked Katie.

'Not much; just chilling as we do on a Sunday. Andy's downstairs making me a breakfast. Yeah, I know, it's nice,' said Caroline.

'Make sure you are, Caro. You are your own worst enemy. Andy is good for you so don't mess things up.'

'Mmm…,' harrumphed Caroline. 'That's great coming from you.'

'True! I think my new surroundings make me so wise' chuckled Katie.

'I'll leave you to your breakfast. Keep in touch Caro and I will let you know how I get on.'

'Always. Take care of yourself.'

'I will. You too'

Katie hung up. Caroline was right, she was not going to sort everything in one day, so she decided to go for a walk and take in some sea air. If anywhere was open on a Sunday she could stock up on a few provisions. She opened the door to test the weather. It looked a bit grey and gloomy but did not feel too cold. She popped upstairs to get her jacket and stepped out onto the high street.

She walked straight across the road and down a narrow alleyway between the buildings towards the sea. She found herself on the path which ran alongside the beach and she plonked herself down on the shallow wall. The memory of her childhood holidays here came back to her again. Perhaps today would be a chips for supper day. She got up and walked along the path with the sea and beach on her left. It was late March; the skies were grey, and the expansive North Sea reflected that colour. The view and the salty sea smell made Katie's heart expand. It was fabulous to be here. As she walked along the path her mind drifted to thinking about the shop. It was a light bulb moment. The thought of having to leave here and move back to a dead-end job in London or somewhere else seemed just too awful to contemplate. She would have to make the bookshop work. With no time to lose, Katie turned back onto the high street. She saw the local supermarket was open, so she was able to stock up on some provisions to keep her going.

By the time she got back to the shop it was about midday. She unloaded her shopping and made herself a large mug of tea which she took down to the shop as she continued exploring. She remembered there used to be large table in the middle of the shop which had wooden boxes filled with "special offers" or "reader's choice". That was gone now, and the space was empty. She turned around and moved towards the back of the shop. There was a smooth wooden top counter on which Katie remembered the till used to sit. There was no sign of that. At the back and to her right was an area she had forgotten about. It was sectioned off with a faded screen that looked Victorian in style. She pulled it aside. Behind was a small kitchen area which she remembered now was used to make tea for her uncle and the staff. It all looked a bit tired but there was a small sink and a work top big enough for a kettle and mugs. She could get that going again. She turned around and noticed what looked like a storage area at the back of the shop. It was so filled up with junk she couldn't get an idea of the space or what lay behind it.

She turned back to survey the whole shop. There was a lot to do to get things tidied up. But the real challenge was how to make this a viable business again. Times were different now and people didn't buy or use books as they used to when her uncle was running the shop. First things first, she would collect the books left on the shelves and start opening up the boxes on the floor to see what was in them.

She started with the shelves on the right. There was a mixture of reference books with topics like Suffolk wildlife, local history and walks as well as a collection of large hardback art books. On the shelves on the other side were a range of cookery books, some about crafts and gardening. She dusted them off. They were unused, she couldn't sell them because they were slightly damaged but were still lovely books. She piled them carefully at the back of the shop and went to open the boxes.

For Katie there was always that thrill of excitement when she sniffed the smell of new books. The boxes were full of them, but they were past their sell-by date. They were fiction paperbacks, summer bestsellers from at least a couple of years ago. They were in pristine condition but as they were not the current "must reads" she would struggle to sell them at full price. She resealed the boxes to protect them and piled them up next to the reference books. They must have been the last order her uncle made before he shut the shop. She collected up the rest of the books which were randomly left on the floor and lower shelves and made another pile.

By the time she had finished, it was almost evening, and she was really hungry remembering she had not eaten since morning. She went upstairs for a shower and then settled on the sofa with some soup and a sandwich. An early night was in order. She had done some of the grunt work but tomorrow she needed to start coming up with some sort of business plan.

The following day the grey skies had cleared, and the sky was blue. She was drinking a cup of tea staring out of the front window. She was tempted to head out into the sunshine for a stroll by the sea, but she decided no, she had to crack on. Today she would start cleaning the shop and see how it looked.

Armed with a bucket and an array of cleaning stuff she went down to the shop. It was such a bright day she just had to pull up all the blinds at the front of shop. Passers-by would probably look in at her with curiosity but so be it, it was lovely to have the light flooding in.

She shrieked as there was a face already peering in. She immediately calmed down and recognised the face belonged to Peter Blankfield, the solicitor dealing with her uncle's affairs and who she had met a few weeks ago in London to sign the papers and collect the keys. He beamed at her and signed to ask if he could come in. Katie unlocked and opened the door

'Come in,' Katie welcomed.

'Thank you,' replied Peter as he strode in. 'Oh, I can see you have made a start, did the bed arrive okay?'

'Yes and thank you so much for organising the clear out of the flat as well. I was expecting the flat to be piled up with boxes, but I was able to make it habitable and homely enough in no time. Down here I have just tidied up really. I am still getting a feel for things and haven't quite worked out a strategy for opening.'

'That's understandable,' Peter replied. 'This has all happened very quickly for you and things had been let go a bit.'

'Yes, I can see that' said Katie. 'I wondered if you would be able to tell me some more about my uncle and why he had run things down so much. I can pop upstairs and make you a cuppa if you fancy one?' suggested Katie. 'I haven't got things organised down here yet.'

'A coffee would be nice. Don't go to the bother of having to make one upstairs. Why don't I go and get us one from the deli over the road? When I get back, I can fill you in on what I know about your uncle and listen to any ideas you have about the shop and see if I can help.'

'That would be lovely, thank you. I'll see if I can find something for us to sit on.'

'Okay,' said Peter. 'What would you like?'

'A latte please, no sugar'

'Right you are,' he replied. 'See you shortly'

Katie watched him leave. He seemed like a nice man. He must be in his early to mid-fifties. She hadn't really noticed when she had met him in London as she had been so excited about signing the documents and collecting the keys. His light brown hair was starting to grey. He was slim built with blue eyes which had a twinkle in them and a striking pointed nose.

Katie went to the back of the shop and saw two bar stools stacked behind the counter. She pulled them out and dusted them off. As she did, Peter returned with two steaming cups of coffee. Katie beckoned him to come and sit on the stools. As they began to drink their coffee Peter began to explain.

'As I said to you before, I knew your uncle. He was a well-known and valued member of the Broxburgh community. Up until the last couple of years I expect he was much as you remember, a kind generous man with a wry sense of humour. I know because I advised him on various matters. He had been successful in other areas of business which meant that he could live comfortably in his house on the Terrace and run the bookshop as more of a hobby. That doesn't mean the bookshop didn't make any money, it did, mostly from the summer visitor trade buying books for their holiday reading. I didn't know much about his personal life. I knew that you and your mother were pretty much all his family. I also knew that he did not keep in touch with your mother as much as he felt he should. As I understood it, he was very close to your father, and he found his sudden death particularly hard to deal with. As you mother's grief was just as deep, he found it too difficult to be in touch much. I think it was the same for your mother.'

He paused as he saw Katie's expression sadden.

'I'm sorry,' he said. 'I didn't mean to upset you, Katie, or drag up painful memories.'

'You haven't upset me' she replied. 'It's more that I have upset myself. I have come to realise in recent months how selfish I had become. I blame my ex, Gary, for being a bit controlling and sweeping me up into his world, but it wasn't all him. I should have made more effort. I am just so thankful that both my Mum and it seems Uncle Simon cared enough about me to see through that. It's why I am determined not to let him down and make a success of this business.'

'Good for you. From what I've seen so far, you seem like you have the drive and personality to pull it off,' said Peter.

'Thank you,' said Katie. 'I feel determined, but a vote of confidence certainly helps! Can you tell me a bit more about my uncle and what happened in the last couple of years?'

'Of course, I can try. I am not sure of the details, but the town grapevine suggests that he started to retreat inside himself a bit. He was never very sociable, but he started not to attend things and was not seen out and about. The shop started to close more often and then eventually shut. I think from the bits and pieces I have picked up he may have started to feel not quite himself and it was the start of an illness which led to his heart failure. We'll never know for sure.'

'That makes me feel even worse,' said Katie.

'Look, he had a close group of friends who supported him and was very popular in our community here. I know he wasn't unhappy.'

'Yes, you must be right. I met some of his friends at his funeral and they all seemed nice and upbeat about him. Well, nothing can be achieved by dwelling on all that, onwards and upwards with the refurb,' said Katie.

'That's the attitude. So, any ideas?' asked Peter.

'Honestly, no,' replied Katie. 'I haven't got as far as an action plan. As you say, everything has happened so quickly.

I just feel it is the right decision to come here. So, as you can see, I have collected up the books which were left here and put them into piles. There are some new books, but they are last year's bestsellers so the opportunity to sell them at their full price has passed. I thought I could sell them as "holiday reads" at a reduced price. It's free stock so anything would be a profit. There are also some lovely reference books. As they have been left on the shelves, they are not fit for selling, but I want to keep them.'

Katie pointed to the last pile. 'I don't know what to do with these ones. They are a mix of fiction and non-fiction and are a bit tatty. The thing is I can't bear to throw books away' she said sighing.

'There are a couple of secondhand shops in Broxburgh. Perhaps they would take them?' suggested Peter.

'That's a great idea,' said Katie. 'I'll check that out tomorrow.'

'I'd best leave you to it,' said Peter. 'I'll keep in touch and will be interested to see how you get on, so I'll pop in again soon.'

'Thank you, Peter,' said Katie. 'You have been a huge support already.'

'No problem,' he replied, 'my pleasure.'

After Peter had left, Katie got back to work. She boxed up the books ready for the secondhand shop and then carried on cleaning. She brought a radio down with a sandwich at lunchtime, so she had Radio Two to keep her company during the afternoon. She wasn't lonely. Over the past few months, she had found that she was quite happy in her own company. She was just finding it difficult to stop herself from pulling out one of the fiction books and giving herself up to reading. By the end of the day the shop was looking clear of dust. She had cleared and cleaned the little kitchenette area and the counter. It was starting to get dark, so she pulled down the blinds and switched on the lights. The place looked much better than it had that morning but still the shelves were chipped and scratched, the wooden floor looked dull and worn and the painted walls were faded and in need of freshening up. She decided to call it a day and indulged herself by going out and buying chips for supper. Once she was back, she locked up the shop, poured herself a glass of wine and sat down on the sofa. She fired up her laptop. She would do some research on bookshops in small towns and see if she could get some ideas. She only managed about an hour before the day's hard work started to catch up with her, so she shut down her computer and went to bed still thinking of ideas.

Chapter Eight

Katie woke up after another good night's sleep. It must be the combination of physical work and the fresh sea air. She got up and made tea and toast. This morning she planned to visit the secondhand shops and see if they would like her "not good enough to sell as new" books. But before that, she was going for a walk along the path by the sea. She set out after her breakfast. She mulled over the ideas she had picked up from her research last night. There had been no real surprises. The traditional independent book shop was a difficult proposition to make profitable these days. The bookshop chains and supermarkets could sell books and associated products much more cheaply. People downloaded e-books onto electronic devices. But Katie refused to believe there wasn't still a market for the experience of choosing a book and the pleasure of turning pages. Broxburgh was a popular holiday and visitor destination. She had to tap into that market and somehow make visiting her shop a pleasurable experience and more than just buying a book to read.

She got back to the shop and collected a couple of boxes of books and headed out into the high street. There was a charity shop only a few doors down. She punched open the door with her elbow and faced a cheerful assistant standing behind the counter.

'Hi,' said Katie

'What have you got there?' asked the assistant.

'Some books,' replied Katie. 'I'm not sure if you would be interested in taking them.'

'I expect so,' said the assistant. 'Let's have a look. What sort are they?'

'Mostly fiction paperbacks,' Katie answered. 'I've just taken over the bookshop. These were left as part of the stock.

They aren't in good enough condition to sell, so I thought you might be able to. Oh, I'm sorry that sounded awful. I didn't mean that I am dumping rubbish on you,' said Katie apologetically.

'Don't apologise,' said the assistant laughing. 'They're fine and yes we would love to have them.'

'That's good, I have a couple more boxes to bring another time. Shall I take these through to the back?' asked Katie.

'Yes please,' said the assistant. 'That would be great. One of our volunteers is sorting stuff, so she can take them off you.'

Katie went through to the room at the back and put the box down. As she lifted her head up, she saw a woman taking clothes out of a black plastic bin liner and sorting them into piles. Katie recognised her. It was Sally, the friend she had made all those years ago, Joe's sister. Sally looked much the same to Katie. Older, obviously, but she still had a head of curly blond hair. When she turned to look at Katie, she saw the same blue eyes Katie remembered and her round welcoming face. She recalled the stark difference in colouring between her and Joe. It had been the source of some friendly banter about their parents. Joe, there he was in her mind again. Well, if she was honest with herself, he had been in her head a few times since she had arrived in Broxburgh. She was being daft, she knew, but she wondered if she would bump into him again and if she did how she would react. She could feel herself flushing at the thought. She needed to get a grip. He is probably married with kids by now. Lucky him if he was. She would be envious though. She bent down to put the boxes on the floor.

As Katie stood up, she heard Sally say 'thanks for those. I'll be able sort them out from there'. Then she heard Sally gasp. 'Katie, Katie Lewis, is that you?' exclaimed Sally. 'I don't believe it. How many years has it been?'

'Too many,' answered Katie 'at least ten.'

'I don't know where to start. Why are you back here?'

'A long story,' said Katie. 'In short my uncle left me his bookshop and I decided to move here and try and turn it back into a viable business again.'

'Wow,' said Sally. 'That sounds brave. I remember that shop and your uncle. He was friend of my Mum's, wasn't he? I heard he had died. I am sorry.'

'Thanks, and yes he did know your mum although I have to confess, I had not seen much of him over the past few years, my fault,' said Katie.

'You used to help out in the shop that summer you were here. It's all got a bit run down now,' commented Sally.

'I know,' sighed Katie. 'I'm still trying to work out what I am going to do but I am determined to do my upmost to repay the confidence my uncle had in me.'

'Good for you,' said Sally. 'I am so pleased to see you again. I always regretted not keeping in touch. Crumbs we have a lot to catch up on. Are you here on your own or is there a "Mr." Katie?'

'Just me,' replied Katie. 'I had a boyfriend for a while, but things didn't work out. That was one of the reasons I decided to do this. I was miserable in London and had nothing really to lose. How about you? Married? Kids?'

'I have two children, Sam and Jenny. Sam is eight years old now and Jenny is ten. I married young to Jim. I doubt you remember him, but he was part of that summer crowd. He's not around anymore. I'm a widow. He died,' Sally blurted out.

'Crikey, Sally. I'm so sorry', said Katie shocked.

'It's fine, well it's not fine but I find it easier just to say it,' said Sally.

'If you don't want to talk about it, please don't but what happened?'

'I don't mind, I like to talk about him. He died in a terrible accident. He was a volunteer for the lifeboat crew. It happened over four years ago now. He responded to a distress call. Then there was the old lifeboat which had to be winched down the beach into the sea. On that night, one of the chains broke and dragged Jim underneath. He didn't stand a chance. There was an investigation, but I still don't really know how he fell. He probably just slipped. It's why we now have a spanking new lifeboat in Broxburgh and why I help out here' explained Sally as she glanced around the room. 'This is a charity shop for the RNLI.'

'Oh Sally, I am so sorry. There is not much I can say to that. I didn't think about which charity shop I was donating to when I came in. It would be great to have a proper catch up. Would you be able to find some time for that?' asked Katie. 'I can't imagine how hard it was for you to lose Jim like that. It's not the same but I do understand grief and can be a good listener.'

'Ah yes, your Dad. I remember now,' said Sally. 'I would love a proper catch up and perhaps we can find more cheery things to chat about,' said Sally smiling. 'I was only going to do another half an hour or so here. Why don't I come down to the bookshop when I have finished up here? I am curious about how it looks now. We could have a catch up over a cuppa there.'

'That sounds like a great idea. I'll leave you to it. Come whenever you are ready. I'm not going anywhere this morning.'

'Okay, I will see you later,' said Sally 'bye.'

Katie reflected on what had just happened as she walked back to the shop. She remembered Jim as Sally was going out with him back then. She recalled he was a lovely guy, one of the quiet and gentle types. How sad. It was lovely to see Sally again though. It looked like it was one of those friendships which just picked up where it left off. She hoped so.

About an hour later Katie heard a knock on the door downstairs. It was Sally. Katie let her in.

'Gosh, I haven't been back in here for years. My, it has changed a bit. What a shame.'

'Yes, it is. I have found out that my uncle went into a bit of a decline in the last couple of years. I am struggling to come up with a concept which would work for this place. It is not enough just to sell books. I want to make it more of an experience visit.'

'Mmm…interesting but challenging though,' said Sally.

'Tell me about it,' exclaimed Katie. 'Let's go upstairs to the flat and have that cuppa I promised while I am waiting for inspiration!'

They sat on the sofa with mugs of tea and Katie was amazed as they settled comfortably back into the friendship, they had started over ten years ago. Sally talked about her happy days with Jim. Sam and Jenny had kept her going after his death. She was so proud of them and how they had coped and adjusted. She lived in a house on the outskirts of Broxburgh just down from her mum and dad. Katie remembered them. She recalled Maggie was a bit bossy but with good intentions and her dad was on the surface bossed around but had strength of character beneath that. Sally explained she had a widow's pension and she worked part-time at the supermarket in Broxburgh. She wanted to make sure she was around for the kids. They got by and her parents obviously were a support. She liked to help out and keep busy which is why she gave some hours to the charity shop. Katie remembered her warm generous nature and was so pleased that they had met up again.

Katie filled Sally in with her news. She told her about how she had worked in a café not long after she went back to her mum. Then she joined the publishers where she met Gary. She went on to explain how she felt she had wasted time hanging on to that relationship. She found herself sharing with Sally her longing for a baby and that she was slowly giving up hope that being a mum would be something that happened to her.

'Never give up hope,' Sally. 'I know I had mine young, but I thank the lucky stars every day that they are in my life. Who knows Katie, you've been through a lot too and changes have happened, so keep that dream alive.'

'I'll try. Talking of dreams, why don't we go down to the shop and you can have a proper look around.'

Katie and Sally stood in the middle of the bookshop. Sally walked towards the window.

'You could configure this area differently to give you more space if that's what you need,' suggested Sally.

'What do you mean?' asked Katie.

'Well, the shop window is very traditional. It was used to display books for sale. If you took away the display structure you would have a lovely bright space by the window looking out over the high street. It would lend itself to some sort of seating area, for example' explained Sally.

'Yes, I see what you mean. I am not sure what sort of experience I want to create but you know when you go into the children's section in the library, it's fun. There is usually a low table with books scattered on it for the kids to pick up and look at. It's colourful and inviting. I am not thinking I would run something similar, but I am looking for a concept which would complement the pleasure of buying a book.'

Sally then went to the back of the shop and scanned the counter and kitchenette area.

'This has potential to be used differently as well. It would need knocking out and refitting, but it may be worth thinking about,' commented Sally.

'You're right. Perhaps if I start thinking about how I could change the layout and space, I might get more of an idea about what to do. I have to remember that this has to be a viable business not just a nice place to hang out in,' said Katie.

'Oh gosh,' said Sally looking at her watch. 'Is that the time? I better dash. I could help you take the rest of the books you want to get rid of to the charity shop and then I need to head home.'

'That sounds great responded Katie. They picked up the boxes and set off. As they were leaving the charity shop Sally turned to Katie and said, 'what are you up to at the weekend?'

'No plans so far,' said Katie.' More sorting out, research and thinking I expect.'

'Do you fancy having lunch with us on Sunday and meeting my lovely kids?' Sally asked.

'I'd love to,' replied Katie. 'There is probably only so much sorting out I can bear. What's your mobile number? Then I can text you, so you have mine.'

They exchanged numbers and said their goodbyes.

When Katie got back to the shop, she decided to spend the rest of the day researching ideas. Armed with tea and biscuits, she sat at the table by the window in her flat, so she had the benefit of the view over the high street. By the end of the day, she had reviewed several book businesses. She was learning that selling books needed to be combined with selling something else. The question was, of course, what? She had pretty much decided the types of books she would stock, popular ones targeted at the visitor market. So, holiday reads with maybe some foodie books as well as some tourist books about where to visit in the area. She had made a list of potential suppliers. She had kept the details from the time she had worked at the publisher. After a couple of hours, she decided to call it a day and shut down her computer. She heard her phone ping. It was a text from Sally.

'*Spoke to my Mum. Told her you were back. She's offered to cook lunch on Sunday. We can go to her. She's a better cook anyway!*'

Katie stared at the message. That wasn't quite what she had expected when Sally had invited her. They were all being so nice and welcoming that she couldn't really say no. She couldn't help herself wondering if Joe would be there as it seemed lunch was turning into a bit of a family gathering. She felt a bit foolish about how excited that made her feel. It was a summer romance years ago. Sally hadn't said what he was up to now. They had been caught up with each other's news. She had specifically stopped herself from asking about him. She didn't want to embarrass herself by acting like a girl with a teenage crush. She was making far too much of a memory.

'*That's sounds lovely*' tapped Katie '*time, address*?'

'*About midday. 12 Linden Road. Know where it is*?'

'*Yes. Think so. See you then*' replied Katie.

She decided to call Caroline.

'Hi Katie, how good to hear from you. How's it all going?' asked Caroline.

'Okay so far, hard work though. I bumped into an old friend, Sally, who I met all those years ago. She is helping by letting me bounce ideas off her. In fact, I am going to her parents for lunch on Sunday.'

'Isn't she the sister of that teenage lover you had that summer?' Caroline said teasingly.

'Yes, but he wasn't my lover as you so crudely put it,' said Katie brusquely.

'Ooh, have I touched a nerve?'

Katie paused before replying,' not really.'

'What does that mean?' asked Caroline, sensing the pensive tone in her voice.

'Nothing, I'm just being a bit silly. I've been thinking about Joe and what might have happened if I hadn't left and gone back to my mum at the end of that summer. It's stupid. I don't even know what he is up to now. I expect he is married, or something with kids.

'Sounds like you should get yourself there for lunch on Sunday and find out before you waste any more time daydreaming,' said Caroline.

'Practical as ever,' said Katie. 'You're right. I need to stop dwelling on what might have been and concentrate on the shop. Anyway, enough of me. How are you?'

'Good thank you, work is going well. Andy and I are still pretty good too. I need you to get things sorted out as we are looking forward to a weekend by the sea and seeing your shop,' said Caroline.

'I would love to see you and show you around. I guess I had better come up with something soon. I'll let you know.'

'Make sure you do and let me know how lunch goes on Sunday,' said Caroline.

'Okay, I will. Speak soon. Bye,' said Katie.

Katie made a cup of herb tea to take to bed with her. Caroline was right, mooning like a teenager over something that happened years ago was a waste of time. The thing was, for her, it hadn't just been a holiday romance. Since she had been back here in Broxburgh, she remembered the depth of her feelings. Maybe she was making too much of it. Anyway, she would almost certainly find out on Sunday what Joe was doing now and she would be incredibly surprised if he wasn't settled with someone. That would put an end to her daydreaming for good. With that resolution, she picked up her mug of tea and went to bed.

Chapter Nine

It was Sunday morning, the day she was off to Sally's mum's, Maggie, for lunch. Katie was pottering about in her flat. Sally had texted her to ask if she wanted her to come and pick her up. Katie had said no as she fancied the walk. She would have to think about getting a car. It was the cost that put her off. She expected she would need all the money her uncle had left her to get the shop up and running and to cover living expenses before she generated any income. Anyway, today she would have a break from thinking about that. She locked the shop door behind her and set off.

She arrived at Sally's parents' house just before midday. It was a bungalow in a quiet road on the edge of Broxburgh. She rang the doorbell. Sally opened the door.

'Hi,' she said, 'come in.'

'Thank you,' said Katie as she walked into the hallway.

'Hang your coat up with the others behind the door and then I can take you through.'

Katie followed Sally into a large kitchen at the back. She recognised Maggie at the cooker. She turned from whatever she was doing and came over to Katie smiling.

'Well, well Katie, how lovely to see you again. I am sorry to hear about your uncle and that I wasn't able to make his funeral.'

'Thank you,' replied Katie. 'It was well attended, so he had a good send off.'

'I'm pleased to hear that,' said Maggie. 'Sally has told me all about the bookshop. It sounds like you have an exciting project on your hands.'

'That's one way of putting it,' replied Katie laughing.

Then Sally's dad came in from the garden.

'Reg, you remember Katie, don't you? Simon's niece. She came to stay here one summer a few years ago and was pally with our Sally,' said Maggie.

'Yes, I do,' he replied. 'Lovely to see you. Go sit yourself down at the table over there and I will fix you a drink. What would you like?'

'A glass of white wine would be lovely, if you have one?' said Katie.

'Right you are, coming up. Anyone else?' he asked

As Reg was sorting out drinks, Katie went over and sat at the table.

'Mum, mum' she heard someone shout. 'Sam's just pulled my hair again' shrieked what had to be Sally's daughter Jenny. Sam walked in behind looking as though nothing had happened.

'Now, now,' said Sally. 'There was me telling my friend what lovely kids you are, and you make a scene like that. This is my friend Katie. Come and meet her properly.'

'Hello, you must be Jenny and you Sam?' said Katie. 'Pleased to meet you.'

As she looked at Sam, she drew a sharp intake of breath. He had the look of his Uncle Joe for sure. Damn, she had been trying her best not to think about him.

'Hi,' they said in unison and then turned to rush back to whatever they were doing. Maggie bustled over with a pile of cutlery and started laying the table.

'Let me help,' insisted Katie.

'Thank you love,' she said. 'There are six of us. Joe can't make it today. You remember him, don't you?' Katie could feel the heat of a flush rise to her face. She kept her face down and concentrated on laying out cutlery.

'Yes of course,' she said.

'It's a shame he cannot make it for lunch as I am doing one of my lasagnes, his favourite, but he is off coaching the kids at football today and having lunch at the club.'

Katie couldn't help herself as she asked, 'Joe's children play football then?'

'Oh no, Joe doesn't have any children. They are a local under-fourteens' team. I am still waiting for him to provide me with more grandchildren but that could be a long one. Goodness knows he seems to have had enough girlfriends but none of them seem to stick.'

'Hey Katie?' said Sally. 'Didn't you and Joe have a bit of a thing that summer?'

Katie dropped a knife noisily on the table, plainly flummoxed. She regained her composure and trying to sound casual, replied.

'Yeah, it was nothing; just a bit of a summer thing as you say.'

Much to Katie's relief, the conversation moved on to how the table should be set out and whether lunch was ready. Jenny and Sam reappeared.

'Gran, is it ready yet?' whined Sam. 'I'm starving.'

'Yes, it is. Come and sit down.'

As Katie took her seat, she was annoyed at how pleased she was at finding out that not only Joe wasn't married and didn't have kids but also that it looked like he didn't have a girlfriend.

Maggie served up generous portions of lasagne.

'Mmm…this is really delicious,' said Katie.

'I'm glad you like it,' replied Maggie. 'As I said, it's a bit of a family favourite. I'm sorry to be a bit nosey but I was wondering what you are going to do with the shop. Simon always kept it so nice, it is a shame for the town that it has become so neglected.'

'Well, I will be renovating the shop but into what I am not yet entirely sure. I want to sell books but not everyone in the world is as passionate about reading as I am. So, I am trying to come up with a concept where I can sell something else as well which compliments books. I also want to make it something else other than just a shop, more of a visiting experience. There is a decent amount of space, particularly if I open up the back where there is a storeroom and kitchenette.'

'If you need any help with shelves and such like you could ask Joe to help. He is a skilled carpenter and works for himself,' said Maggie proudly

'I'll keep that in mind, thank you,' replied Katie.

A carpenter, hmm … she remembered he had lovely hands. She could feel the heat of that flush rising again. She was relieved to hear Sally interrupt.

'Anyone for pudding? What have we got, Mum?

'Apple crumble,' said Maggie 'not very Italian but another family favourite.'

Judging by the squeals of delight from Sam and Jenny that was obviously true. After pudding Katie offered to help clear up.

'Don't worry, I'm better off left to myself. It all goes in the dishwasher anyway but thank you for offering. Why don't you catch up with Sally?'

'Okay, thanks. Lunch was really lovely.'

'I was thinking of dragging the kids off for a walk this afternoon, otherwise they'll spend their time doing all sorts of rubbish on their tablets. We could walk back with you, Katie and have a stroll by the sea? It's dry and bright out there,' suggested Sally.

'That sounds a great idea,' replied Katie. 'I can work off some of Maggie's lasagne.'

Sally rounded up Sam and Jenny and they said their goodbyes to Sally's parents. They chatted amiably as they walked back down into Broxburgh. Jenny and Sam skipped ahead.

'I'm sorry if Mum was a bit nosy about the shop. She can seem a bit blunt sometimes.'

'That's okay. She's right really, it's such a shame the shop fell into neglect. I am going to spend some time doing some more research about concepts and hang out in the shop generally, so I get to understand the place.'

'That sounds all a bit zen but might work,' said Sally as they reached the high street.

'I'll leave you to your walk, Sally,' said Katie. 'Thank you for inviting me today, but I need to get back. I have work to do and I haven't been in touch with my mum for a bit, so a phone call is overdue.'

'That's okay. It was a pleasure. Look I know we have just met up again, but we do get on well. I can't bear being idle and am a bit restricted with what I can do given Sam and Jenny take priority, but I could help out a bit in the shop for a couple of hours next week if you could make use of me.'

'You're right, we do get on well and I would welcome your company, if nothing else. So yes, great, thank you Sally. I would love that.'

'How about Wednesday?' said Sally 'I can be with you at about ten o'clock in the morning after I have dropped Sam and Jenny off at school and tidied up at home.'

'Perfect. I shall think of some jobs for you to do.'

Katie gave Sally a hug and turned to walk back to the shop. Once she was back at the flat, she kicked off her shoes and curled up on the sofa. She reached for her phone and called her mum.

'Hello sweetheart,' answered Susan. 'What a lovely surprise. How are you?'

'I'm good thank you. How about you?'

'I'm fine. Not much to report. Work is busy and I get tired but don't we all.'

'How's John?'

'He's fine too, thank you for asking. It is good to have him around.'

'I know Mum. I like him. I really do and you seem good for each other.'

'So, how are you? Not getting too lonely on your own?'

'Not at all. I bumped into an old friend who I met that summer I was here, Sally.'

'I remember you talking about her when you came home but you didn't keep in touch.'

'No, and we both regret that, but we have seemed to have picked up where we left off. I'm just back from having lunch at her parents.'

'That's good. Didn't she have a brother as well. I seem to remember you were a bit sad he didn't keep in touch either?'

'Yes, Joe. He's a carpenter now, apparently. He might be able to help with my refurbishments.'

'Aah, that's what you call it now is it?' teased Susan.

'It's nothing like that,' Katie said back a little too sharply.

'Whatever you say love. I just want to make sure you are okay.'

'I am, I promise. I'll keep in touch and let you know when I come up with a plan.'

'Bye sweetheart. Take care.'

'You too and say hi to John for me.'

Chapter Ten

It was Wednesday morning. Katie was at the back of the shop surveying the contents of a storage cupboard. It was another bright day, and she was feeling energised after an early morning walk along the coast path. An early morning walk had become a regular routine which was a good thing. She had opened the blinds at the front of the shop. Now that she had tidied up a bit and cleaned the shop front, she was not so bothered about people looking in. It still looked empty and faded but to outsiders there were signs of activity and change. It couldn't do any harm to start generating some curiosity about the shop. She just had to make sure she developed a good enough plan to live up to any expectations.

Sally would be here soon. Katie hoped they could tackle the storage cupboard. There were more boxes of books in there as well as a load of other stuff which looked like it needed to go to the tip. Without a car she might have to blag another favour to do that. She cleared away a load of rubbish stacked up in front of some French doors at the back of the shop. Once that was done, she could see the doors opened out onto a small courtyard. There was a side gate to an alleyway which led back up to the high street. The courtyard was private and enclosed by an attractive old brick wall, definitely potential for something. The morning sunshine lit up one side of the courtyard. There were a couple of tatty wooden chairs out there and a small table. Despite looking a bit dilapidated, it looked like a good spot for her and Sally to start the day with drinking coffee in the morning sunshine. She opened the door to let the fresh air in. She breathed in the warm salty sea air and listened to the mournful cries of sea gulls above. She had been in Broxburgh now for two weeks and was still pinching herself to check it was all real.

She heard a muffled knock at the shop door. Katie walked over to let Sally in and in she marched carrying a large flat cardboard box.

'Sorry,' she said. 'I'm glad you heard me. I had to knock with my elbow.'

'I can see why. What have you got there?'

'Let me put it down and I can show you.'

'Come to the back and you can put the box on the counter,' invited Katie.

'Perfect,' said Sally as she walked briskly to the back of the shop. She opened the box.

'Wow,' exclaimed Katie. 'They look amazing.'

Katie was looking at a range of colourful small cakes and bakes carefully laid out in rows inside the box. There were little mini sponges decorated with mixed pastel coloured icing, chocolate brownie slices scattered with what looked like bronze sugar, mini pavlovas filled with cream and topped with a bright red raspberry sauce.

'Did you make these?' asked Katie.

'Yes, I did. I bet you thought I couldn't cook given I swerved my invite for lunch to my mum. I can cook okay but bake so much better.'

'Are they for me?' asked Katie.

'No,' said Sally laughing. 'I often do a batch and donate them around the town. I give some to the RNLI shop, some to the doctor's surgery and some to the library staff. I don't get enough time to bake what with the kids and working at the supermarket, but it is my absolute passion. I would do it for a living if I thought I could make any money out of it. I did think about it after Jim died but it would have needed time and investment to set up a business and my priority obviously was to look after Jenny and Sam and provide for them.'

'What a shame,' said Katie. 'You clearly have a gift for it. Why don't you go and distribute them to who you want to, but leave a couple of them here? When you get back, we can have a coffee and sample them with a coffee. You have given me an idea.'

'Okay, I'll only be thirty minutes or so,' said Sally as she selected some of her bakes and left them on the counter.

Katie couldn't wait for Sally's return. She picked up the mini-pavlova and went out to the courtyard and sat in the warm sunshine. She bit into the crispy outside and found the light marshmallow centre, before tasting the delicious mix of cream and raspberry. It was lovely. There was a connection between the pleasure of relaxing with a good book and the indulgent experience of eating a sweet homemade bake. Perhaps there was the beginning of a concept here. Sally was back so Katie invited into the courtyard while she made mugs of coffee for them both.

As they sat in the sunshine, Katie said 'I know you offered to help me with some of the sorting out, but I want to chat something through with you. It's a germ of an idea but it may have some legs.'

'That sounds interesting,' said Sally. 'Go on. I'm listening.'

'Well, I have eaten one of your bakes. It was delicious. Eating it was a moment of pure pleasure just like reading a good book; a pleasure in the moment if you like. There is something about reading books and munching on a delicious cake together. I am starting to think there is a package I could put together around my visiting experience idea. What I thought was maybe a combination of books and bakes so people can come and enjoy a cake and browse though some books. I kept those reference books which are more what I call sofa table books. I could use those to scatter on low tables. It is like an upgrade of my example of the children's section in the library. Then I could have books for sale as well. A relaxing experience might encourage people to buy one on their way out.'

'A books and bakes shop,' Sally blurted out.

'That's it!' exclaimed Katie. 'Not "a books and bakes shop" but "The Books and Bakes Shop" that's what I'll call it!'

Katie was excited now. She jumped up from the chair she had been sitting on.

'Come on Sally, let's have a look at the space and have a think about how this could work.' She grabbed Sally's hand and pulled her inside.

'This could be quite a spacious seating area if you took out that big cupboard,' said Sally as she walked in. 'What's in it?' she asked as she opened the door.

'Some more books and all sorts of junk which needs throwing away,' replied Katie. 'I could make some room upstairs in the flat to store stuff. I see what you mean about the space. This could be a relaxing seating area with a couple of coffee tables. I could arrange a selection of books to browse through.'

'You could put shelves up on the wall behind and there would be enough space for people to access them,' suggested Sally.

'I have already thought that I would stock books that visitors either day tripping or staying in Broxburgh might like; fiction obviously, but also food books and books about things to do locally.'

Sally turned around and walked towards the counter.

'If you turned this round,' she said tapping her hand on the top 'so it faced out into the main shop, you could move the kitchenette area to the back wall. Then you could have a coffee machine and make hot drinks there and display the cakes on the counter. There would be room for storage underneath.'

Katie turned around and started to walk towards the middle of the shop. She stopped and went to open a door on her left which led into the small hallway where the stairs led up to her flat. Sally followed her.

'There's a loo on the right down here. It is a bit grim but could be done up,' said Katie.

Sally peered in. 'Hmm..., I see what you mean' she said grimacing. 'But a loo is always a draw for day trippers!'

They went back in the shop and moved towards the window at the front. The light was pouring in and passers-by turned their heads, curiously looking in.

'See,' said Sally, 'interested punters already.'

'This would also make a nice seating area,' said Katie. 'It catches the light and would look welcoming from the outside. Maybe I could have a window seat rather than the window display platform.'

'Yes, I think that is a great idea. You would still have room for display bookshelves on the walls in the middle of the shop and you could perhaps have a low-level display in the centre. That would mean that people could see through the shop to the back.

'I guess I could create different types of mood for the seating areas. The front could be more chilled, more of a quiet zone. I could put out more serious reference books. The back area could be more active with children's books and the foodie section and tourist books.'

'You could also include gardening books at the back as they would link to the courtyard,' said Sally.

'Gosh Sally, I'm really excited now. I just have to come up with a plan of action.'

'Talking of which, I mentioned to Joe yesterday that you had taken the bookshop and might need some help. He was surprised to hear you were back but said he would help if he could. I said you weren't expecting him to do anything as a favour for old times' sake,' said Sally.

'Oh,' said Katie. 'Thank you.'

'Is that okay?' said Sally. 'You look a bit startled.'

Damn, she really had to stop this silliness. She couldn't bear the embarrassment of Sally working out she was having teenage crush thoughts about her brother. She also didn't know what to make of Joe's reaction   He obviously remembered her.

'Of course it's okay,' replied Katie. 'I'm just a bit overwhelmed by how quickly we have come up with the idea of The Books and Bakes Shop and what I am going to have to do to get it up and running.'

'Yes, it is quite daunting. I'm sorry Katie, but I must go. I'm working this afternoon. I can come back another time and help sort out that storage cupboard. You can arrange a special collection of rubbish by the council. That will save you worrying about trips to the tip.'

'That's a good idea, Sally. I need to think about stock and displays so I have plenty to get on with.'

'Okay, I'll be in touch,' said Sally as she left the shop.

Sally hadn't stayed very long, but what a difference she had made. Katie had the framework for her business. She needed to get on with the detail. She shut and locked the courtyard door and pulled the blinds down. She need fuel for thinking, so she went up to her flat and brewed a large mug of tea. She grabbed a pack of biscuits and settled down at her table and fired up her laptop. She was ready to start preparing a proper business plan with costings. Where to start? She looked again at the notes she had made about suppliers. She wasn't ready to contact them yet. She needed to get the layout of the shop ready first. She had got the categories right though. Maybe some more baking books if she was selling the bakes and cakes idea. She then started looking at sofas and matching chairs. She certainly had ideas about the look she wanted, with warm colours for the front seating area decorated with maybe gold and rust. For the back of the shop perhaps a fresher look with turquoise green and beige to connect with the outside. As late afternoon turned to evening Katie sorted out a bite to eat and poured herself a glass of wine. She had started to think about the cakes she could sell. The suppliers she had looked at online did not inspire her. The problem was that she had been captivated by Sally's cakes. Finding a supplier with cakes as good as those was going to be difficult. She wanted Sally to supply the cakes, but Sally might not want to or would be too busy to find the time. The only thing she could do was ask her. She decided to call it a day and continue planning tomorrow. She would go to bed and lose herself in a bit of reading if she managed to stay awake long enough.

Chapter Eleven

It was Saturday morning. Katie was busy taking out the contents of the cupboard at the back of the shop. She had already filled up half the courtyard with stuff to be thrown away. She had arranged a special collection for next week. Sally was due to pop in this morning. Jenny and Sam were swimming or something with her parents. There was a knock on the door. Katie realised she had not put the blinds up that morning but that must be Sally, so she hurried to open the door.

'Morning,' said Sally breezily as she bustled in. She walked briskly to the back of the shop.

'My, you've been busy,' commented Sally as she continued out into the courtyard. That left Katie staring at a second visitor, Joe.

Her heartbeat picked up and could feel the warmth of a blush creeping up her neck.

'Hello Katie,' he said softly. 'Can I come in?'

'Yes, yes of course, I'm sorry,' she replied, stammering a bit.

Joe walked into the shop and stopped to cast his eyes over Katie before looking round to see the inside of the shop. She watched him. He had obviously matured given the years since she had last seen him, but he was just as handsome. He still had that thick brown hair. He was well-toned and looked strong. That must be because of his physical work as a carpenter. He turned towards her and she saw that face that had once meant so much to her. She noticed he now had a couple of wrinkles at the side of his eyes which added character. His eyes were the same deep brown, twinkling with warmth and humour and when they were turned on her, they still had the power to make her stomach flip. Seeing him again had done nothing to quash that teenage crush feeling.

'So, how are you?' said Joe, breaking Katie out of her spell.

'I'm okay,' she spluttered, wishing she hadn't pulled back her hair into a tight ponytail but had left it hanging free. She also realised she had on an old baggy grey tee-shirt making her look shapeless and frumpy. If only she had put on that baby blue one which hugged her figure so nicely.

'Sally said you might need some work done. Now I'm here, I can see that you do.'

Katie foolishly felt deflated. He was here about the job not because he wanted to see her. Well of course he was. It was just stupid to think that he remembered their time together let alone that he might still regret they had not kept in touch.

'Yes, you're right. I am going to need some shelves ripped out and a refit. Did Sally mention to you what I had in mind for the shop?' asked Katie.

'Sort of, something about books and cakes.'

'The Books and Bakes Shop,' announced Katie rather grandly.

'That sounds good. Anything involving cakes gets my vote,' said Joe smiling. 'It runs in the family. Talking of which, have you tried Sally's cakes?'

'Yes, I have,' replied Katie enthusiastically. 'They are what gave me the idea.'

'It's a shame she can't do more with them,' said Joe. 'She talked about trying to bake as a business after Jim died. That was her husband,' said Joe.

'Yes, I know,' said Katie. 'She has told me all about Jim.'

'Oh right, but I don't think she could come up with a viable plan which would generate enough income and still leave her enough time to be with the kids. They needed so much support.'

'I expect they did, and it looks like they got it. Jenny and Sam seem lovely children.'

'They have their moments,' said Joe, grinning.

'I'm sure they do,' said Katie.

At that point Sally returned from the back of the shop.

'So, Joe, has Katie explained what she needs done?' asked Sally.

'Give us a chance Sal, I've only just put my foot in the door.'

'If you have time to fit my work in along with your other jobs that would be great, but I think there is a fair amount to do and I am not sure it will all fall within my budget,' said Katie nervously.

'Tell me what you have in mind and then I can work out some costings,' said Joe.

Katie started at the front and walked round with Joe, explaining what she had planned. As she talked and pointed things out, she felt more relaxed. She could just stick to talking about the job in hand and put aside any other thoughts. As they got to the back of the shop Sally produced three mugs of tea.

'Thought these might be welcome,' she said.

Katie and Joe took them gratefully.

'So, what do you think?' Katie asked Joe.

'I will need to come back and do some proper measuring up. The work is quite straightforward. Assuming we don't find anything wrong when we start ripping shelves off the walls, I reckon it would take two to three weeks to do. I will prepare a more accurate quote but if you want a ballpark figure, without holding me to it, maybe between six to eight thousand.'

'Oh,' said Katie. 'That is not as much as I thought. Perhaps I shouldn't have admitted that before you have done your quote!'

'Don't worry, I won't fleece you,' said Joe. 'Look, I have to go, but I'll get back to you as soon as I can.'

Katie walked with him back to the front door feeling mortified at her comment. He seemed very keen to leave after it. She hadn't meant to imply he would bump up the price. Oh well, what did it matter what he thought of her. She just had to remember he was interested in the work, not in any long-forgotten fling.

She said goodbye and Joe confirmed he would be in touch in a day or so.

Katie turned back into the shop and joined Sally.

Seeing Katie's crestfallen face, she said 'don't worry, he can be a bit sensitive about his pricing. Some local traders think he doesn't charge enough for his work which makes them look less competitive. But he will stand by his word. You can trust him, you know.'

'I'm sure I can. I didn't mean to imply he would give me special treatment. I'll wait and see what he comes back with. In the meantime, I need to have a word with you.'

'That sounds serious. What's up?'

'The thing that really sparked off my idea was eating your cakes. I have been doing some research for potential suppliers. I'm fine for the books but struggling to find a cake supplier that has the look and quality of yours and could supply the limited amount I would need at a reasonable cost.'

'So, what you're trying to ask is would I make them for you?'

'Well yes, I am. I just thought it might put you under too much pressure, what with working and looking after Jenny and Sam.'

'They're a bit more self-sufficient these days and Mum and Dad are always willing to help. Joe helps too. You know I wanted to bake as a business, and this is a chance for me to do that. To be honest, I would have felt resentful and put out if someone else supplied them, given, as you say, it's my cakes which provided the inspiration. So, yeah, I will make them for you.'

'Oh, thank you Sally,' said Katie, enthusiastically wrapping her up in a hug.

'Now I'm as excited as you,' said Sally. 'Assuming Joe takes on the work which I'm sure he will, it will be only a few weeks before you are ready, so I have time to work out a plan. I must go now and relieve Mum and Dad from looking after Jenny and Sam. I'm sorry I haven't helped much with sorting out today.'

'Don't apologise, I can carry on with that. I am so pleased you want to help and thank you for bringing Joe round.'

'Hmm…' mused Sally raising an eyebrow. 'It must have been interesting for you to see him after all this time.'

'I don't know what you mean,' blustered Katie. 'He was just here to quote for a job.'

'If you say so,' replied Sally. 'You looked a bit thrown off balance to me, but I could be imagining things.'

'It's only that I'm a bit caught up with the plans and everything,' said Katie hastily, making an effort to put on an expressionless face.

'Yes, you must be. It is all rather scary but exciting too. I'll be in touch,' said Sally as she walked out of the door.

Katie locked the door behind her and pulled the blinds back down over the windows. She went outside into the courtyard and sat down on one of the chairs in the middle of the rubbish she had cleared out of the cupboard. What a morning! She was feeling a bit shaky. She wasn't sure if it was because things seemed to be moving forward fast or whether seeing Joe again had affected her. Both, probably, if she was honest. She had to nip this in the bud now. Joe had come around because Sally had asked him to, and he was interested in the job not seeing her again. With that thought firmly in her mind she set about finishing emptying out the cupboard ready for the collection next week.

Chapter Twelve

Katie was in her kitchen making toast. It was Wednesday and she was about to go down to the shop and wait for the special collection of the rubbish. She was thinking about what else to do with her day. She had pretty much sorted out as much as she could now. She had found space for the books she wanted to keep, and the shop was now clear. Her mum and John had helped with that when they had visited for the day on Sunday. They had also found the time to go out for the day and had driven inland to a lovely old town with a castle and wandered around before having a tasty roast lunch in a pub they found on the way back. She loved Broxburgh, but it was nice to get out for the day. She would have to have a think again about a car, but she couldn't decide about that until she knew how much the renovations would cost. She hadn't heard anything more from Joe. She guessed he was busy, but she did need to get going with the project. Perhaps she should think about getting someone else to quote but she didn't want to do that. She wanted Joe to do the job.

As she was finishing the last bit of toast, she could hear the rumble of a dustbin truck. The rubbish collectors had arrived. She rushed downstairs to open the side gate to let them in.

'Morning,' she said brightly. 'Here it all is,' she said, pointing to the pile of rubbish in the middle of the courtyard.

'Cheers love, I can see that,' replied the collection man cheekily. 'Just leave us to it and we will have all this loaded up in no time.'

'Okay and thanks.'

An hour later they were still loading up. So much for, no time, Katie mumbled under her breath. She bent down to pick up an old bit of rag which had missed the last load. As she looked up, she saw Joe standing over her.

'Oh hello,' she said.

'Hi, sorry I didn't mean to surprise you. I saw the gate open, so I came down the path,' said Joe.

'You didn't,' lied Katie. 'I was just tidying up.'

'Right, well I have some time to do some measuring up. Have you got time for me to do that now?' asked Joe.

'Yes of course. Why don't I make a cuppa and by then the refuse guys should have finished? It looks like there is only one more load to go.'

'That sounds good, coffee please.

'Okay, coming up.'

Katie's timings were spot on. Just as she handed a mug of coffee to Joe the bin men returned.

'Right, we're all done here, love.' The '"Boss"' said winking at her.

'Thank you,' said Katie as she walked out to lock the side gate. When she came back in Joe was smiling.

'Looks like you've got yourself a fan there.'

'Mmm… not sure it's the sort of fan base I would want to build up,' replied Katie chuckling.

'What sort of fans would you like?' asked Joe.

'Oh, I don't know, rich handsome ones probably,' she said.

'That rules me out then,' said Joe turning around towards the counter. He put down his empty mug and picked up his tape measure. 'Right, let's crack on, then, shall we?'

What was that about? His comment puzzled Katie. She followed Joe to the front of the shop. Nothing, just a bit of banter.

'Let me open the blinds so we have more light,' said Katie.

'I'll do it,' insisted Joe.

'Okay,' said Katie, standing back to let him get on with it. She noticed his broad muscular back and toned upper arms as he pulled the cord to raise the blinds. She dragged her eyes away, she had to concentrate on the job, not him.

Joe opened a small notebook, ready to take down measurements. Katie joined him as they moved round the shop working out the detail. Joe made suggestions about how the shelving could work to maximize display space. It took them about an hour to finish.

'Okay,' said Joe. 'That's about it. I have enough to draw up some sketches and work out some proper costings.'

'Great,' replied Katie. 'Thank you so much. I know you must be busy, but I was just wondering when you might be able to get back to me? I need to get going with this so I can be open to catch the summer visitors.'

'I have a couple of jobs on the go. I'll see what I can work out. I don't mind putting a few hours in at weekends, as long as I can fit in coaching the lads at football.'

'Yes,' said Katie. 'Sally told me about that.'

'They're great kids but can be a bit boisterous. Good practice I guess, in case I ever have any of my own.'

Katie didn't know what to say to that. The thought of Joe being a dad hit her with a punch along with her familiar longing for her own baby. Would it ever get any easier?

'Shall I take your mobile number? I can then let you know when I'm ready with the quote and arrange a time with you rather than just turning up unannounced again,' said Joe.

'Oh, I don't mind,' said Katie enthusiastically.

'I'll call you soon,' promised Joe as he opened the door to leave.

He looked at her, his eyes smiling as he said goodbye. He hesitated, as if he were about to say something more.

'Was there anything else?' asked Katie. 'Er no, no, bye,' he replied hastily and walked out the door.

Katie was left wondering if she had caused offence to Joe in some way. Had she been too keen to say she did not mind him coming around unannounced? He must have thought she was desperate. A walk and some fresh air were what she needed. She went upstairs to get her coat. Her phone pinged. It was a text from Caroline.

'*Just wondering how you are getting on?*'

'*Okay.*' replied Katie. '*Will call you later for a chat?*'

'*Yup fine, Am home tonight.*'

Katie set out on what had now become her usual route along the coast path. Today there was a bracing breeze coming off the sea. She spotted a familiar figure walking towards her. It was Peter Blankfield, the solicitor.

'Well, hello there,' he said brightly. 'I am sorry, I had meant to pop by to see how you were getting on. But I seem to have got caught up in all sorts of things.'

'That's okay. It's good of you to be interested. I have come up with a plan. In fact, I have just been with a carpenter who is going to help with renovations, I hope.'

'Who's that?' asked Peter. 'I might know him.'

'Joe Parker' replied Katie. 'He has his own business.'

'Oh yes I know him, he's a jolly good chap. Seems to have a constant stream of work with holiday lets. He has a good reputation so I hope he can help you. I know his sister, Sally, as well. I helped her out with sorting things out after her husband so tragically died.'

'Sally is a friend of mine. I first met her years ago when I spent a summer here when I was a teenager. We lost touch but seemed to have picked up where we left off.'

'That's good. Look I have half an hour, or so free know. Do you fancy a coffee, and you can tell me about your plans and see if I can help?'

'Yes, that would be great. In fact, there are a couple of things I would like to run by you, although I am not asking for free advice, just something to keep in mind in case I need some!' Katie hastened to say.

'I am sure we can sort something out,' he reassured her.

They found a cafe and Katie outlined her plans to create The Books and Bakes Shop.

'I just wondered whether there would be any planning issues I need to think about?' Katie asked Peter.

'I wouldn't have thought so,' said Peter. 'The shop is already classed as a commercial premises, and it is not restricted, so it means you don't have to just sell books. As you are not preparing food on the premises you won't need a health and safety licence. You might have to think about labelling your cakes for allergy reasons. Are you going to put tables out the front on the pavement?'

'I hadn't thought about that. Maybe, if there is room.'

'You would need permission for that, so let me know a bit further down the line and I can look into that for you.'

'Thank you,' said Katie. 'Now' she said as she finished her coffee 'I mustn't keep you and I need to get back and finish tidying up after the bin men came and took a load of rubbish away this morning.'

'Okay,' said Peter. 'You know where I am if you need any advice. My office is just as you go out of Broxburgh next to the cinema.'

'Yes, I saw it a week or so ago as I was walking up to Sally's for lunch. Thanks for the coffee.'

'No problem.'

Katie spent the rest of the afternoon sweeping up in the courtyard. She could imagine three or four tables out there. She could put some hanging baskets on the wall and maybe some pots with flowers which might inspire people to look at and buy garden books. There was so much to think about and plan. It was early evening, time for a glass of wine and a chat with Caroline.

Katie sat at her usual spot at the table by the window and looked out over the high street. With a glass of wine at the ready, she called Caroline.

'Hi' answered Caroline 'what's happening?

'Quite a bit since we last spoke,' said Katie as she went on to explain about The Books and Bakes Shop.

'Wow, that is a great idea, and you sound so excited,' said Caroline.

'I am. Sally has agreed to supply the cakes and Joe has been round to measure up for the refit.'

'How did that go?' asked Caroline quizzically.

'What do you mean?' asked Katie, taken aback.

'What's it like being with lover boy again?'

'He's not my lover boy,' insisted Katie.

'Maybe not yet but if I am reading you right that might not be far off.'

'Okay, yes, I can't seem to shrug off the teenage crush I had. He is still amazing, but he has only shown interest in quoting for the job. He hasn't given any indication that he even remembers we were together when I was eighteen. I expect he has forgotten all about it, it obviously wasn't important to him. If it had, he would have kept in touch.'

'I thought it was you who left suddenly and didn't keep in touch,' said Caroline.

'To be honest, I can't exactly remember the details,' said Katie, ducking the issue. 'Anyway, I need to focus on getting my shop up and running rather than dreaming about what might have been.'

'If you say so,' said Caroline laughing.

'Let's stop talking about me, how are you?'

'All good here, thank you. Andy and I were talking about having a long weekend away soon so we might book ourselves into a cottage or something and come and see what you are up to.'

'It would be lovely to see you any time,' said Katie. 'I might ask you to bring your tool kit and put a few shelves up!'

'Not sure my or Andy's DIY skills are up to that, but we would be happy to help if we can.'

'Thanks Caro let me know. I can ask around for some recommendations for somewhere to stay,' said Katie.

'Will do and take care.'

'Same to you, bye.'

She had just hung up from speaking to Caroline when her phone rang again. She didn't recognise the number.

'Hello, Katie speaking,' she replied.

'Hello Katie, it's Joe.'

'Oh hello,' said Katie.

'I have managed to put together some costings. I know you want to get going quickly, so I thought I would call and see when you are free to go through them.'

Katie was thrown off guard by Joe calling so quickly.

'Yes of course, anytime really,' she said trying to sound casual. 'What time would suit you?'

'I know it's short notice, but I am free now if you are?'

'Yes, that's fine, what time can you get here?'

'I am actually already in Broxburgh, I had a couple of things to do, so about five minutes or so?'

'Okay, great, see you in a bit.'

Katie hung up and threw her phone on the sofa. She had about five minutes before Joe turned up. She had already finished her glass of wine. What would Joe think of her drinking alone? She couldn't pretend she hadn't, so she just had to stay cool and calm and make sure she did not show how flummoxed she was about the thought of him in her flat. She looked around. It was tidy enough. She then dashed into the bathroom to check her face and quickly brushed her hair. Then she heard a knock on the door downstairs. He was here. Katie went down to meet him, trying hard to appear relaxed and casual, but not convinced she had succeeded. She opened the door.

There was Joe, smiling gently at her as she beckoned him in. As well as carrying his notebook, he was holding a bottle of wine.

'I thought we could have a glass of wine whilst we go over the plans,' announced Joe.

'I am ahead of you and have already have one on the go,' admitted Katie. 'But another one would be lovely. Come on up and I will find some glasses.'

Joe followed Katie upstairs to her flat. Katie wandered into her kitchen and fetched some wine glasses and set them down on the table by the window. Joe unscrewed the bottle and poured the wine.

'Please sit down,' said Katie indicating to a chair opposite her. 'Things are still a bit basic in the flat. I haven't really got around to thinking about furnishing and that sort of stuff, as I have been preoccupied with the shop.'

'Looks nice enough to me,' said Joe 'great view of the high street.'

'Yes,' agreed Katie. 'This has become one of my favourite spots.'

Joe sat down opposite Katie and opened up his notebook and took out some folded paper.

'I've done some sketches of what I think it could look like. See what you think' he said nervously as he smoothed out the drawings with his hands.

'Wow,' exclaimed Katie as she looked over the sketches trying not to get distracted by his strong broad hands. 'These look great.'

Katie saw that Joe had absolutely captured her vision of the shop. He must have listened closely to what she had been describing when they had walked round the shop measuring up. Katie had thought he was just being tolerant of her going on about what she wanted but he had managed to create, in his drawings, exactly what she had in mind. After he had left today, he must have spent the rest of the afternoon preparing the plans.

'Well, what do you think?' asked Joe. Katie looked up to his face. Joe looked nervous, almost as if he wanted her approval.

'They're brilliant,' said Katie. 'You've completely captured what I had in mind.'

'Oh good,' said Joe, obviously relieved.

Katie took a sly look at his face. Why was he so bothered that she liked what he had done? Surely it was not her good opinion which mattered to him. He was just being professional.

'So,' said Katie looking straight at him. 'The burning question is how much all this is going to cost.'

Joe took a deep breath, then said 'I think I can get some of the wood as off cuts which should help with the price. It will probably take about three to four weeks to complete given I have a couple of other jobs to finish off. Assuming there are no surprises, I reckon I could bring the job in at about six thousand. I am a one-man band, so I don't need to charge VAT except on materials.'

'Well, that's less than I thought,' said Katie. 'Are you sure that's right and you are not doing me a favour just because we used to know each other?'

How had she let that out? She looked up at Joe. There was no indication in his face that he acknowledged what she was referring to. Why would he? It was only her who was making something of it.

'No favours, it's a fair price.'

'Okay, let's do it then. I hear you have a good reputation, so there is no need for references.'

'Been checking up on me, have you?' said Joe laughing.

'No,' said Katie, embarrassed. 'It's nothing like that, I just happened to mention you to Peter Blankfield, the solicitor and he said you had a good reputation.'

'How do you know him?' asked Joe.

'He was my Uncle Simon's solicitor. He sorted things out after he died, and he's been kind to me since I moved here as well as giving me some advice.'

'I see if you're talking reputation you need to watch out for him,' said Joe sharply. 'He's certainly got one. He divorced a few years ago and since then seems to have been trying to recapture a lost youth which is a bit daft as you can never go back.'

Katie sat back in her chair reflecting on what he had said. It was clear that even if he did remember what we once meant to each other, that comment makes it plain he's not thinking about rekindling anything.

'Even if he has, he has not shown any of that sort of thing with me,' said Katie.

'Just watch out,' said Joe.

'Thank for the heads up,' replied Katie, a little sarcastically. 'But it's not really any of your business.'

'I guess not,' replied Joe, cutting her short. 'I'm sorry, I didn't mean to cause any offence.'

'Especially to a new client,' said Katie smiling, to try and relieve the tension which seemed to have bubbled up between them.

'Quite, so let's get back to business. If you are happy to go ahead, I should be able to start this Saturday. As I said, I don't mind working a bit at the weekends. I know you need to get up and running as soon as possible.'

'That would be great. Thank you, Joe,' said Katie.

'Right, I guess I had better leave you to the rest of your evening,' he said, standing up preparing to leave. 'I'll leave the sketches with you. I have the measurements, so I can get started with those.'

'Okay. I'll show you out' said Katie as she moved towards the stairs down to the shop. As she opened the door to let Joe out, he hesitated and had that look again as though he was about to say something else but thought better of it.

'Bye,' he said. 'I'll be in touch and see you Saturday.'

'Bye Joe and thank you for the wine.'

'No problem' he said and left.

Katie went back up to her flat. There was still some wine left. Sod it, she poured another glass. She didn't have Joe down as a wine drinker, more of a beer man. Maybe she was wrong. Surely he hadn't chosen the wine specially to please her? He had made it clear he was not doing her any favours and even if he did remember that summer it didn't mean as much to him as it did to her. But then why had he got so touchy about Peter Blankfield. The wine was making her maudlin. Time to stop that, she told herself. She sat and looked over the sketches again. They were really good. He had even drawn in the sofa and tables. If he was right about the timing of the works, she could start thinking about ordering stock and sorting out cakes with Sally.

Chapter Thirteen

It was a Saturday morning. Joe was coming to start work today. Katie was up early, full of a mix of anticipation about both seeing Joe and the fact that the refit was finally happening. She had spent the last couple of days contacting book suppliers. She was due to meet with the two she had selected next week in Ipswich. She wanted to make personal contact before ordering, as she might need to pull in a few favours with delivery dates, if the works went on longer than anticipated. Suddenly, she heard a loud clanking noise outside coming from the front of the shop. She walked over to the window and saw Joe on the pavement below directing the delivery of a skip. It was really starting. She grabbed a pint of milk from the fridge anticipating tea would be on the cards and went downstairs to greet the workers.

Katie had cleared the shop of all the books she wanted to keep and was ready for action. She opened the door and stepped out to meet Joe.

'Morning,' she said brightly. 'Kettle's on.'

'Great,' said Joe. 'I'll be with you in a minute.'

He was true to his word and almost followed her in. He was so close behind her when she turned around, she bumped into him.

'Sorry,' said Joe. He seemed a bit confused.

'Err no, my fault,' corrected Katie.

'Right,' said Joe looking uncomfortable.

'So,' said Katie. 'What's happening today?' once again breaking an unexpected tension between them.

'I am going to strip out the display area in the front window and the cupboard at the back. That will leave a clear space to rebuild the shelves and display area in the middle of the shop. I have only hired the skip for today so if you are around to help that would speed things up.'

'Of course,' said Katie. 'I'm all yours.'

'Really?' said Joe. 'You're all mine?'

At that moment, there was another huge clanking noise outside.

'Oh crikey,' said Joe. 'What now?' as he rushed out of the door.

Katie ran out too. It was all okay, just the truck driver clumsily lowering the skip.

And so, the day started. Joe got stuck in and began to rip out the front window. They worked together in an almost silent partnership, he confidently ripping out the shelves and old fitments and she, picking up the debris left behind and taking it out to the skip.

At the end of the day, Katie looked round the shop. It was stripped of all the old shelves and fittings. It was sad in a way as that was Uncle Simon's shop and her memories. But it was exciting as well because now she could see how it was going to look. It was early evening and after all the physical work she was really hungry. Joe was still there collecting up his tools.

'Right then,' he said. 'I guess I am done for today.'

'Yes. Thank you, we have achieved a lot.'

'Yup. Not bad. I can come back tomorrow afternoon after I have coached the lads in the morning. You could always come along and watch if you fancy it?' he said.

'Oh,' said Katie, rather taken aback by the invitation. 'I think Sally is planning to pop in tomorrow morning to talk about the cakes she can supply. Your mum and dad are taking Jenny and Sam swimming, I think.'

'Right, of course. You wouldn't want to hang about on the edge of a draughty playing field anyway. Silly of me for suggesting it.'

'No, it wasn't. It's just that I need to sort things out with Sally.'

'I get it. No problem,' mumbled Joe. 'I'll see you tomorrow at about two-thirty.'

'That's fine with me, and Joe' she said looking straight into his eyes, 'thank you.'

His face broke into a broad smile. 'You're welcome Katie' he said gently.

Katie sat curled up on her sofa. Well, what a day. She was exhausted but in a good way after all the lifting and carrying she had done. She was trying not to, but the thing was she couldn't stop thinking about Joe. She couldn't work out what he was thinking. They had worked well together without the need to fill gaps of silence with chatter. They seemed to anticipate what needed to be done and she had felt comfortable working with him. As she thought of him, she could not pretend to herself any longer. It was not a teenage crush she had. Her feelings for him had revived in full. They hadn't ever gone away she now realised. They were just pushed to the back of her mind. The thing was, she wasn't sure if Joe was just being friendly or whether he remembered how they had once been. Was his invitation to watch him coach football a sort of date or just Joe being nice because she was on her own? Perhaps she should call Caroline and see what she thought, but it was a Saturday night. She would leave her alone and not take up her time with her romantic dreaming because that was what it had turned into, but she could feel herself falling for him. It seemed that, as hard as it was going to be, she would have to keep her feelings under wrap. She couldn't allow Sally to guess. It would be so humiliating if Joe found out and she was rejected. He may not even want to carry on with the work if it got all too awkward. So, she would have to suffer in silence and concentrate on the shop. She had loads to sort out. She had to think about the range of cakes she would sell, get a website up and running, as well as books to order and furniture. She flicked on the television in the hope it would distract her. It didn't. She gave up and went to bed.

Despite her angst over Joe, she slept well. It was mid-morning on Sunday. She had been for her daily walk along the sea path and was waiting for Sally. The blinds were up and she saw Sally's face suddenly peering in. Katie beckoned her to the door and let her in.

'Morning,' said Sally perkily, marching straight to the back of the shop and dumping a pile of cookery books on the counter. 'Crumbs, you have been busy. Joe said he had had a first go at stripping out, but I didn't think he had done this much.'

'I helped a bit,' said Katie.

'A bit more than that if what Joe said is true. He said you worked like a trooper all day lifting and carrying. He made some comment about not knowing where a "city" girl got such strength.'

'Oh, so you've spoken to Joe about me?' said Katie trying to sound casual.

'Yeah. We had a chat this morning as he was leaving to take Sam and Jenny to Mum's before he went off to coach. He seemed a bit preoccupied. He's coming round to do some more work this afternoon, isn't he?'

'Yes, I think so,' said Katie.

'I asked him if he wanted to join me at Mum's for tea later, but he said he had something planned for this evening,' said Sally.

Katie tried not to let it show how much that affected her. He probably had a date lined up with one of the girls Maggie had referred to when she had been for lunch that time. It was none of her business. She needed to get a grip and treat things on a working relationship basis only.

'You okay, Katie?' asked Sally. 'You look a bit distracted.'

'I'm fine. Let's put on the kettle and start talking cakes,' she said cheerily. She was a better actress than she thought.

Sally turned to the counter and started to open the boxes she had brought.

'Okay,' said Sally. 'I have tagged the ones which I make the best for now. We have mini-pavlovas, banana pies, apple and cinnamon upside-down slices, chocolate brownies with a salted caramel centre.'

'They all sound lovely and fit in with what I had in mind,' said Katie. 'I want to recreate the experience I had when I first tasted your cakes. I want to bite into a smooth soft marshmallow feeling. It is the sensuous experience which makes me want to relax and have more.'

'I get it,' said Sally. 'I guess we just don't know how much take-up there is going to be. If things take off, we can have a re-think and maybe I will add a cupcake that looks pretty on the top but has a soft surprise filling.'

'Good with me,' said Katie. 'It's all so much of an adventure. I swing from being so excited to being so scared.'

'I can understand that' said Sally. 'Look, I don't want to get too sentimental, but it feels to me that it has been great that we have been able to become friends again and also for me to be involved in a business opportunity. I had given up thinking it might be possible. So, hold your nerve. I feel you can do this, and it has given me a jolt in my tummy thinking about how things could grow. What's the timeline on this?'

'Joe reckons three to four weeks as he is trying to fit me in around other jobs. Add another week to decorate and get all the furniture in. I really want to be open for the end of May to catch the beginning of the summer season. It should be half term that week and so popular with families for visiting.'

'Well, Joe seems pretty keen on this job, so I think you should be able to do it. I know him and he is good as his word,' said Sally.

'Really' said Katie trying not to show any interest in her voice. 'What has he said? He seemed quite keen to get away,' said Katie.

'That's not the impression I got. He is eager to get on with this job. Who knows, men eh? I miss Jim terribly and wish he was around to enjoy Sam and Jenny but sometimes I think I am better off on my own. Men are so hard to read sometimes!'

'I'm with you on that one. I read Gary completely wrong. What a waste,' said Katie.

'Not really because you thought you loved him at the time. All you can do is live in the moment,' said Sally wisely.

'I know, but as I have said before I feel I have wasted so much time waiting around for a baby that was never going to happen with him. Anyway, no more feeling sorry for myself, I have so much going for me at the moment. I want to embrace it.'

'Too right and I am so thrilled, as it means I have a lot going for me too.'

Katie and Sally turned around and saw a few people looking through the shop window. Katie and Sally smiled and waved at them.

'Oh, crumbs,' said Katie.' What will they think? It looks such a mess in here.'

'No, it doesn't,' said Sally. 'It's stripped out and you have tidied up. It's a good thing that people are curious. Perhaps we should put a "coming soon" notice outside to see if we can get an idea of interest.'

'Yes, maybe when some of the shelves are up so people can get a better idea of how it might look.'

'Right, I need to go and rescue my parents from Jenny and Sam,' said Sally laughing.

'Okay but thank you so much,' said Katie.

'No, thank you,' replied Sally. 'I know you are caught up with working on the shop, but we should try and get you round for lunch again or do something fun.'

'That would be nice. Perhaps we could do something with Jenny and Sam?'

'If you have enough energy for that, then yes, they would like that too, I'm sure.'

It was midday. She had an hour or so before Joe was due, so she decided to shut up the shop, buy a sandwich and have a walk on the beach. It was a warm spring day. She should make the most of it while she could. She pulled down the blinds and locked up.

She bought a sandwich and rather than taking her usual route along the path by the sea she walked the other way, away from the town. She didn't think it was intentional, but Katie reached the spot which had triggered the memory of Joe earlier in the year. There was the shelter with the pew benches. She sat down facing the sea and could feel the warmth of the sun on her face. She could hear the crunching noise of children running on the pebble beach, squealing as they ran away from the waves which rolled in catching their feet. It was lovely here, but still the noise of children made her sad. She thought about what Sally had said that morning about Joe being keen on the job. She shouldn't read too much into that. Perhaps he was just keen to get it finished because he had so much other work on, nothing to do with her. He would be round soon, so she got up to head back.

To her surprise he was waiting for her when she returned to the shop. He beamed at her as she approached.

'Hi Katie, sorry I am here a bit earlier than expected. The football session finished early today as a couple of the lads had family things to go to.'

'That's fine. I was just taking a moment by the sea.'

'It is a lovely day. I don't mind working on my own if you want to spend more time on the beach,' said Joe.

'No, not at all, I want to help if I can,' said Katie eagerly. 'What are you planning to do this afternoon? I am not sure how much time you have as Sally said you had arrangements this evening,' said Katie trying to sound casual.

'No, not really, nothing fixed. I like to keep Sunday evenings free just in case I fancy a pint at the pub with a mate. So, I told her I had something on just so she knows I might not be around if Jenny and Sam need looking after. It's a bit sneaky of me but sometimes I need some time to myself. This afternoon I was planning on doing some sanding down and making good, ready to fix up the shelving' he said changing the subject.

'I can help with that, surely?' said Katie.

'Well, I'm not sure about that,' he replied teasingly. 'What experience do you have, Ms Lewis?'

'What experience do I need?' she replied.

'That depends on the job in hand,' he said, his brown eyes twinkling at her.

Were they flirting? Katie felt herself blush but carried on facing him.

'You tell me?' she couldn't help grinning at him.

'Actually,' he said, suddenly turning serious. 'I don't really know much about you. I guess we just need to start and see how we get on.'

'Okay,' said Katie somewhat, deflated and she turned away from him quickly to hide her disappointment.

'I'll put the kettle on, shall I?'

'Yes please. I'll just grab my tools and stuff from the van.'

Katie walked to the back of the shop to put the kettle on. In that moment, if it was a moment, had definitely passed. Joe returned and seemed to have resumed his professional role.

'You can start by helping me sand down the walls. I'll show you what to do and we can work round the room together.'

'Right you are. Here, drink your tea first,' said Katie handing him a steaming mug, 'milk, no sugar.'

'That's it. You remember,' said Joe.

Katie sighed. She remembered everything. That was the problem. She shrugged off her thoughts and picked up a piece of sandpaper, ready for work.

'You start at the bottom and I can use the ladder to get to the top,' said Joe.

'Okay,' said Katie and she crouched down and started gently sanding the walls. Joe watched her.

'Mmm...not bad for an amateur,' commented Joe.

'I have done some decorating before; I'll have you know' said Katie defensively.

'When was that?' asked Joe.

'In a flat in London where I lived in a few years ago.'

'Was it yours?'

'No, I just lived there with my boyfriend at the time.'

'What happened? Sorry, I didn't mean to pry. You don't have to answer that.'

'It's all history now. It didn't work out. I guess there was a bit of a misunderstanding about where we were going with our lives. I thought we were growing up and settling down. So, I made an effort to do up the place and make it nice. That's when I learnt my decorating skills. Gary didn't make any effort and seemed to carry on gallivanting. As it turned out with a younger colleague from the office where we both worked' explained Katie.

'Oh, I'm sorry. Sounds like a bit of an idiot to me and you are better off without him.'

'Probably, particularly now with my bookshop but it was a kick in the stomach at the time,' said Katie.

Joe climbed up the ladder saying, 'I'll start up here,' suddenly changing the subject.

Katie watched him as he climbed. That's put him off, she thought. He obviously does not want to know anything about me. She looked up and thought he was scowling. He was certainly rubbing the sandpaper furiously. That unexpected tension seemed to have built up between them again. She decided there was nothing else to do but carry on working so she refolded the sandpaper and carried on. They continued to work without speaking for an hour or so and were pretty much halfway round the shop. She looked up to see how Joe was getting on and saw him staring at her. When she met his gaze, he faltered and almost fell off the step ladder. He dropped the sander he was using which narrowly missed Katie's head. Joe scampered down the steps.

'I'm so sorry Katie,' he exclaimed. 'I'm not usually so clumsy. Are you okay?'

'I'm fine Joe. No need to fuss.' She was grinning. She couldn't help herself as Joe had looked so panicky as he came down.

Joe grinned back. 'No need to make me feel worse. I must have looked a bit of an idiot?'

'Just a bit,' she teased 'but you made a good recovery.'

With harmony restored she went to put the kettle on again. 'How much longer do you want to work?' she asked.

'I reckon another couple of hours if we both stick at it. If we could finish the sanding today, then I can start the structural work sooner.'

'Fine with me. Before you start, here's another cuppa,' said Katie as she handed him another mug of tea.

'Thanks. Look, I am sorry, I didn't mean to offend you earlier. What you did and with whom before you came here is none of my business. So, forget I asked,' said Joe.

'Okay' said Katie. She was not sure if she was relieved by his apology or bothered because he had clearly said he wasn't interested in her life. Ah well, she finished her tea and went back to sanding. They resumed their companionable working arrangement and by early evening they had finished.

'That was a good job, Katie,' said Joe as he surveyed the walls all now smoothed down. 'We work pretty well as a team.'

'Yes, we do,' said Kate wistfully and then remembered he would probably want to get away for his pint at the pub.

'I had best not keep you,' she said more brusquely.

'Oh, I'm not in a rush,' said Joe.

'I thought you were keen to have your Sunday pint?' said Katie.

'Oh yes' mumbled Joe. 'I had forgotten I said that. Guess I best be off then and leave you to your evening.'

'I need to be out and about a bit next week, so I was just wondering when you planned to come back next?' asked Katie.

'What are you up to?' asked Joe.

'Well, on Tuesday I need to go to Ipswich for the day. I am meeting a book supplier I know, and I want to get some ideas for furnishings for the shop.'

'How are you going to get there? You don't have a car, do you?'

'No, I don't but that's not a problem. I can get the bus to Saxmundham and then take the train,' said Katie.

'Just a thought' replied Joe. 'I could give you a lift to the station and then you could leave me the keys. I can spend the day fitting shelves. I don't mind picking you up later and returning the keys.'

'That seems like a bit of a bother for you,' said Katie.

'Not really. Tuesday is a good day for me to work here so it kind of works for me.'

'Do you live nearby?' Katie asked.

'I thought Sally would have said something. I live with her and Jenny and Sam. When Jim died it seemed to make sense. I wanted some independence away from my parents and Sally needed help with looking after Jenny and Sam. We are probably all a bit too close together, but Jenny and Sam came first,' said Joe.

'Don't knock it. I've never had that, and I would love a close family,' said Katie suddenly, feeling sad. She turned away from Joe as she did not want him to see the tears that threatened to well up in her eyes.

'Are you okay?' asked Joe gently.

'I'm fine,' said Katie turning back, towards him and putting on a smile. She was determined not to reveal her pathetic longing for a baby to Joe. That would just look so desperate and put him off her even more.

'Look I've kept you hanging around too long,' said Katie. 'Thank you for your offer. A lift on Tuesday would be great. What time do you think?'

'About eight-thirty?' said Joe, looking a little disappointed at his sudden dismissal.

'That's fine with me.'

Joe picked up his tools and walked towards the door. As he opened the door, he turned towards her.

'Bye then. See you Tuesday,' he said, lingering a bit as if he was not ready to leave.

'Bye' said Katie. Joe then quickly turned and left. Katie watched him go. He'd had that look again like he was about to say something more but changed his mind. She locked up. Another confusing day with Joe, she thought. She pushed thinking about him out of her mind and resolved to have an early night ready to carry on with research tomorrow before her trip to meet the suppliers on Tuesday. She could always read. That should distract her from daydreaming about Joe. No chance!

Chapter Fourteen

It was Tuesday morning and Joe arrived early. There was a knock on the door at eight-fifteen. Katie was up and ready, of course. She hadn't slept well. She had had a good day yesterday preparing for her meetings, but she had been fretful in the night. She kept waking up trying to banish thoughts of Joe from her mind. He had made it clear that he was not interested in her life before she had come back to Broxburgh and he had showed no recognition that he remembered how close they had been that summer. In fact, if she was honest, he had not shown any indication that they had been together at all.

She was also bubbling with excitement at the thought of her meeting today. By the end of it she hoped to start ordering books and have an idea of colours for the interiors. Her mum and John were coming to stay in Broxburgh this weekend to help with ordering furniture. There were a couple of great home furnishings shops nearby. John was going to play a round of golf at the club while she and her mum looked for sofas, tables and chairs. Once that had been decided the project would really feel like it was in sight.

She went down and opened the door and stepped out to meet Joe.

'Morning, sorry I'm a bit early. Hope that's okay?' he said.

'No problem. I am raring to go and meet the supplier, so I can start placing orders,' said Katie.

Joe opened the passenger door of his van for her.

'Hop in,' said Joe.

He gently shut the door behind her. Katie watched as he walked round the front of the van. It was kind of him to be so considerate with the door. She was pulled out of her thoughts as he sat down in the driver's seat with a thump.

She could feel the strength of him as he turned on the ignition and grabbed the steering wheel. She couldn't help but sigh and hoped Joe hadn't noticed.

The journey to the station was about twenty minutes. Joe asked her about the types of books she was going to stock in the shop. Katie enthusiastically described the categories, but she found her eyes irresistibly drawn to his hands on the steering wheel. They were wide and strong and gripped the wheel firmly. She admired his wide wrists and the brown hairs which swept down his forearm.

Her sneaky gazing stopped as Joe turned into the station and pulled up in front of the entrance.

Katie turned to him and handed him the keys to her shop.

'Thanks Joe. I'll text you later and let you know what train I am on so you can pick me up,' said Katie.

'Fine with me. Have a good day,' he replied.

'You too,' she said.

The train set off on time. It was scheduled to stop at every station on the way to Ipswich. Katie didn't mind. She had plenty of time. She wasn't due to meet the book supplier until late morning. Life certainly moved at a different pace out here in Suffolk. She stared out of the window. She couldn't keep Joe out of her head. She seriously fancied him and had so wanted to stroke those strong forearms she kept staring at on the drive to the station. But it was more than physical desire. She was drawn to him just as she had been all those years ago. Then she had felt the intensity of a teenage summer romance but now, all grown up, her feelings overwhelmed her. Was she falling in love with him? If she was, she couldn't stop herself. How she felt about Joe was not the same as how she had felt about Gary. She understood now how she had been overwhelmed by Gary in a different way. He had been confident and pushy and had relentlessly pursued her. She had been taken in and flattered by his attention. Gary hadn't loved her. He has desire to control and a need to give him exclusive attention. She had given him that attention and misinterpreted it as love.

The train arrived on time and so she was in Ipswich with time to spare before her meeting at 11 o'clock. She wandered around a few shops and found the coffee shop where she had arranged to meet Sheila, the book supplier.

Katie scanned the cafe but could not see her, so she ordered a coffee and found a table to sit down and wait. No sooner than she had sat down, Sheila appeared. She was as Katie remembered; a smart middle-aged woman dressed in a black trouser suit and bright cerise blouse. Her brown hair cut in a clean bob shaped her face. She smiled at Katie as she shook her hand.

'Hi Katie. Good to see you. I'll just grab a coffee and then you can tell me all about your project.'

'Okay, no rush,' said Katie.

Sheila returned and sat down opposite Katie. 'So, spill the beans' said Sheila as she took a sip from her coffee.

Katie explained her idea about The Books and Bakes Shop. When she had finished, Sheila said 'Right Katie, I've got a clear idea about what you need. I will email you with a list of recommendations and prices and we can take it from there.'

'Brilliant and thank you for taking the time to meet with me today.'

'No problem, I had other appointments in the area anyway.'

It was lunchtime now, so Katie decided to take a walk down to the quay. She picked up a sandwich on the way and found a bench to sit on looking out towards the estuary. She munched on her sandwich and watched the small boats bobbing about on the water. Things were starting to come together. There was no doubt she loved living in Broxburgh but it was good to be away from the town for a bit and it felt even better to be making decisions about her business. It was a welcome distraction from thinking about Joe. She had to throw herself in to her business and forget about getting together with Joe. Easier said than done probably, but she had to try. After a while, she roused herself and set off back into town to look at some rather posh furniture and interior design shops. They were way out of her price range but got her thinking about styles and colour schemes.

By the time Katie had walked back to the station it was late afternoon. She texted Joe.

'*Hi. Will be at station about 5pm. Is that okay?*'

He texted back almost immediately '*Yup. No problem.*'

He was there parked up outside the entrance when she came out of the station. As she got in the car Joe smiled.

'Hi, how was your day?' he asked.

'Good, thank you,' replied Katie. 'I met with a supplier. She seemed really enthusiastic about my project and will be able to supply me with the range of books I think I need.'

'That sounds great,' said Joe. 'Looks like you should be up and running soon.'

'Yeah, I hope so. Talking of which, how did you get on today?' asked Katie.

She turned to look at Joe. He was grinning, looking really pleased.

'I managed to pull someone in to help me today, so I made really good progress.'

'I can't wait to see how you have got on,' said Katie picking up on his enthusiasm.

A few minutes later they were back in Broxburgh and Joe dropped Katie off outside the shop.

'I'm just going to park. I've still got the keys, so you can't go in until I get back,' he said excitedly.

Katie was left standing on the pavement feeling a bit anxious. Joe seemed terribly pleased with himself. She hoped she liked what he had done. She couldn't peer through the window as he had put the blinds down. She saw him walk towards her. Her stomach flipped over watching him. Before she could linger over her longing for him anymore, he was in front of her, opening the door to the shop.

'Close your eyes,' he said. Then he took her hand and led her into the shop.

She heard the door shut. He was still holding her hand and she had an overwhelming feeling that she didn't want him to let go, but he did and said, 'okay, you can open your eyes now.'

When she did, she was stunned by the progress he had made.

'Oh, Joe that's amazing. I can't believe you have achieved so much in one day.'

She scanned the shop and turned towards the front. Where the platform had been in the shop window there was now a seat built into the bay window. On the walls to each side, she could see the first fixings ready for the shelves. She walked towards the back of the shop.

Joe had moved the counter, so it now faced out into the shop. Behind it were the carcasses of cupboards just waiting for their doors to finish them off. Katie ran her hand over the work top. It was a lovely piece of polished wood.

'Where did you get this from?' asked Katie. 'It looks like a countertop from an old shop.'

'It is,' said Joe. 'I've a mate who does reclaim stuff. It comes from an old draper's shop which was ripped out years ago. It has been hanging around for a while, so he was pleased to get rid of it.'

Katie turned away from Joe. Looking at what he had done, his craftsmanship overwhelmed her, and she could feel tears welling up in her eyes.

'Are you okay?' said Joe. 'Don't you like it?'

'I love it' said Katie with a croak in her voice. 'It's just…'

'What?' asked Joe.

Katie turned around to face away from him so he would not see the tears in her eyes.

'Hey,' said Joe softly. 'Are you crying?'

Oh no, she didn't want him seeing her being so pathetic. She could feel him step towards her and reach out his hand as if he were about to draw her to him. Her heart was pounding, she knew she would collapse into a teary emotional mess and blurt out something she would regret if he touched her. Suddenly her phone rang. Joe dropped his hand back to his side. Katie reached inside her bag and grabbed her phone. It was her mum.

'Hi Mum. Is everything okay?'

She saw Joe signalling to her that he was leaving and would call her. Katie raised her hand to beckon him to stay. He shook his head and signed again with his hand that he would contact her. Before she could do anything else, he had walked out of the door.

'It sounds like you have got someone with you. I am sorry to interrupt. I can call back later,' said Susan.

'No, it's fine. He's just left'.

'Who?'

'Joe, the guy who is doing the work for me.'

'How's it going?'

Katie recovered herself.

'Really well, thanks. I've been to Ipswich today to meet a supplier, so Joe was able to bring in some extra help and he's made great progress. You'll be able to see this weekend when you come up.'

'Aah,' said Susan. 'That's why I called. There is a bit of a snag about that. I'm not used to having to think about someone else yet and so I didn't consult with John about coming up this weekend. As it turns out it is his best friend's sixtieth birthday bash on Saturday night. I could of course not go to that and still come up to you, but John looked so disappointed. It turns out he was looking forward to "showing me off" as he put it. Could we fix another time?'

'Don't worry about it. Of course you should go to the party. Actually, it will give Joe more time to get on with things here. At this rate we could be ready to open in two or three weeks. I would much rather you were here for my launch event.'

'Oh sweetheart, we wouldn't miss that. What have you got in mind?'

'Nothing specific yet, I just thought about it as we were speaking.'

'Well, keep me updated,' said Susan.

'I will,' said Katie.

'Other than that, are you okay?' asked Susan.

'I'm fine, a bit shattered after today, that's all.'

'I'll leave you to it and thanks for being so understanding.'

'No problem, I'll speak to you soon.'

She felt deflated after she had finished speaking to her mum. She went up to her flat and poured herself a glass of wine and curled up on the sofa. She thought about calling Caroline, but she was well and truly shattered. She would have something to eat and see if there were any follow-up emails from the supplier, she had seen that day.

Katie opened up her laptop whilst finishing off a cheese sandwich. That was all she could be bothered to eat. There were no new emails. She wasn't surprised. Doubtless Sheila would be in touch as soon as she could. She sat back and reflected on the day. She realised that if Joe was able to carry on working at the pace he was, then she would be ready to open in a couple of weeks or so. She also realised that once the job was finished, she wouldn't see Joe anymore. That thought sent a thud to her stomach. Her phone pinged. It was a text from Joe. Her tummy flipped.

'*Hi, sorry I dashed off. Looked like you needed to speak to your mum. Will be round tomorrow afternoon to put in shelves. Ok?*'

'*Fine. Thank you, Joe.*'

What was the point of saying anything more? Joe was plainly just treating her as a client. He was just a nice person and giving her a lift to the station was just general kindness, nothing more. It was the same thing when he had been concerned, when he had seen her being a bit emotional earlier on that evening. She had to pull herself together. She had a business to get going. So, she had to stop dreaming of things that aren't going to happen. She shut down the laptop and headed off to bed.

Chapter Fifteen

Katie woke up excited, thinking about what she had to get done. The opening of her shop was in sight. After the success of her meetings yesterday, the selection of books was well under way. She saw an email from Sheila. She would look at that in a bit. She had to think of a plan "B" for furniture as her mum was not coming this weekend. As it turned out, there wasn't going to be much time for browsing. She had to make some decisions. Thank goodness for online shopping. She also had to decide which coffee machine to buy as well as mugs, plates, the type of coffees and teas she would serve. She really needed another opinion and wondered whether Sally would be up for helping to make decisions. She grasped the moment and texted her.

'Hi Sally. Joe is doing such a good job I might be ready to open in a fortnight or so. I need to buy furniture and coffee machines etc. Can you help with deciding?'

'Shopping with someone else's money! Of course. Will sort out a time to discuss.'

'Great. Thank you,' replied Katie.

She opened Sheila's email and selected a variety of books from the lists she had provided. By lunchtime she had ordered the books. They would be delivered in the next couple of weeks. Her tummy rumbled. What better way to conduct some research on coffee machines than to visit one of the cafes in Broxburgh and have some lunch. She packed up and walked down the high street. She selected the cafe and ordered a latte and tuna baguette. She sat at a table near the counter so she could watch the barista make the coffees. The coffee machines looked smarter than the ones she had used when she worked in a café but the mechanics didn't seem too different. She needed a revision course before she let herself loose on her customers. She smiled to herself.

She didn't think the owner of the cafe would take too kindly if she asked to have a go here, given she would be training her up to set up in competition. She would have to find someone to give her some refresher training. Sally might possibly have an idea if there was anyone not so local who might be able to help.

Lunch was over and she was walking back to the shop. She saw Joe standing outside. He waved at her. She waved back and hurried to meet him.

'I got away sooner than I thought. Hope that's okay?' said Joe.

'Of course,' said Katie as she opened up the door to let him in.

'You know where everything is now so help yourself to coffee if you want one. I need to head back upstairs. While I think of it, are you able to give me an idea of how long you think it will take you to finish the works? You seem to be getting on really well.'

'Yeah, faster than I thought. I hope to finish the shelves and fixtures by the end of this week. I've got an electrician coming in tomorrow to put in some power points. After that there is just the decorating, so possibly by the end of next week.'

'That soon? Wow, I need to crack on then. I'll just be upstairs if you need anything,' said Katie.

Katie retreated to her table by the window and opened her laptop once more. She searched coffee machine supplier sites and loaded details into a spreadsheet to do a price comparison. She searched for YouTube videos on how to use commercial coffee machines to start off her revision. She could hear Joe banging about downstairs. It took a lot of resolve not to find an excuse to pop down and see him. Then she heard Joe call up the stairs.

'Err, Katie can you spare a minute to look over something for me?'

'Yup, of course, on my way.'

Joe was at the bottom of the stairs looking eagerly up at her.

'Okay,' said Katie, 'what's up?'

'Nothing serious, don't worry. I just wanted your opinion on the shelving. You see I managed to get some reclaimed wood from the mate I told you about who gave me the work top. I thought I had better check you approved before I started making shelves and fixing them on the wall.'

'Let's have a look then,' said Katie walking past him and towards a stack of wooden planks in the middle of the room. She stroked her hand over the wood.

'I love them,' said Katie 'You seem to really get what I like, Joe.'

'Yes, yes I do,' said Joe. She turned to look at him and he wasn't smiling but was staring at her intently. He stepped towards her and then seemed to stop in his tracks.

His tone suddenly changed as he said, 'right you are, I'll just get on with putting them up.'

'Oh,' said Katie. 'I'll get back to work too then.'

That's me dismissed, she mumbled to herself as she climbed back up the stairs to her flat. It was starting to look like he was driving hard with the job to get it finished as soon as possible. Perhaps he couldn't wait to be away from her.

Once back upstairs her phone rang. It was Sally.

'Hi, Katie. How's it going?'

'Good thanks. Joe is here putting up the shelves. He has sourced some lovely old wood and polished it all up. It looks really lovely.'

'Well, he seems to be spending every spare minute doing stuff for your shop,' said Sally.

'He certainly seems to be really keen to get the job done he so he can move on to something else. I sometimes get the impression he will be glad to see the back of me and my shop.'

'Oh no,' said Sally. 'I think it is more like showing off to try and impress you, classic bloke behaviour. Anyway, about shopping, would Sunday morning suit? I can dump the kids with Mum and Dad. Mum said if you wanted to, you could come back and have lunch with us again. What do you think?'

'That sounds absolutely great. Thank you Sally,' said Katie.

'No problem, particularly as I am going to be part of this business. I can come and pick you up about ten o'clock in the morning. There are a couple of places we can go. One is only about a ten minutes' drive away. The other one is a bit further away but all do-able in a morning.'

'Okay. See you then and thanks again Sally.'

Katie heard Joe call again. She went down. He had finished the shelving on one wall. It looked amazing. The colour and texture of the reclaimed wood added depth and character to the space.

'Oh, Joe thank you. They look amazing, they really do,' exclaimed Katie as she walked over to admire them more closely. 'You've done a wonderful job.'

'Thank you. They do look great, even if I say so myself,' he said grinning and looking very pleased.

'I've done about as much as I can for today, so I'll head off if that's okay?' said Joe.

'Yes of course it's okay. You've done a brilliant job. I couldn't be more pleased,' said Katie.

Katie noticed he seemed almost relieved as she said that as his face broke out into a huge smile.

'I aim to please,' said Joe.

120

Katie gazed at his handsome face. She desperately wanted him to stay but found herself unable to find the words to ask him. So, she watched as he packed up and made his way to leave.

'I'll be in touch about when I'll be in next,' said Joe as he walked out the door.

'Okay and thanks again,' was all Katie was able to say. 'Bye'.

Chapter Sixteen

Katie was enjoying a morning cup of tea. Today she was going shopping with Sally. Katie heard the knock at her door at nine-thirty. She was ready and excited. She had a good day to look forward to.

'Hi Sally,' said Kate as she got into the car. 'Thank you so much for this.'

'Nothing to thank me for, I love shopping. Much as I adore Sam and Jenny, it is nice to have a break and have some adult company,' said Sally.

'So where are we off to first?' asked Katie.

'I thought we would go to the furnishing shop which is a bit out of town first. We can then come back to the one nearer to Broxburgh. We'll be back in time for lunch which is of course a priority.'

'Sounds like a plan,' said Katie. 'Let's go.'

As they drove off, they chatted about progress to the shop.

'Joe has done a great job. I never expected he would find such lovely materials to make the shelves and counter,' said Katie.

'He is a craftsman that's for sure, but he seems to be a bit obsessed with this job. I think it might be the client,' said Sally chuckling.

'I didn't think I was that demanding,' said Katie defensively.

'Oh no, it's not that. It's as I said to you on the phone, he's trying to impress you,' said Sally.

'Why would he want to do that? He seems just keen to get the job finished.'

'If you say so,' said Sally, raising her eyebrows and tutting. 'Here we are,' she announced as they turned off a roundabout and into a large business park. Katie could see a large barn conversion type which was the soft furnishing shop.

'Crumbs, this looks a bit above my budget,' said Katie.

'It is,' said Sally bluntly. 'The idea is to get ideas about styles and colours. You can source what you want online. It should be cheaper that way.'

'Whatever you say, boss,' said Katie smiling.

They wandered in and slowly moved round the displays. There was a range of sofas and chairs as well as throws and cushions. Katie was starting to get a good idea about what she wanted. She thought a three-seater sofa flanked by two smaller sofas facing the window at the front of the shop. That arrangement would bring in the window seat. She could have a low-level square coffee table which would be big enough for putting mugs and small plates on as well as room for reference books for browsing in the middle. Sally came to stand next to her.

'Getting some ideas?' she asked.

'Definitely,' said Katie as she explained to Sally her ideas for the seating at the front of the shop.

'I think that would work very well. What about at the back? Let's go over and look at the dining furniture. You should get some ideas from there.'

Katie ran her hand over the surface of a long wooden dining table.

'Isn't this lovely,' she said to Sally. 'Way too big for what I need but I love the finish on the wood.'

'Yes, it is,' said Sally. 'You could have wooden tables though.'

'They would have to be good quality. Otherwise, they will look shabby next to the shelves Joe has made.

'Yes, they would,' said Sally. 'Look there's a nice cafe area over there' said Sally pointing. 'Let's have a coffee break.'

123

'Good idea. We can examine the tables and chairs they use!'

Sally and Katie made themselves comfortable at a table with two lattes.

'These are a nice touch,' said Sally pointing to a posy of fresh flowers on the table.

'They are,' said Katie. 'But I don't want the shop to look too much like a cafe. Maybe some wildflower posies would be good. It might be another inspiration to customers to buy a gardening book. I want to create a more at home feel. You know, kind of like you grab a cuppa and a cake and sit down to browse books and maybe start a conversation about them. The focus is on the books. The coffee and cakes are to create the environment to make it easy to buy books.'

'I get that,' said Sally.

'I know. Maybe I should go for mix and match furniture and make the area look a bit more relaxed and casual.'

'You could try and find some secondhand furniture. That should be cheaper and perhaps fit in better with the reclaimed wood Joe has made the shelves with.'

'I am still amazed he has managed to work out my taste and what I like,' said Katie.

'Really Katie, have you not worked it out?' said Sally rolling her eyes.

'What do you mean?' asked Katie.

'He's never actually said anything,' replied Sally. 'But you know what blokes are like, not great at talking about emotional stuff, especially with his sister. I know it is a long time ago, but he was really messed up when you left that summer. I told him at the time he should try and find you or contact you to work out why you left. But his stubborn male pride wouldn't let him.'

'I had no idea,' said Katie quietly.

'Why did you leave so abruptly?' asked Sally.

Katie didn't answer immediately. She drew in a deep breath and then tried to explain to Sally.

'If I am honest, I am not entirely sure why I left so suddenly. As you say it is a long time ago now. As I remember it, I was torn between staying longer in Broxburgh and returning home to my mum. I wasn't facing up to things. I realized I had abandoned my mum to her grief, and we should have been bearing it together. Hiding away in a Broxburgh bubble wasn't the right thing to do. I remember I was crazy about Joe in that intense way you can be as a teenager. Part of me didn't trust my feelings. I was young and damaged with grief for my Dad. Joe was so wonderful but didn't tell me how he felt. I thought at the time that he didn't feel the same way as I did. So, I guess I ran away. Looking back, I guess I didn't tell him how I felt either. In my young romantic mind, I think I thought in some way he would follow me, but he didn't. I heard nothing from him, and I didn't contact him. Seems a bit silly now but I interpreted Joe's failure to get in touch as rejection. I am not blaming Joe as I certainly played a part, but to an extent I think his rejection, as I saw it, made me settle for second best with Gary and look where that got me.'

'Not very far,' said Sally in her matter-of-fact way.

'Exactly,' replied Katie. 'Anyway, that was over ten years ago now. Maybe there was a misunderstanding, but he hasn't mentioned anything to me about that time, so I guess we should let sleeping dogs lie.'

'Whatever you say,' said Sally, shrugging her shoulders and rolling her eyes again. 'Come on, it's eleven o'clock already. We need to head off to the other shop. It has more soft furnishings and fabrics so you can get more of an idea about colours.'

'Sounds good to me,' said Katie. She was relieved they did not have to continue the conversation about Joe. She was in danger of confiding her growing feelings for him to Sally.

As they walked out of the shop and back to the car, she couldn't help thinking about what Sally had said. Surely it couldn't be that there had been such a misunderstanding. She had convinced herself that Joe had not felt the same as her and wouldn't have been troubled by her leaving. He certainly, as far as Katie was concerned, hadn't given any indication that she had been wrong. She wasn't going to dwell on it now. She was excited about the next shop and started thinking about colour schemes.

They drove back towards Broxburgh and arrived at the second shop. As they walked in Katie could see the fabric and throws were arranged in different areas with coloured themes.

'What do you think, Sally?' asked Katie.

'About what?' replied Sally.

'Oh sorry, I am not making myself clear. I was thinking that the area in the front of the shop should be relaxed seating. It will be visible from the window and I want it to look warm and inviting,' said Katie.

'Yeah, I get that' replied Sally.

Also, 'I think there should be a connection to the outside from the café area, so perhaps some green colours to link to plants in pots in the courtyard. May be a connection to the sea and the sky, so bright blue and turquoise as well,' said Katie.

'Katie, look over there,' exclaimed Sally pointing to some garden furniture. She pulled Katie by the arm in that direction.

Katie saw the display of small round and square wooden tables painted in a variety of colours.

'How about if we were able to source some secondhand chairs and tables, as I suggested earlier? We could paint them a mixture of vibrant colours, then set them out in a mix and match arrangement. I think it would look fab,' said Sally.

'So do I,' said Katie. 'Once again you seem to have come up with an inspirational idea. Let's take some colour samples and I can see what works when I get back to the shop.'

'There are some secondhand furniture shops around locally, but they tend to be geared up for the tourist trade and can be a bit overpriced. They brand things with the "vintage" label so they can add an extra mark up. Fair enough if people are prepared to pay. You would probably do better on eBay or something.'

'I am already there with that plan. That's my job this afternoon.'

'Well then, we had better head to Mum's and get a decent lunch inside you. Looks like you will need the energy,' said Sally.

'Sounds good to me. Do you know what she is cooking? I'm starving.'

'Full Sunday roast I believe, possibly chicken.'

'Lovely,' said Katie as her tummy rumbled in anticipation.

Katie and Sally chatted amiably on the way back to Broxburgh.

'Thank you so much for today Sally,' said Katie. 'You have been really good to me with the shop and everything.'

'I don't mind helping at all because I enjoy it. Anyway, there is a benefit to me. With your project you have given me an opportunity to do something I have wanted to do for a long while. As well as baking I love all that interior stuff. Seriously Katie I feel part of The Books and Bakes Shop already, and I want to be, so let me help. Sam and Jenny are getting more self-sufficient every day. I feel the timing is right somehow and I don't want to lose this chance.'

'Amen to that, Sally. I know what you mean about timing. Uncle Simon's legacy came at a time when I was ready to look for something new in my life. Finding my friendship with you again has been such a bonus. We seem to work well together. Let's make this a success for both our sakes.'

Sally grinned at her as they pulled up outside her parents' house.

'Oh' said Sally. 'That's Joe's van. I didn't know he was joining us. I bet he found out you were coming and couldn't help himself.'

Katie didn't know what to say to that and could feel herself blush. She delved into her handbag to find a tissue so Sally couldn't see her face.

'Let's go and find out, shall we?' said Sally laughing at Katie's discomfort.

As they went into the house, Sam and Jenny came rushing up to hug Sally.

'Steady' said Sally. 'You're nearly pushing me over. What's all this? Normally a couple of hours away from you both doesn't meet with this greeting. Are you after something?'

'No' they said in unison.

'Mmm...' said Sally smiling 'I'm not convinced. We'll see.'

Katie then noticed Joe coming out of the kitchen.

'Oh hi,' he said nonchalantly. 'How are you, Katie?'

'I'm good, Joe, thank you,' replied Katie. 'Sally and I have had a great morning.'

'Well, come in and tell us about it. Mum's nosiness won't wait much longer.'

'I heard that, Joe' Maggie shouted from the kitchen.

Katie went into the kitchen and saw Maggie looking flushed and warm by the cooker. She was enthusiastically basting a large chicken. She turned around as Katie walked in.

'Hello Katie love, good to see you again.'

'Same to you and thank you for inviting me. Gosh, that chicken smells delicious.'

'I hope there's enough. I wasn't expecting Joe. Not to worry though. I can do extra spuds and veg.'

'So, Joe,' said Sally as she came into the kitchen, 'to what do we owe the unexpected pleasure?'

'Nothing special,' said Joe, looking a little uncomfortable. 'Coaching finished early again, and Mum happened to mention that you were going out with Katie this morning and coming back here for lunch. So, I thought why not swing by and take advantage of one her Sunday roast lunches.'

'Ah I see,' replied Sally patting Joe on the shoulder.

Katie watched Sally tease Joe and saw her turn around to raise her eyebrows at her with a "told you so look". Suddenly Katie wasn't hungry anymore. Surely Sally couldn't be right, and she was the reason Joe had crashed lunch? She was spared dwelling on that for too long as Reg came in from the garden.

'Hello Katie,' he announced. 'Good to see you again. Joe mentioned you were coming for lunch.'

Sally looked at Katie and winked. Joe moved awkwardly from one foot to the other and said, 'can I help with anything Mum?'

'Crumbs,' Maggie replied, almost dropping the spoon she was using to baste the chicken. 'That's a first. You're not known for offering to help in the kitchen. I'm fine, love. Why don't you see if Katie wants a drink and set about laying the table?'

Before Joe could say anything more, Jenny and Sam raced into the kitchen.

'Uncle Joe,' they screeched. 'Come and see what we've found,' and dragged him out into the garden. As he left, he turned to face Katie and shrugged his shoulders smiling apologetically at her.

'Come on, Katie,' said Sally. 'Let's sort the table out. Goodness knows what those little monkeys have dragged Joe off to.'

As Sally passed a pile of cutlery to Katie, she leaned forward and whispered in her ear. 'See, didn't I say you were the attraction.'

Katie didn't have the chance to answer as Maggie turned around and announced that lunch was ready.

'Sally, can you call Joe and the kids in from the garden?'

'Yup' replied Sally as she walked towards the back door.

Katie then sat down at the table and watched as Jenny and Sam clattered in from the garden. Joe followed, looking ruffled but grinning.

'What was all that about?' asked Sally.

'Oh nothing, just stuff between me and Sam and Jenny,' replied Joe as he tickled Sam in the ribs and winked conspiratorially at Jenny.

As they all helped themselves to vegetables and Reg carved the chicken, Katie sat back in her chair and watched the scene. Jenny and Sam plainly adored their Uncle Joe. He had such an easy, relaxed way with them. There it was again, that imagining about what a great dad he would be. She hadn't had a chance to really process what Sally had been saying. Had she got it wrong and maybe Joe was interested in her after all? Her thoughts were interrupted as Maggie couldn't keep her curiosity under control and was demanding details of Katie and Sally's shopping trip that morning.

'Well,' said Katie, 'we certainly got a few ideas. With Sally's help, I think we have got the colour schemes worked out. Sally suggested a fabulous idea of finding some secondhand chairs and tables and painting them in a range of mix and match. This will bring some vibrant colour to the cafe area linking to the outside space. It will also enhance the vintage feel that Joe has created by using reclaimed wood.'

'Well, that sounds great,' said Maggie. 'How's Joe been working? Do you like what he's done?'

'Oh yes' said Katie enthusiastically. 'He's really captured the style and look I was aiming for.'

'Looks like you've got yourself a fan there, Joe,' said Reg.

'I am glad she approves,' replied Joe softly.

For Katie, it seemed that conversation around the table was suspended for a moment. She saw Joe staring at her. There was a look in his eyes she could not quite read. It was as if they were searching for something from her. What was going on? One thing was for sure, the way Joe was looking at her made her stomach swirl. It was a good job she was sitting down as she could feel her legs go weak. She was almost trembling.

The moment was broken in an instant as Jenny said 'Uncle Joe, when are we going to visit Katie's new shop? You've spent a lot of time doing stuff for it. I want to see it.'

'That is not for me to say. You will need to ask Katie and if you want to be invited, I suggest you ask a little more politely.'

'Sorry Uncle Joe,' said Jenny meekly. 'Katie, I would love to visit your new shop and I wondered when it would be a convenient time to call, please.'

Katie tried not to smile at the change in tone in Jenny's request, but she saw Joe wink at her.

'You would be most welcome. I would be delighted to show you around. However, we would need to sort out a suitable time with your mum as you have school during the week,' said Katie.

'I could come after lunch?' said Jenny eagerly.

'I want to come too,' added Sam.

'Woah,' said Sally 'you can't just impose yourself on Katie, she has things to do this afternoon.'

'That's true, I do because I need to start looking for tables and chairs, but I am sure I could spare an hour or so to entertain guests. Joe were you planning on doing any work there this afternoon?' asked Katie.

'No, sorry, Katie I haven't managed to talk to you about that,' replied Joe. 'The job I had booked in for next week cancelled on Friday which means I am free then. If it is okay with you, I can work in your shop instead and should be able to get most of it finished by the end of the week.'

'Oh my, that would be great Joe. Thank you. So, guys,' she said turning to Jenny and Sam 'it looks like I am free this afternoon. So, as long as we can sort things out with your mum, I guess you can visit.'

'It's not ideal, my lovelies,' said Sally. 'I have all those Sunday afternoon jobs to do rather than toing and froing with you two.'

Katie could see the disappointment on Jenny and Sam's faces. How wonderful children are with their simple views of excitement. I mean, how could they be so upset that they might not be able to visit her shop that afternoon.

'Well, you could walk back with me and I could walk you home later if that is any good?' suggested Katie.

'Don't be daft,' said Joe. 'I'll run you back after lunch and hang around to make sure these two little terrors behave themselves and then I can bring them back later. That means you can do your jobs in peace, Sally.'

'Crikey Joe what's wrong with you? You don't usually give up your chilled-out Sundays,' said Sally.

'There's nothing wrong with me,' said Joe defensively. 'I just thought I would help out. You should be grateful that I have freed you up, so you have the afternoon to yourself.'

'Alright you two,' said Maggie interrupting. 'No squabbling, please. You are setting a bad example.'

'Okay, okay' said Joe holding his hands up in a gesture of surrender. 'Just saying.'

'Now, who's for pudding?' said Maggie. 'It's apple crumble and I have cream or ice cream.'

'Yes please,' squealed Jenny and Sam.

'Am I allowed cream and ice cream?' asked Sam appealingly.

'Now there's an idea,' said Joe, 'the same for me please, Mum.'

As Maggie got up to clear the plates, Sally prompted Jenny and Sam to help.

'So' said Reg, 'if my lad cracks on this week it sounds like you might be ready to open soon.'

'It does, doesn't it?' replied Katie. 'I am getting anxious now, to be honest, but excited as well. There is so much to do. I need to order furniture and things such as cushions. I also need to finish off the courtyard ready for the tables and chairs. There is the decorating as well. I am not too bad at that but it's just getting it all done. I need to open as soon as I can to make the most of the visitor season.'

'Yes, I can see that 'said Reg. 'Look, I know I am a bit past it these days, but I am a dab hand with a paint brush. I wouldn't mind helping out. Now I am retired I am at a bit of a loose end and I am sure Maggie would like it if I cleared off from under her feet for a bit.'

'I agree to that,' she said, laughing as she returned to the table armed with a golden-topped apple crumble.

'Thank you, Reg, that's very kind of you. I will keep your offer in mind,' said Katie.

Katie looked across at Joe. He looked a bit put-out. She wondered how she had managed to offend him again.

Maggie valiantly served out the crumble. Katie watched as Sam tried not to look at how much cream and ice cream Joe was piling on to his crumble. He obviously wanted to match his uncle. Katie's heart flipped as she saw Joe recognise Sam's dilemma. He quietly leaned forward and picked up Sam's bowl. Katie watched as he loaded small amounts of cream and ice cream on to Sam's crumble with exaggerated movements. Katie could see that Sam was wide eyed with anticipation because, for him, the portions were the same as Uncle Joe's.

As Sally tucked into her crumble she said, 'It looks like I will be baking sooner than I thought if Joe carries on making progress.'

'Is that going to be a problem?' asked Katie anxiously.

'Not at all,' said Sally. 'I can't wait to get cracking. The one thing you haven't talked about is what coffee and other drinks you will be serving.'

'You've hit my weak spot, Sally. I am in a bit of a dilemma about it. I went to the cafe opposite the beach the other day to have a look. I couldn't ask if I could have a go at using the machines because that would have been a bit cheeky as I am setting up in competition! A few years ago, before I got the job at a publishing company, I worked in a café back in Sudbourne. I ended up working there for about a year and became quite good at coffee making, but the style of the machines has moved on since then. What I need is a revision course.'

'Hang on a minute,' said Maggie 'I might have an idea about that. I have an old friend, whose son, runs a café in a village inland. It's out of our area so there is no problem about being the competition. I'll ask her and see if her son would let you have a go at refreshing your skills on his machines.'

'Oh, thank you so much. That would be great if you could. He may be able to advise me on the make and type of coffee machines as well.'

'I'll give her a call later and let you know.'

'Tony' said Sally out of the blue, 'that's his name isn't it Mum?'

'Yes, I think it is. How do you know him?'

'Because he is known for being quite a dish and most single women round here would fancy their chances at hooking him. So, Katie girl, I would get yourself up there sharpish,' said Sally.

Katie saw Joe glare at Sally.

Sam tugged at Katie's arm 'is it time for us to go to your house now?'

Katie laughed. 'Let's check that's okay with everyone else first, shall we?'

'I'm ready if you are,' said Joe.

'And me,' said Jenny, jumping up from her chair.

'Katie turned to Maggie and said, 'thank you for a lovely lunch yet again. Hopefully if I am up and running soon, I will be able to return the invite to you and Reg, even if it is only for tea and cakes.'

'I am sure that would be lovely Katie. As I said before it was such a shame the shop got so run down, I would love to see it all done up again.'

'I am going to have a launch party. You and Reg will definitely be top guests on that list.'

'Oh gosh that does sound grand. We would be honoured,' replied Maggie. 'You run along now with Sam and Jenny, Reg and I can sort out the tidying up.'

Katie stood up and looked across at Joe. 'Are you ready?' she asked.

'As I will ever be, facing the prospect of an afternoon with these monsters,' he said, making a face at Jenny and Sam who squeaked with delight.

'What time do you want them back, Sal?' Joe asked.

'You will only probably last an hour or so with them running around the shop. So, when you have had enough, any time this afternoon will be fine,' replied Sally.

'It's turned out to be quite a nice afternoon, so we could always go for a walk on the beach or something as well,' said Joe.

'I'm sure they would love that if you can put up with them,' said Sally.

Katie moved to the hallway followed by Joe, Jenny and Sam.

Once outside Joe pointed across the road. 'My van's just over there. As Sam and Jenny are littluns, I reckon you can all squeeze in the front with me.'

And they did. Katie got in first and Jenny and Sam squeezed in next to her. Joe jumped into the driving seat and Katie found herself almost wedged up against him. That set her blood pumping.

'Have you got enough room, Joe?' she asked. 'I can always get out and walk.'

'Don't be daft,' he replied. 'It's only a short run back to your place. We'll be fine.'

As they set off, Joe moved into second gear and in doing so brushed the side of Katie's right thigh. Her reaction to that touch felt like a jolt of electricity. She instinctively drew away.

'Oh, so sorry,' said Joe, looking offended she had moved away from him so quickly. Katie was saved from having to say anything more as Sam shouted, 'are we there yet?'

'Nearly,' said Joe. 'We just need to find somewhere to park. 'What luck, there's a spot just outside the shop.' He parked and they all got out of the van and Katie opened the front door.

'Wow,' said Jenny as she stepped in and looked round. 'This looks amazing.'

'Joe,' said Katie. 'Could you pull up the blinds, so we have more light, please?'

'Sure thing,' said Joe. 'As I'm here I might as well get my tools. I can do a quick bit of finishing off on the shelves.'

'Can I help Uncle Joe?' said Sam, obviously not finding the bare interior to the shop in any way exciting. Helping Uncle Joe obviously was.

'Of course,' said Joe.' You can start by helping me in with my tools.'

'Come on, Jenny,' said Katie. 'I'll show you round and then we can make a drink for the workers.'

Jenny walked towards the back of the shop and traced her hand along the counter. 'This feels nice' she said. 'Is this where you will be serving mum's cakes?'

'Yes, that's right,' said Katie.

'She is so excited about working with you. She has promised me I can help her. Uncle Joe seems really keen on working with you too. He always seems to be talking about this shop. It's why Sam and I wanted to come and see it. I was surprised when Uncle Joe said he would come down with us. He usually can't wait to get away on his own on Sundays,' said Jenny.

'I expect he just enjoys hanging out with you guys,' said Katie.

'I think he likes hanging out with you,' said Jenny giggling. 'I think he wants to be your boyfriend. I'd like you to be his girlfriend. I sometimes think he gets lonely on his own. Mum has me and Sam. I miss my dad a lot. I remember him more than Sam. I know my mum misses him a lot too. I wish she had someone to give her special hug sometimes, like Grandpa gives Grandma.'

'Oh sweetheart,' said Katie 'I know you must miss your Dad. I miss mine too. He died when I was young as well. I was older than you, but I do know how it feels.'

Jenny suddenly put her arms around Katie and gave her a big hug. Katie nearly sobbed out loud, not just because of the sadness of both her and Jenny feeling the grief of losing their fathers but perhaps also because of the feeling of being hugged by this lovely little girl. There it was again, that longing for a child of her own. The moment broke when Joe and Sam came clattering back.

'Come on love,' said Katie gently to Jenny 'let's sort those drinks out for the boys.'

Joe looked across to Katie.

'Everything okay?' he asked. Katie glanced at Joe's face. She felt a tug in her stomach at the look of concern in his eyes. There was a connection between them. She could feel it.

'Yes, everything's fine. We were just having a girlie moment,' said Katie. 'I'll tell you later' she mouthed at Joe silently.

'Okay,' he mouthed back with a nod.

Joe and Sam set to work, and Jenny recovered her mood and helped Katie make some drinks. She took them over to Joe and Sam.

'How long do you think you will be working?' asked Jenny.

'Not too long,' said Joe. 'I just wanted to finish that last bookshelf.'

'Okay,' said Jenny. 'I'll have a look round with Katie.'

'Perhaps we can go for that walk along the front in a bit?' suggested Katie.

'Sounds good,' said Joe.

'Come on Jenny. I'll give you the guided tour. Let's start at the front,' said Katie.

Katie took Jenny round the shop, explaining to her what colours she had planned for each area and how she hoped it would look. Jenny took it all in and by the time they had completed the tour, Joe declared he had finished.

'Okay,' said Katie. 'Shall we go for that walk on the beach and then Joe can take you home?'

'Oh, trying to get rid of me, are you?' said Joe jokily.

'No that's not what I meant,' said Kate defensively. 'It's just I expect Sally will want them home to get ready for school tomorrow.'

''I know, Katie,' said Joe gently. 'I was only joking.'

'Sorry,' said Katie. 'I didn't mean to be snappy. Let's head off and get some sea air.'

As they walked along the coast path, Jenny and Sam ran off to the beach and raced down the pebbles towards the sea. Katie looked on anxiously.

'Hey,' said Joe 'they're fine. We can keep them in our view as we walk along.'

'Sorry again,' said Katie. 'I am behaving like an over-anxious parent. Silly really as I am not.'

'Not what?' asked Joe.

'A parent,' replied Katie.

'Nor am I,' commented Joe 'but I think we are doing okay this afternoon.'

They continued walking in companionable silence. Joe kept checking Sam and Jenny were in sight. Katie kept taking a sneaky look at him. She still couldn't work out if he was trying to spend time with her or whether it was just coincidence. After the comments they had made about being parents, she started daydreaming. To the outside world anyone might think that they were Jenny and Sam's parents.

She yawned. It was turning into a long day and the emotional strain of being with Joe but unable to work out how he felt was taking its toll. Not only was she dealing with all of that, but also, she had so much to sort, order and organise as her opening date was getting much closer. Joe must have picked up on her mood as he turned to her and said, 'you look tired, Katie, maybe it is time to call it a day and get those ragamuffins back to their mum.'

'It seems a shame as they look like they are enjoying themselves so much but yes, the day is starting to catch up on me and I still have so much to do. So, let's get them home.'

'Jenny, Sam time to go,' shouted Joe. Sam and Jenny obediently ran towards him.

'Do we have to?' pleaded Sam.

'I am afraid so,' replied Joe. 'Your mum will be missing you.'

'Okay,' said Sam as he took Joe's hand. Katie felt Jenny's hand reach for hers. She took it and gave it a squeeze.

They walked back to the shop where Joe had left his van.

'Right, you two, say thank you to Katie and then hop in the van,' said Joe.

'Thank you, Katie,' said Sam hopping from one foot to the other. 'Thank you from me too' said Jenny who rushed towards Katie and gave her a hug round the waist.

'You're most welcome,' said Katie as she gently stroked the top of Jenny's head. 'I will take you up on your offer of help. I am sure your mum and I can put you to work.'

'I'd like that. It would sort of be like being part of a club,' said Jenny.

'Looks like you've got another member of your fan club there, Katie,' said Joe as he indicated to Jenny to get in the van.

'What are you talking about Joe? I don't have fans,' said Katie.

'Oh, I don't know about that. There are a few of us around,' said Joe.

Before Katie could press him more about what he meant, he turned away from her to shut the passenger door of the van.

He then turned back to Katie. Katie gazed at his face. He had that look again. It was if he was about to say something but couldn't quite get the words out. Damn, he looked gorgeous. Joe eventually spoke.

'Right then, I'd best be off,' he said. 'Thanks for letting Jenny and Sam come and see your shop. They seem to have enjoyed their visit. I have too.'

Katie felt her stomach flip as Joe spoke to her. His deep brown eyes bore into hers. The words 'I have too' seemed to hang in the air between them. She didn't know how to respond to that without blurting out something she might regret. So, she took the easy option and ignored the comment and breezily said, 'No problem, Joe. It was fun hanging out with Sam and Jenny.'

Katie thought Joe looked a little disappointed at her reply but seemed to brush it off by saying 'I'll see you soon. As I mentioned earlier, I should be able to spend some time here this week.'

'Great,' said Katie. Once again, there was that sense of suspended silence between them. She longed to reach out and touch his face. His expression suggested he wanted her to. Katie wasn't sure and the moment passed as Sam banged on the window and then opened the door saying, 'are we going now Uncle Joe?'

'Yup buddy. On my way,' replied Joe.

'Bye, Katie' said Joe again as he got into the van and shut the door. Katie watched as they drove off. She felt deflated and empty. She went into the shop and locked the door behind her. It was late afternoon now. She shrugged her feelings off and decided to distract herself by getting to work on ordering furniture in time for the opening.

Chapter Seventeen

Back upstairs she settled herself at her usual spot at the table in front of the window and with a large mug of reviving tea next to her. She fired up her laptop and began searching for suitable sofas after her trip that morning. She became engrossed in the task. It gave a welcome break from overthinking the afternoon with Joe. Her work was a success and she had found some good deals with reasonable delivery times.

She looked at the time. It was nearly eight o'clock. Enough for today, she was done in. Time for a Sauvignon Blanc pick-me-up. She went into the kitchen to pour herself a glass. She sat on the sofa as she sipped the wine. Maybe there was something on catch up which would be sufficient to distract her. There wasn't. In addition to thoughts of Joe, there was so much else to think about. She still hadn't sorted out the coffee machine and other kit for the shop. She would speak to Sally tomorrow and see if she could sort out a trip to that café Maggie had mentioned today. She should think about an early night, but her mind was whirring. She was still full after Maggie's lunch, so she didn't have to bother with getting anything to eat.

The phone rang. It was Caroline. It seemed a while since they had spoken.

'Hi Caro, what a nice surprise,' said Katie. 'How are you?'

'I'm fine. Andy has his feet up and is watching football so I thought I would take the opportunity to have a catch up with you. So, what's been happening?'

'Crumbs, where to start. Well today has been a bit full on.'

'On a Sunday?' exclaimed Caroline.

'I know but things are moving so quickly. It's all a bit scary at the moment. I seem to be spending money all over the place and I've not finished. You know me, I am super organised, so I am keeping tabs on what I am spending, and I am on budget which is great.'

'I don't doubt you've got all that in hand. Your uncle left you a generous budget and I expect you will shave off a few bits and keep some for a rainy day. But you know Katie, I've got a good feeling about this. It's going to be a success. You're not aiming for the sky; you just want to make a living so you can stay in Broxburgh.'

'Exactly, and I do so want to stay here for all sorts of reasons', said Katie.

'Ah, which brings me to my next question. How is he?'

'Who?'

'Don't be coy Katie, it doesn't suit you, Joe of course.'

'I had lunch again with Sally at her mum's today and Joe was unexpectedly there. We ended up spending the afternoon visiting my shop with Sally's kids and then taking them for a walk on the beach' garbled Katie.

'Quite a member of the family now,' observed Caroline.

'I don't know what you mean!' said Katie

'Yes, you do. You like him, Katie, don't you?'

Katie lacked the energy to pretend anymore so she said, 'I think it has gone beyond "like". All those feelings I had for him as a teenager are still there and some. I keep getting moments when I think we have a connection and then the moment disappears. Sally says he likes me, and even little Jenny said so, but I have had nothing from Joe.'

'What did Jenny say? Kids usually pick up on things better than us grown-ups,' commented Caroline.

'She said that her Uncle Joe wants to be my "boyfriend".'

'Aww sweet,' said Caroline.

'Yes, it was,' said Katie wistfully, 'she is very sweet.'

'I don't know what to say. I reckon it will have to be you who makes a move. Remember you bolted before without an explanation. Blokes tend to hang on to memories like that. He may not want to get hurt again if what Sally says is true and he was really gutted when you left.'

'Maybe, but I haven't got the guts to do anything. What if it all backfired? Who would finish the renovation of my shop then?' laughed Katie nervously.

'Good point,' replied Caroline. 'Look, I know it is easier said than done, but just try and chill a bit and things will work out one way or another.'

'I know and I have plenty to distract me at the moment.'

'I am keen to come up some time and see what you have been up to, but things are a bit hectic,' said Caroline.

'It would be lovely to see you but don't worry. I am planning a launch party at some point. I would love you and Andy to come to that,' said Katie.

'Of course,' said Caroline emphatically. 'I really wouldn't want to miss that. Let me know as soon as you fix a date, and I can arrange a trip. Andy and I can make a weekend of it and find a cottage or something. We can be a bit romantic!'

'Sounds perfect and I am pleased things seem to be working out for you and Andy.'

'They are, actually. It's good.'

Katie was about to quiz Caroline about why exactly things were so good with her when she heard a rap on the door downstairs. Who could that be? It was gone eight o'clock.

'I'm sorry, Caro, but I am going to have to hang up. Someone's knocking on the door downstairs. I'm not expecting anyone, so I am going to see who it is.'

'Oh, take care, Katie,' said Caroline.

'I will, bye.'

Who on earth could that be at the door at this time? She was a bit anxious as she went down the stairs. Since she had been in Broxburgh she had been in a sort of holiday mentality and never thought of a threat to her safety. But horrid things can happen anywhere. There wasn't a peep hole on the door, but she could lift up the blind on the side window to have a peek and see if she could work out who her visitor was. She crept up to the window and looked cautiously behind the blind. It was Joe. He had his hands deep in his pockets. He was frowning and looked troubled as he shifted from one foot to the other. What's he doing here? Crumbs, she was exhausted but seeing him kicked off an adrenaline reaction. It had been such a long day. What she really needed was a shower and an early night. She didn't want Joe seeing her looking drawn and pale, but it looked like she didn't have much choice. She smoothed down her hair which she hadn't brushed since the morning. Perhaps if she relied on the evening light and didn't switch the lights on, she might not look so bad. Of course she would let him in.

'Hi Joe,' she said as she opened the door, 'did you forget something?'

'Sort of,' said Joe as he dramatically pushed the door open, stepped inside and pushed the door shut behind him. Before Katie could say anything, he added, 'I need to talk to you about something.'

'Oh, that sounds ominous. Is everything okay? Are you in difficulty in finishing the work on my shop?'

'No, no, not at all. It's not that,' he replied rather impatiently.

Then there was silence. Katie felt herself start to tremble. The feeling was there again, as if there was something hanging in the air between them. She was grounded to the floor staring at him. He was so gorgeous. His eyes were staring into hers as if he was trying to reach out to her. She was aware of the click of the feet of passers-by outside and the muffled conversations as they walked past. But inside it was like the world was happening somewhere else. Then he stepped forward towards her.

'Katie, I can't carry on like this,' and before he could say anything else Katie felt him lean towards her and slide his hand round her waist. She felt the pressure of his hand in the small of her back and then the pull as he drew her to him. She took a short intake of breath before he brushed her mouth with his.

Then his lips were on hers. Not a cursory brush but a full drag, tight and tantalising. Woah, his taste and touch shot a jolt of excitement through her body.

She pulled back. She wasn't sure why. She had wanted him to kiss her so much and her body's reaction had been electric, but she suddenly felt protective of herself. So much had happened today she couldn't quite take on anymore.

'Oh, I am so sorry', said Joe. 'I've got this so wrong.'

'No, no, you haven't,' said Katie urgently. 'I just don't know what to say. I am so tired after today. I don't know where my head is. I'm shattered.'

'I'm sorry Katie. I didn't think. I just went away after this afternoon and thought about you so much. I have tried to be professional and just concentrate on renovating your shop, but I can't help remembering us as teenagers. That was an amazing summer we had. But then you left so suddenly without saying anything.'

'Oh Joe, that was over ten years ago.'

'I know and I remember it, still.'

'Do you?'

'Yes, Katie, I do.'

'Don't be silly,' said Katie. 'We were so young and from what Sally and your mum have said you have not been lonely.'

'What have they been saying about me?' asked Joe defensively.

'Don't look so alarmed. They just mentioned that you have had a string of girlfriends but never settled for any of them.'

'That's true, I guess. None of them ever seemed quite right.'

'Look' said Katie. 'I've got a bottle of wine open upstairs, why don't you join me for a glass?'

'I'd love, to thank you,' replied Joe looking relieved.

As they walked up the stairs Katie's mind was in meltdown. She was trying to process what had just happened. Joe had kissed her and pretty much admitted that he had not forgotten her just as she hadn't forgotten him even after all these years. If she had succumbed to what her body had told her, she would be in bed with him right now. But something had held her back. It was not a reluctance to be with him, far from it. She instinctively felt she should hold back and test whether what appeared to be happening was real or not. She was sure of her feelings for Joe, but she couldn't risk getting it wrong now. There was too much at stake, not just her heart but the shop too.

As they reached the top of the stairs and went into her flat, she turned into the kitchen to fetch the wine from the fridge and get Joe a glass. Joe moved into the sitting room and she watched him as he walked towards the window.

'It's white wine,' said Katie. 'Is that okay?'

'That's fine. Here let me,' he said as he took the glasses and bottle from Katie and poured the wine. Then he took her hand and guided her to the sofa. They sat down and each took a big gulp of wine. Katie cradled the glass in her hand.

She felt tense and could feel the trembling starting again. It wasn't the wine. Joe broke her mood by saying, 'I know it is a long time ago now, but I still would like to understand why you left that summer without any explanation.'

'Sally asked me the same question today. She said you were really upset. I had no idea. The fact that you didn't try and contact me sort of confirmed what I suspected at the time that you didn't feel the same way as I did. It was a difficult time for me after my dad died.'

'Yes, I remember that too,' said Joe softly.

'You really helped me deal with all of that, but I thought I was pushing my grief for my dad to one side by being with you. I also came to realise, mostly because of the talking to from my Uncle Simon that I had been really selfish and not thought about how my mum was feeling. I felt guilty, I suppose, that I had been wrapped up in you. We were only what, eighteen or so? I took the easy option and ran away. I'm so sorry if I hurt you.'

'Well, that's an explanation, I guess. Maybe I should have had more courage and tried to contact you but, as you say, we were very young and didn't understand or know the rules we were meant to play. I still don't,' said Joe.

'What does that mean?' asked Katie.

In response Joe put his glass down on the floor and reached for hers. He placed her glass carefully on the floor too. He then cupped his hand behind her neck and gently drew her to him. This time there was no cursory brush of the lips as his urgency took over and his lips pushed onto hers. This time Katie's body couldn't resist, and she gave herself up to his embrace. His hand moved slowly up her body and she longed for him to touch her. This time, he pulled back.

'Shall we take this somewhere more comfortable?' he suggested.

'Yes,' said Katie, breathless. They got up from the sofa and this time Katie took Joe's hand and, turning the lights off on the way, she led him into the bedroom.

Chapter Eighteen

Katie woke the following morning to find Joe breathing deeply and still asleep next her. She turned to look at him. He looked so peaceful. She wanted to stroke her hand across his chest and trace around the toned muscles. She couldn't believe what had happened last night. Their lovemaking had been gentle but intense and deeply pleasurable. She was suddenly unsure what to do. If she woke him, the blissful bubble she was in might burst. What would happen next? She was anxious that Joe might have a change of heart and how awkward would that be?

She carefully crept out of bed and gathered up her clothes which had been discarded on the floor last night. She collected her dressing gown from behind the bedroom door and went into the sitting room. Sunshine flooded through the window as shutting the blind had not been on her mind yesterday evening. She closed her eyes and took a deep breath. Please make it work out with Joe, she whispered to herself.

She went into the kitchen and made tea and took the mugs into the bedroom. She found Joe awake and he lifted himself up to lean against the pillows. Katie was suddenly shy. In the "moment" last night and in the evening light she had not been conscious of her body, now she was. She handed Joe his tea and placed her mug on the bedside table and tried to get back into bed with her dressing gown still on.

'Hey, what's going on?' asked Joe. 'Now you've had your wicked way with me, are you ashamed to come back to bed with me?'

'No,' said Katie. 'I don't know, I just felt a bit different now it is daylight.'

'Katie,' said Joe. 'Last night was amazing and beyond my expectations when I turned up uninvited last night. You're gorgeous. So, get back into bed and let me explore that brazen behaviour again.'

Katie smiled and said, 'okay, have it your way.' Her shyness gone, she took off her dressing gown and slipped back into bed with Joe. They didn't drink the tea.

Afterwards Joe said, 'what's the time?'

Katie looked at the clock on the side table next to the bed and said, 'about five past eight.'

'Ouch,' said Joe 'I need to get moving. I'm working for this beautiful and talented woman at the moment who has a strict deadline. If I don't turn up on time, I may be sacked as she is very demanding.'

'Ha ha,' said Katie thumping him with her pillow. 'You're welcome to use my shower and stuff if you want.'

'Thanks,' said Joe. 'But I need to get my tools, so I'll head back to mine.'

'Okay,' said Katie. 'Can you see yourself out?'

'Sure' said Joe as he got out of bed. Katie watched him as he put his clothes back on. She felt the stir of desire all over again as she gazed at his broad lean back. She tried to pull herself together. Joe bent over and lightly kissed her.

'See you in about an hour.'

'Okay, bye' said Katie and watched him as he left the bedroom. She waited till she heard the click of the front door downstairs shut before she got up and headed for the shower. Relishing the feel of the hot water washing over her body, she reflected on the night that had passed. If it wasn't for the way her body felt, she might not have believed it had happened. The big question now was what's next? What if he got back home and had a change of heart? Katie was clear in her mind what she wanted, the question tormenting her was what did Joe want? She had got herself in deep and she knew she was serious about him. She had a lot to lose now.

She had cleared away the cold mugs of tea and the wine glasses from last night and was sitting again at her table with some toast and a fresh mug of tea. She picked up her phone. There were two missed calls and a message from Caroline. She had understandably forgotten in the heat of the moment that when she had been speaking to Caroline last night there had been a knock at the door. Caro would not know who it had been. She opened the message.

'*You okay? Worried about you now.*'

'*Sorry' Katie replied. 'It was Joe. He has just left.*'

She got a text back immediately. '*That was quick work. You okay? On my way to work. Details later. Xx*'

'*I'm fine. Just worrying what will happen next. Defo a chat later. Call me when you can x*'

Katie looked at the time. Joe wouldn't be back for another half an hour or so. Katie decided it was time for a blast of fresh air to collect her thoughts. She looked out of the window. It was misty and damp, so she grabbed a jacket and went out. She walked to the beach path. She breathed in the fresh sea air. She realised she had neglected her morning walk along the path and picked up her pace. So, what was last night all about? Katie stopped and stared out to the sea. She let the memory of the feel of Joe sweep over her. She sighed. She was fed up with angsting over what may or may not happen. Her life had turned around so dramatically in the last few months she would just go with it. If she got hurt again, so be it. She had dealt with that before and was stronger now. Anyway, she had so much to occupy her with the shop and she needed to focus on making that work, but the thought of having Joe by her side and in her bed sent a fresh tingle of excitement through her. She turned around and headed back, thrilled at the thought of seeing Joe again so soon.

There he was, waiting for her outside the shop sitting in his van with the window down. He jumped out when he saw her.

'Hey' said Katie, 'sorry, I thought you would be later than this.'

'As I explained earlier, I currently work for a very demanding client. I wouldn't dare be late.'

'Well,' replied Katie. 'You may find she gets even more demanding.'

'I am more than capable of dealing with extra demand,' said Joe gleefully as he moved towards her to kiss her.

'Not out here,' said Katie.

'Why not?' asked Joe, looking slightly petulant.

'Let's go inside,' said Katie as she opened the door.

As Joe shut the door behind him, he drew Katie to him. 'Look' he said. 'Last night wasn't a one off as far as I'm concerned. Was it for you?'

Katie was caught a little off guard by his directness. 'No, no, not at all,' she blurted out.

'Then why do you want to stay behind closed doors. Are you ashamed to be with me? Is a common carpenter not good enough for you?'

Katie raised her hands up to his face and placed them gently on his cheeks. 'Oh Joe,' she said. 'You couldn't be more wrong. The thing is, last night came as a bit of a surprise for me. I guess I am taking a bit of time to believe that you feel the same way as I do. I don't know, maybe I am being a bit silly, but I felt a bit shy out there.'

Joe put his arms around her and hugged her tightly. Then he pulled away and rested his hands on her shoulders. He stared straight into her eyes and said 'There is nothing silly about you, Katie. When I knew you all those years ago you were brave and strong, trying to come to terms with the death of your dad. I guess it was that strength which made you go

154

back to your mum to support her and face up to things. And then, when you so unexpectedly came back into my life, I have seen how brave you have been again, having the courage to take on this shop. I want to be around you Katie.'

'That's good because I want you around me too.'

Joe leant down to kiss Katie deep and long. She could feel the strength of his body hard against hers. Then there was a knock at the door. Joe released Katie as she went to open it. It was Sally who strode in and went straight to the back of the shop and put a box of cakes on the counter.

'Morning, Katie,' she said. 'While you were canoodling with my brother last night, I made a batch of cakes for you to try. Don't look so shocked. It's no surprise to me. I'm just more surprised it has taken so long for Joe to get his act together. You can put that face away, Joe. You've been mooning over her since she arrived and she over you, though she would never admit it.'

Katie laughed and holding up both her hands said, 'Okay, okay it's a fair cop. We've been rumbled, Joe. Let's look at those cakes. What have we got, Sally?'

As Katie moved over to look, she heard Joe say he would fetch his stuff from his van.

'Right,' said Sally 'I've made some chocolate brownies for you to try. I'll leave them with you as I have to dash.' Sally paused and took Katie's hand. 'Look, about Joe,' she started. Katie suddenly felt anxious. Sally might be about to tell her something she did not want to hear.

'He's really keen on you. He hasn't said anything specifically, but I know him. You're both single so what's the problem?'

'None really, I guess. I just don't want to get hurt or given the run around again like Gary did. The thing is, Sally I'm really keen on him too.'

155

'I know he has had a few girlfriends, but he never treated them badly or two timed. Anyway, remember it was you who ran away last time. So, from where I am standing it is more likely Joe is the one at risk!'

'A low punch, Sally but I hadn't thought about it like that.'

'Well hurt him at your peril. I can be a bit protective of my big brother,' said Sally.

'Warning noted,' replied Katie laughing.

Then Joe came back in.

'Talking about me?' he asked grinning.

'Of course we were. What else is there to talk about?' said Sally, smiling and rolling her eyes. 'Right, I'm off. Joe, remember I'm working the late shift tonight, so you are on duty with the terrors.'

'No problem Sally. I'll be there.'

Then he turned to Katie. 'Right then, best get on. What are you up to today?'

'Well, I need to research coffee machines and crockery. I still haven't ordered any and if we are ready to open in a couple of weeks that could be a problem. Where is that cafe your mum mentioned? The one owned by the son of one of your mum's friends. Maybe I could go and visit.'

'It's in Framsted, only about a fifteen-minute drive away. I've got some free time this week, so I could take you if you like.'

'That would be great. Maybe tomorrow? I should have more knowledge about coffee machines by then.'

'It's a date,' said Joe.

Katie walked over to Joe and kissed him gently on the lips. 'I'll be upstairs if you need me.'

'Mmm… I'll be up in five' he said jokily.

'Don't you dare,' replied Katie. 'I need you to be getting on with the job I am paying you for.'

'Yes boss,' said Joe, clicking his heels together with a mock salute.

The day passed and Katie made sandwiches and had a happy lunch sitting with Joe in the courtyard.   In the afternoon she sat reviewing coffee machines and amending her comparison spreadsheet whilst listening to the sounds of Joe working downstairs. Late in the afternoon he came up to see her.

'Hey, I am going to have to finish for the day. I need to get back to look after Jenny and Sam' he said.

'Of course, no problem. Let me come and see how you have got on today.'

Back down in the shop Katie walked round the shelving island Joe had built in the centre of the shop.

'It's fabulous, Joe, like all your work,' said Katie.

'Pleased to hear it,' Joe replied, grinning. 'Another day or so and we will be ready to decorate. I'd best be off, but I am sure Sally wouldn't mind if you came over later,' said Joe. Katie was tempted as he pulled her towards him and looked down at her.

'I know she wouldn't but given I was so distracted last night I have things to catch up on. So, I'll see you tomorrow, Joe.'

'Okay' said Joe, looking disappointed. Katie was pleased by his reaction.   He went and Katie returned to her flat thinking she had to put Joe out of her mind and start planning her launch event. The way things were moving she would have to have a plan and send out invites in the next week or so.   Her phone rang.   It was Caroline.   Katie smiled to herself. Caroline just couldn't help herself. She had to call at the first chance.

'Hey, Caro'.

'Hi, lovely. Spill the beans. I can't wait.'

'Gosh Caro, I am still in a bit of a daze. When we spoke last night, there was that knock on the door. Joe launched himself in and said something like "can't carry on" and the next minute he was kissing me.'

'So how was the sex?' asked Caroline bluntly.

'Aah romantic you,' said Katie sighing. 'Amazing, actually. Not surprising though, he is gorgeous, and Caro I love him.'

'I know,' replied Caroline quietly. 'That's been obvious to me for a while.'

'So, what next?' asked Caroline.

'I don't know. I spent some time fretting over whether this was real, but I have decided just to go with it. Joe seems really keen. Anyway, I have more than enough to distract me, planning for the opening of my shop. You are coming, aren't you?'

'Of course, wild horses and all that!' said Caroline.

'Fab. I had better go. I have stuff to get on with. I need to do some research as Joe is taking me to look at coffee machines tomorrow.'

'Well, he certainly knows how to show a girl a good time!' said Caroline.

'Cheeky. I'll speak to you soon.'

'You will. Take care, Katie, bye.'

Katie woke after an unexpectedly good night's sleep. She had been tired yesterday even before Joe had unexpectedly turned up. What with the shock of that and their blissful lovemaking she was not surprised she had gone out like a light.

She heard a knock at the door. Joe was here. She was ready for her "date" to the cafe to try and start her coffee revision course.

Joe opened the door of his van to let her into the front seat. She leaned forward and kissed him firmly on the lips.

'Missed me huh?' asked Joe.

'Maybe,' replied Katie coyly. 'Now let's get going. I am keen to crack on with my training.'

They drove off companionably. Katie remembered the last time she had been in the van with him that time when he had given her a lift to the station. She turned and looked at his strong hands once again gripping the steering wheel. This time she reached out and stroked his arm.

'Steady,' said Joe. 'You'll make me drive off the road!'

'It's nice Joe,' said Katie.

'What?'

'Just being together like this.'

'Yes, yes, it is,' replied Joe while still keeping his eyes firmly on the road.

They reached Framsted and Joe parked in the town square. As they walked uphill, Joe took her hand and pulled her into a cafe just at the bottom of a road leading up to the castle. It was in a good spot to catch the passing visitor trade.

The guy behind the counter turned around to greet them. Sally was right thought Katie. He was good looking but in more of a classic model way with his bright blond hair and blue eyes, not like her brown eyed rugged Joe.

'You must be Katie and Joe,' he said.

Mmm..., Katie and Joe. She liked that.

'My mum said you might come and visit. I'm Tony. Welcome to my cafe. Katie, come around here next to me and I can show what to do. The visitors usually start turning up about ten o'clock, so I've got an hour or so to show you what's what.'

Katie was stupidly nervous as Tony fired up the coffee machine. She made a few dud lattes for Joe but after about twenty minutes she exclaimed, 'I've got my mojo back! Here, Joe, taste this.'

'Not bad. Yup I would pay for this one.'

After that customers started to come in. Tony let Katie make a few more drinks so she could increase her repertoire before she declared during a lull in customer flow, 'thank you so much, Tony. It is all starting to come back to me now. Once I have bought a machine and with some more practice, I think I might be safe enough to be let loose on the public. Joe and I will head back now and leave you to it. Thank you so much for the training. If you ever get a day off, come out to the seaside and visit my shop in Broxburgh. Actually, I am having a launch party so it would be great if I could invite you.'

'Sounds good to me. You know where I am, so send me an invite. I would love to come. It is always good to see what my competition is up but Broxburgh is far enough away for it not to be a threat to my café,' said Tony.

Joe and Katie left and went back to Broxburgh to continue work and start to get ready for opening the shop for business. Katie had never been so scared but excited all at once.

Chapter Nineteen

Today was the day of the launch event. Katie woke up and turned to look next to her. She remembered Joe was not there. She missed him. Crumbs, she was so far into him. But today was her day, the day of the opening of her shop. It was only eight weeks ago she had started work. Joe had worked so hard to get everything ready and, in that time, she had fallen completely in love with him. She felt a bit queasy with the anxiety about the day ahead. This was not just one day; it was the start of her future. She breathed deeply and launched herself out of bed. Her mum was staying in a hotel nearby with John. They had been so supportive, but she couldn't help wishing that her dad was here to see what she had achieved. She was being fanciful but suddenly she could feel her Uncle Simon with her willing her on. She needed to get herself together and face the day.

The party didn't start until midday. Katie was pleased that her late nights and hard work and planning meant that she was ahead of the game. She was standing in her shop. Not just a shop but The Books and Bakes Shop. She looked round to see how it all looked. Gosh it was good. There at the front was the open window with a full view into the shop and beneath it the comfy sofa area. Her meticulous research into colour schemes had paid off. She had got it so right. She had used rust and gold at the front to create a relaxing, cosy autumnal feel. There were a mix and match set of scatter cushions for customers to relax into as well as throws laid on to the backs of the sofas to warm knees on chilly days. In the middle was the shelving island Joe had built with smooth rolled edges and stylish wooden book displays on top.

Then she walked to the back. This area was more vibrant than at the front. She had sourced a mix of wooden tables and chairs. They had all been painted in a range of colours between green and turquoise. Inside was the beautiful counter Joe had made facing out to the front of the shop. She opened the patio doors and breathed in the fresh morning sea air. The hanging baskets looked vibrant and full of colour. The pots were full of herbs and other plants.

Katie took a moment to pause and think about how far her life had changed in the last few months. That scared her a lot, as she had so much to lose. Not just the shop but Joe, Sally and their family which she had now become part of.

There was a knock at the door. She went over, expecting Joe. It was her mum and John. She tried not to look disappointed.

'Hey, sweetheart,' said Susan as she came through the door,' I thought you might need some help in getting things sorted.'

'Morning Mum. Yes, please come in.'

John followed her in. 'Wow Katie' he said. 'This is amazing. I can't even begin to recognise the place since we dropped you off a couple of months ago. You have worked hard.'

'Thanks John, it's not just me, I have had some help from my friend Sally and Joe of course.'

'Ah yes, Joe. Your mum mentioned him. I hope we get a chance to meet him today.'

'Of course,' said Katie. 'It's an opportunity for him to showcase his work.'

'Your mum seemed to think it was a bit more than that, but whatever you say,' said John smiling. Katie could see her mum glaring at him and John mouthing "what"?'

'Let's get on, shall we?' said Katie, changing the subject. 'We need to sort out some posies for the tables. There are some wildflowers outside in the courtyard as well as some

162

jam jars I have decorated. Would you be able to help with that, Mum?'

'Of course, it's a lovely day,' said Susan, 'good to see the doors are open already. John be a love and put the kettle on, would you?'

'It won't suit me,' he replied chuckling.

'Ignore him,' said Susan to Katie. Katie noticed how her mum grinned as she spoke. Since she had met John Katie had noticed how confident and happy, she had become. John seemed to look out for her, and it was good to see.

John dutifully brewed up and they sat outside sipping their drinks.

'What can I do?' asked John.

'Well,' said Katie, 'if you could sweep the courtyard and give the chairs a wipe that would be great. I was also wondering if you could be in charge of the prosecco. The glasses are in boxes just underneath the counter. Mum could help with washing them after you have finished the posies?'

'Sure, sweetheart.'

'There is extra prosecco in my fridge upstairs if you need any,' said Katie.

'Leave it to me,' said John. 'I am very good at looking after prosecco.'

Another knock at the door. It was Sally. Katie smiled as in Sally marched, in her usual strident way, her arms filled with a stack of boxes.

She put them carefully down on the counter. 'I have made smaller versions of the cakes to go with the prosecco,' said Sally. 'That way people can have more than one and get an idea of the range we can offer.'

'What a great idea,' said Katie as she opened the lids of the boxes. Inside was a range of beautiful mini cakes of the types they had discussed.

'Oh Sally,' exclaimed Katie, 'they look lovely and just the right size for a bite with a glass of bubbly.'

'Joe said he would be here in about half an hour. He is just dropping Jenny and Sam off at Mum and Dad's. They can bring them down later for the party. Thanks for freeing him up last night so he could sort out Jenny and Sam while I made these,' said Sally, as she waved her hand over the cakes.

'Actually, as it turned out, I wanted to be on my own. It was kind of a reflective evening. I still need to pinch myself sometimes to check all this isn't a dream. So much has happened to me in such a short time.'

Katie left Sally to sort out the cakes. She saw her mum go up to Sally and introduce herself and John and heard them praise the cakes.

She methodically walked round the shop to check everything was ready. The shelves were all filled with new books set out in the categories she had decided. It all looked and felt great to her. The courtyard basked in sunshine and the tables looked pretty with the posies. She hoped the customers would think so too and perhaps encourage them to buy something. She had kept a careful track of her spending and still had enough left over for her to live on for the next six months or so. Hopefully she would top that up, if she had a good season, to build up a reserve to cover the winter months.

The door opened and in came Joe. Every time she saw him again her tummy flipped over. He had been fabulous this last week. Working late with her to finish off a few snags to the renovations and helping her set up all the stock. He had become so important to her in such a short time. Her insecurity sometimes made her panic that things would not work out. But today she would concentrate on her launch and hopefully enjoy it.

Joe came over and wrapped his arms around her and kissed her full on the lips.

'Morning gorgeous,' he said, 'I missed you.'

'I missed you too and am glad you are here. Gosh, look at the time. My guests will start to arrive in half an hour or so, hopefully.'

'Anything you need me to do?'

'No, just hanging around looking handsome will be fine,' said Katie jokily

'Aah, flattery will get you everywhere, Ms Lewis,' said Joe as he kissed Katie on the head.

'Come and meet my mum,' said Katie, excitedly.

'Should I be nervous?' asked Joe.

'Let's find out,' said Katie, taking Joe's hand and leading him out to the courtyard where her mum was sorting out the posies.

'Mum, this is Joe.'

Susan turned around and Katie saw her face break into a warm smile. She held out her hand and said, 'hello, Joe. It is good to meet you. Katie has obviously mentioned you, not least to talk about the lovely work you have done here. It is a credit to you.'

'Thank you, Mrs Lewis, it has been a pleasure working with Katie' replied Joe returning the smile.

'I have no doubt about that,' said Susan in a knowing way.

Katie looked a little embarrassed and Susan noticed.

'I don't think arranging posies is quite your thing, Joe. Why don't we sit down with a cuppa and have a chat? You can then meet John and help him sort out glasses and prosecco,' said Susan.

'I'll sort the drinks out,' offered Katie, 'tea?'

'Great' they both replied.

As she made the tea, she saw her mum and Joe settle down at a table and start chatting. One less thing to worry about, but she hadn't really had any doubt they would get on.

It was midday and Katie could see her guests start to arrive. Peter Blankfield was first. He walked in and came up to Katie and kissed her on the cheek.

'Well, well, young lady what a splendid job you have done. This looks fantastic' he said.

'Thank you, Peter. I am rather pleased with it, I just need some customers now!'

'Oh, I'm sure that will happen. It is definitely something that will appeal to the visitor trade.'

'Yes, that was the plan, but I still want to encourage local trade too.'

Katie saw Joe coming towards them. He was frowning. Really, he can't seriously still be jealous of Peter? As he approached Katie noticed Peter holding out his hand to shake Joe's.

Joe took it and Katie saw the scowl disappear.

'Hello Joe,' said Peter. 'I was just admiring the craftsmanship of the work you have done here.'

'Thank you. It was a pleasure to work with this particular client,' replied Joe beaming at Katie.

'I'll take a look around, shall I?' said Peter.

'Yes, please do. Make sure you get a glass of prosecco and sample some of Sally's cakes.'

'I will and thank you, Katie', said Peter.

Over the next thirty minutes or so the guests continued to arrive. Katie circulated, chatting to them about the books and encouraging them to sample Sally's cakes. It was a good turnout. The shop was full and spilling out into the courtyard. Then she heard her name being called out.

'Katie, I am so sorry we are late. We had to drive up this morning. The traffic was atrocious coming out of London.'

Katie turned around and there was Caroline trying not to push anyone as she made her way towards Katie. It was the first time Caroline had visited the shop. Caroline's opinion mattered to Katie and she hoped she liked it.

'Oh my god, this is so amazing' she exclaimed reaching out and gathering Katie up into a big hug. 'I had no idea it would be so lovely.'

'Thanks Caroline, I'm so glad to have you here. Hi Andy, good to see you too,' said Katie as she saw him standing behind Caroline. He was always a bit in her shadow but seemed happy to be so. But there he was, tall and lanky with his pale skin and red hair. He smiled warmly at Katie and said, 'Hi to you too. It really is quite something. I'll go and grab a glass of prosecco. I'm gagging for one after that journey. I'll get something for Caroline while I am there.'

'Well obviously I am here to support you for your launch, but my main interest is Joe,' whispered Caroline in Katie's ear. 'So where are you hiding him?'

'Nowhere, he is just behind you.'

'Oh' said Caroline turning around abruptly 'hello.'

'Hi' said Joe. 'I am guessing you are Caroline.'

'You guessed right, and you of course are Joe. Good to meet you at last.'

Katie could see her mum waving her over. She was by the counter.

'Sorry to drag you away but we have few people who want to buy things.'

'Great' said Katie. 'I'll sort it out.'

Katie went behind the counter. Her first customer was Debbie from the library. She bought a cookery book.

'This isn't one the library has, and I doubt I can bake as well as Sally, but it is a lovely book,' she said.

Katie stayed for a while behind the counter so she could see how the party was going. As the party was an afternoon event Sally had allowed Jenny and Sam to come. Sam was sitting on one of the sofas with a drawing book. Katie had left some out on the table at the front of the shop. Something to keep children occupied while their parents browsed the books. She smiled as she saw Jenny carefully wandering round offering mini cakes. There was an expression of studied concentration on her face. She had been so keen to help.

She listened to the lively buzz of conversation around the room. There were familiar faces. Sheila, the book supplier, had bothered to come. There were others who could be useful for spreading the word about The Books and Bakes Shop. She saw David, the manager from the Greendale Hotel. There was also Susie who worked at the tourist information centre. She would make sure she had a word with them all. Susie was chatting or trying to chat up Joe at the moment. Good luck with that. He was well and truly spoken for. Time to break up that party. She left her mum in charge of the till and launched herself out there to network and make the connections.

All the guests had gone, and Katie was sitting in the courtyard with Caroline and Andy. What an event it had been. The number of people who had turned up was a lot more than Katie thought would come. They were probably just nosy, but it was encouraging anyway. She was listening to Caroline commenting on the people who had turned up. They were waiting for Joe to come back with fish and chips for supper.

'Who was that slightly hands-on bloke who kept coming back to chat to you?' asked Caroline.

Katie laughed 'I know who you mean. But he is okay. His name is Peter Blankfield. He was my Uncle Simon's solicitor. I know he seems a bit hands on as you say but he has been kind to me and a real help with getting me set up and settled here. He still manages to wind Joe up though.'

'I can imagine,' said Caroline. 'Talk of the devil, here he is with our chips.'

Katie heard a knock at the gate and got up to let Joe in. He put down parcels of fish and chips.

'Dig in,' he said, 'before they get cold.'

Katie unwrapped the parcels and went in to fetch some cutlery and salt and vinegar. She came back outside with a bottle of red wine as well.

'Who's for a glass?' she asked.

'Yes please,' said Joe and Andy almost in unison.

Katie turned to Caroline and went to pour her a glass. Caroline stopped her and said, 'thanks Katie but I think I will pass and stick to water thanks.'

'Oh, that's not like you,' said Katie.

'It's just I've just been drinking a bit too much recently, so I have decided to have a bit of a break,' replied Caroline rather casually.

Katie watched her. Caroline looked a bit sheepish as if she was hiding something. Then the penny started to drop. Katie cast her mind back over the afternoon. Whereas the Caroline she knew would have been first in line for a glass of prosecco, she hadn't noticed Caroline drink any at all. Also, she knew that she and Andy had been getting on well but now she thought about it they seemed really close. Katie had been so engrossed in the party; she hadn't really taken much notice of them as a couple. The only thing that would keep Caroline from red wine was either because she was ill or pregnant. The penny now definitely dropped. Caroline was pregnant. Wow, that packed a punch right in her stomach. How could she when she knew how much Katie longed for a child? She was angry. She knew she had no right to be but couldn't help it. Stop it, Katie said to herself. Caroline had not done it on purpose to hurt her. She should be happy for her. She locked eyes with Caroline and then suddenly couldn't bear the sight of her. She got up and bolted through the shop and out the front door, leaving a stunned Joe behind. He started to go after her, but Caroline stopped him.

'I'll go,' she said.

'What's going on?' asked Joe. 'Is it something I've done?'

'No, no it's not you. Katie's just worked out something I was hoping to keep from her for a bit longer and not spoil her party,' said Caroline.

'It must be quite something for her to react like that,' said Joe, concerned.

'For her it is but I need to explain to her. Stay here with Andy and I'll go and find her. It will be alright, Joe, I promise.'

Caroline found Katie. She was on the path by the sea staring out. She turned as she heard Caroline approach. She couldn't stop the tears pouring down her face.

'Why didn't you tell me? How could you? You knew how much it would hurt me.'

'Hey,' said Caroline trying to pull Katie into a hug. 'I didn't do it on purpose, and I didn't want to tell you before your party as I knew how much this would upset you. It wasn't planned either. It was just the result of a one glass too many evening. As you know I have never thought about having kids, but now I am pregnant, I am really pleased. Andy is too.'

Katie allowed Caroline to hug her. She pulled away and said 'I'm sorry, Caro. I am being terribly selfish. I am exhausted from today which doesn't help. Oh, crumbs what on earth will Joe think?'

'Well perhaps you should tell him how you feel. He may be sympathetic to the idea' suggested Caroline.

'Are you mad? We have only been together a few weeks and it's going really well. If I start talking about trying for a baby, he'll run a mile. I know I love him, but I am not sure how deeply he feels about me.'

'Mmm…' replied Caroline, 'maybe. Come on, let's get back and think up a plausible explanation before we get there.'

Back at the shop Joe asked Katie straightaway, 'are you okay?'

'Yes, I'm fine. I'm sorry, I just got overwhelmed with today. I am overtired and everything just caught up with me.'

Joe looked suspiciously at her, unconvinced but just said, 'well come over here and have a glass of wine.' Katie did and noticed out of the corner of her eye that Caroline was signalling to Andy to keep quiet.

'Look Katie, we'll head off now and leave you to rest,' said Caroline. 'It has been a great day, but you have to open properly tomorrow.'

'Okay Caroline. Thank you so much for coming and apologies again for my silly outburst.'

'Nothing silly about it,' and as she hugged Katie she whispered in her ear, 'tell Joe the truth about how you feel. I think he can take it.'

Katie watched Caroline and Andy leave. She was anxious that Joe might press her for more of an explanation about her outburst. But then she felt Joe's arms circle her waist. She leant into him and allowed her back to rest against his chest.

'Are you still okay for me to stay tonight?' asked Joe.

'Of course. Why did you think that wasn't okay?'

'Oh, I don't know. You just seem a bit distant after your outburst earlier on.'

Katie turned around and put her arms around his waist. What could she say? She was petrified of scaring him off by telling him the real reason for her outburst but then again it was a big thing for her. If this thing with Joe was going where she hoped it was, then maybe she would have to have to open up to him about how much she longed for a baby. She ducked the issue and kissed him instead.

'Let's go upstairs and finish this day off in our own special way, shall we?' said Katie.

'I'm all for that,' replied Joe and he took her by the hand and led her upstairs.

Chapter Twenty

Katie couldn't believe it was Friday again already. This time last week she had been preparing for the party. Now she was opening up for another day's trading. The past week had gone well. The launch party has spread the word about her shop and she was starting to build up a local, regular customer base who came in for coffee and one of Sally's lovely bakes. The tourist season was only just starting. The schools didn't break up until next week. But it was the weekend and Katie hoped there would be lots of day trippers who might want to come in and enjoy the experience of The Books and Bakes Shop. Sally was due in today with a fresh batch of cakes. If it carried on being this busy, she may be able to pay Sally to manage the shop for a few hours a week. She would probably end up with her looking after Sam and Jenny though. She didn't mind that at all. She had grown so fond of them and spending time with them helped her push back her feelings about having children. If she could get Sally to cover at weekends, she may be able to get Joe along too. They seemed to play happy families rather well. She still hadn't had "that" conversation with Joe. She hadn't spoken to Caroline either. She knew she would nag her about opening up to Joe about the real reason for her reaction to the realisation that Caroline was pregnant. She had fought against it, but Katie couldn't help her jealousy.

She heard a knock at the door. It was Sally.

'Morning,' said Sally breezily stepping into the shop. Katie closed the door behind her and asked, 'what lovely things have you brought me today?'

'More of the same,' replied Sally. 'They seem to be selling well so why change what works?'

'You are so right,' said Katie. 'We want to build up a reputation for the quality of the cakes and part of that will be keeping the brand consistent. Are you working today, or can you stay for a coffee before we open? I want to talk to you about making your hours a bit more permanent and maybe even paying you!'

'Okay, if that's the case I can definitely stay for a coffee! You sort that out and I'll deal with the cakes.'

Settled with their coffees, Katie explained her thoughts to Sally.

'Really I need help at the weekends when we are busiest. The takings have been good this week and if that continues, I expect to see some reasonable profit next week.'

'Well as you know I have more time for myself at the weekends. Mum and Dad are around and Joe usually can help out with looking after Sam and Jenny, although that might not be for much longer.'

'Why,' said Katie in a panic. 'Is he going away?'

'Don't be ridiculous. You're the reason. If you are freed up at weekends, he will want to spend time with you. He was moping about yesterday evening as he was helping with Sam and Jenny, so I could bake the cakes and he couldn't see you.'

Katie couldn't help but smile to herself. It was true they had become almost inseparable. He stayed with her most nights. He was so tender with her and their lovemaking was breathtakingly passionate. They couldn't get enough of each other's bodies. It was reassuring to hear Sally describe Joe's behaviour because she was feeling a bit insecure about the whole thing. She knew she was in love with him and wanted to be with him on a permanent basis, but he hadn't given any indication of his thoughts. He hadn't told her he loved her. When they were together, he certainly seemed as though he did. Then again, she had not been completely open with him about longing for a baby. It was still early days although she felt they had known each other forever.

'You okay?' asked Sally, jolting Katie out of her thoughts, 'you look far away.'

'I'm fine. Sorry. Look, why don't you give me an idea of what hours might suit you and we can take it from there.'

'Well, maybe Saturday mornings as a start. Mum and Dad usually spend it with Sam and Jenny anyway. So, how about tomorrow?'

'Sounds good to me.'

'I'll check with Mum and Dad and let you know if there is a problem. Otherwise, I'll be here about nine o'clock. I have to go now but I'll text you later to confirm.'

'Okay,' said Katie. 'Hopefully see you tomorrow.'

Sally worked things out and started working the extra hours. It made a big difference to Katie, as it had given her more free time to spend with Joe.

It was a Saturday morning. Katie was setting out the cakes ready for the day. She made herself a coffee and sat down in the courtyard to catch a few moments to herself before she opened up. Joe had left early that morning. He was working today. Unusually for a Saturday but it was an emergency job at one of the premier holiday houses. It was changeover day and so they needed the work done by midday. Joe didn't really like doing handyman work, but it was good money. She smiled to herself. He could be a bit precious about his work sometimes. She had laughed with him this morning about it, teasing him that repairs were beneath him. Well, that had led to one thing and another when he pretended to be offended and they had to make things up together in bed. Sometimes the strength of her feelings for him grabbed her like a physical assault. Things had moved quickly between them but then part of it felt like they had just picked up where they had left off. He had pretty much moved in. They had fallen into domestic routine. Joe quite often cooked dinner or they grabbed some fish and chips. She stopped her mind wandering and went to open up.

It was a gratifyingly busy morning. Her regulars turned up and some of them were always keen for a chat. She suspected they may be a bit lonely. They always left a generous tip in appreciation of the conversation. She had some day trippers come in as well. So far, her concept seemed to have taken off. Visitors to the town bought the tourist books as well as the baking ones. Her stock was apparently different to what was normally available in mainstream shops or online.

Katie noticed a rather smartly dressed woman come into the shop. She stood out as she wore a black trouser suit with a crisp white blouse. Not the usual casual Saturday look of her customers. Katie guessed she was about the same age as her, maybe a bit older. She spent some time looking at the books in the front of the shop before coming up to the counter.

'Hello,' she said, 'may I have a skinny latte please.'

'Of course,' replied Katie, 'any cake?'

'Definitely, they look absolutely delicious.'

'They are,' said Katie, 'there's no doubt about that.'

'Can I ask where you source them from because they do look special?'

'A local lady makes them and supplies them. Talking of which here she is,' said Katie, pointing to Sally as she came into the shop.

'Talking about me?' said Sally grinning.

'We were actually. I was just explaining to this customer that you are responsible for these lovely cakes.'

'Yes,' said Sally to the woman. 'I can claim credit for that. Why don't you find somewhere to sit down, then I can bring your coffee and cake over to you,' said Sally.

'Thank you, I will.'

Katie watched the woman in the smart suit drinking her coffee. She had chosen the mini banana pie. Katie watched the woman's face as she bit into the bake. She smiled with pleasure and closed her eyes, so obviously savouring the moment. Katie noticed she was looking round the shop and watching the customers. She finished her coffee and came back with her empty cup and plate to the counter.

'That was utterly delicious,' she said. 'It's a long time since I tasted anything quite so gorgeous as that and in such pleasant surroundings,' she added. 'I think I'll have a look round the outside and at the books you have on sale here, if that's okay?'

'Please go ahead,' said Katie.

Katie watched her again as she went outside and looked at the courtyard. She came back in and browsed the gardening books displayed on the shelf by the door. She selected one and brought it over to the counter.

'I'll take this please. The cookery books look tempting, but I am no baker, so there is no point in me trying to re-create the taste of that lovely pie I had. I do like gardening though. So, this book about herbs for medicinal purposes caught my eye. I've not seen anything like it anywhere else.'

'That's a good choice,' said Katie, 'would you like a bag?'

'Just a paper one would be great, thank you.' Then she paused, as if she was about to announce something.

'Perhaps I should come clean. I'm a lifestyle journalist for the Sunday Press. I'm preparing a piece about Broxburgh as a weekend destination. Is this your place?' she asked.

'Yes, yes, it is,' said Katie trying not to sound too excited. Katie introduced herself. 'My name is Katie Lewis' she said, lifting her arm ready to shake hands.

'I am really impressed with the experience you have created here so, if it is okay with you, I would like to include your Books and Bakes Shop as part of the feature.'

'Of course, it's okay with me,' replied Katie, unable to stop the huge grin on her face.

'Great. My name is Lydia, by the way. Here's my card.'

Katie waited until Lydia had left the shop before she called out to Sally.

'You'll never guess who that was,' said Katie.

'You're right, I won't so tell me,' said Sally.

'She's a journalist from the Sunday Press and she is writing a piece about Broxburgh being a great place to stay for the weekend. She loved our shop and raved about your cakes, so she is going to include a piece about us in the article.'

'No way,' exclaimed Sally. 'Are you sure?'

'Look, here's her card. She looked genuine.'

Then Lydia reappeared.

'Sorry to bother you, but would you mind if I sent a photographer round tomorrow to take a shot of the shop? It looks so lovely I think that it would enhance my article. Oh, and I might ask him to take a shot of you as well, as its owner.'

She turned and left without waiting for an answer.

'Oh, Sally I'm so excited,' said Katie. 'I can't wait to tell Joe. He's coming over this evening. Would you mind covering for me while I pop out and get something nice for supper?' asked Katie.

'Of course, but you spoil him, Katie. You should make him cook for you.'

'He does, sometimes,' said Katie. Sally raised an eyebrow in disbelief.

Katie was in her kitchen preparing supper. In the end she hadn't bothered that much. She was just making a Mediterranean dish by adding tomatoes and peppers to some chicken. Joe was lounging on her sofa watching what sounded like the news on the television. She liked having that domestic noise around her. She didn't watch much television. Most of her evenings had been taken up with planning for the shop or reading. Even now there was work to do in the evenings, checking on sales and keeping up to date with stock, but when she was on her own reading was always her first choice over television

She had told Joe about the visit from Lydia from the Sunday Press. He had been pleased, of course, but warned her not to expect too much until the article was published. He was right. Journalists often ended up printing things that hadn't quite been expected.

As she gazed at Joe, she felt her stomach flip over. Sometimes she had this feeling of doom that something in her life now would go wrong, and she would end up drifting and miserable again. She didn't think she could bear it if anything happened, such that she and Joe split up. What would Caroline say about her mopey thoughts? The news about the article was an excuse to call her. Things had remained a bit distant between them since she had found out Caroline was pregnant. She wanted to repair that. Imagining what Caroline would say stopped her brooding and made her smile. She called out to Joe.

'Hey lazy, how about getting up off that sofa and pouring me a glass of wine, there's beer in the fridge if you fancy one.'

He got up and stood next to her in the kitchen.

'Mmm…I do, but I fancy what's in front of me much more,' said Joe turning her round to face him.

'What, the dinner I'm cooking?' suggested Katie teasingly.

Joe's response was to place his hands on her shoulders and draw her to him. He kissed her deep and long.

'You're a temptress, how can a man choose between those choices?'

'You don't have to make choices, you can have them all but only in a certain order; so, wine and beer first and then dinner. You can have your dessert after that,' said Katie with mock sternness.

Katie and Joe were in bed after "dessert". She lay back against the pillow with her hands behind her head. Joe was asleep. She started thinking about tomorrow and the photoshoot. Not only was Lydia sending a photographer to take shots of the shop, but also possibly of her. What should she wear? Who would see it? Joe was right, she needed to calm down as the article might never be published.

It wasn't that late, but Joe was sound asleep. There was too much buzzing around in her head to allow her to sleep, perhaps it would be a good time to call Caroline. She would probably still be up at this time. She crept out of bed and went into the lounge, gently closing the bedroom door behind her so as not to disturb Joe. She the bit the bullet and dialled Caroline's number. She answered.

'Hey Caro. It's me.'

'Yes, I can see that from my phone,' she answered. 'It's late for you to call. Is everything okay?'

'I'm fine, I just wanted to say I'm so sorry I have not been in touch. I am still struggling, and I know that is not fair on you. So, how are you?'

'We're fine and just so you know we had our first proper scan yesterday and it's a girl!'

'Oh my god, I'm so pleased for you. Can you send me a copy of the scan?'

'Of course, I can, if you're sure?' said Caroline hesitantly.

'I am, Caro. Really, I am interested albeit insanely jealous, but now I've calmed down I want to be involved.'

'Good. I knew you would come around once you had had a bit of time to adjust. So, other news, fill me in. Have you had "that chat" with Joe yet, who is by the way gorgeous and so right for you?'

'No, I haven't. I know I am being a coward, but I think that if I tell him, he will run a mile.'

'I think you're wrong, but it's your call.'

'Anyway, the reason I called was to tell you that today a journalist for the Sunday Press visited. She loved The Books and Bakes Shop so much she is going to feature it in an article she is writing about Broxburgh being an ideal short break destination. Imagine the boost that might give to the business,' said Katie, full of excitement.

'Wow that is good news. You would get nationwide coverage with an article like that.'

'I know. Let's hope I'm up for the challenge. I'm having my photo taken tomorrow as well.'

'Crikey, I had better let you go and try and get some sleep. We want you looking your best for the feature.'

'You're right' said Katie 'it was good to chat, Caro.'

'It was. Call again soon.'

'I will.'

As Caroline hung up Katie put her phone down on the table and went back to the bedroom. She snuck into bed next to Joe. She curved her body against his back and fell into a deep sleep.

Chapter Twenty-One

Katie woke up with a start. Joe was not next to her but then she heard clattering in the kitchen. He was making tea. She got out of bed and headed to the shower. What should she wear today for the photograph? She closed her eyes and smoothed her hair under the running water from the shower. Suddenly she felt Joe's naked body press against her from behind. She turned around to meet his kiss.

'Hey,' said Katie, 'I thought you were making tea?'

'I thought making love would be better,' he replied. 'Oh' said Katie, 'love, is it?'

'Yes, yes, it is. So back to the bedroom with you so I can show you what I mean.' And he did.

Katie was setting up the bakes and coffee for the day. As she laid out the pavlovas and banana pies, she dwelled on what Joe had said in the shower. She hadn't really taken it in at the time as she got swept up in the passion when they went back to bed to complete their lovemaking. There it was, that word again "love". Okay, he hadn't actually said the "I love you", but he had said "yes" when she had asked if it was "love". She knew she was in love with him but hadn't quite plucked up the courage to tell him. She was still holding back about telling him how much she wanted a baby. Maybe Caro was right, and he would understand.

She had no more time to think about it as she was interrupted by a male voice.

'Hi, you must be Katie Lewis,' he said.

Katie looked up and saw a man about her age with slightly messed up brown hair. He had a big black bag hanging from his shoulder.

'Yes, I am,' she replied, 'and judging by the kit you have walked in with you must be the photographer from the Sunday Press.'

182

'I am.'

'Would you like a coffee or something and one of our bakes before you start?' asked Katie.

'Yes please, that sounds great. Just a plain black coffee would be good.'

As Katie busied herself firing up the coffee machine the photographer unpacked his kit.

'I'm Jake by the way,' he said, 'which cake would you recommend?'

'They all look scrumptious but maybe one of the sponges. They have a mystery filling.'

As he bit into the cake, Katie could see the expression of pleasure spread across his face.

'Wow. That is something else,' he exclaimed.

'Just on cue,' said Katie. 'Here is the lovely lady responsible for their creation.'

'You're not talking about me again?' asked Sally as she strode into the shop but then she stopped in her tracks.

'Jake? Is that you?'

'Crumbs, Sally. What are you doing here?'

'That's a daft question. I live in Broxburgh as you well know.'

'It's been a while, Sally. You may have moved on,' he replied rather sombrely.

'Sorry, I didn't mean to be so brusque. In answer to your question, as Katie said, I make the cakes for The Books and Bakes Shop and work here.'

'All I can say is that your cake was absolutely delicious.'

'Are you going to take a picture of me as well, so I can get my mug shot in the paper too?' Sally asked with a grin.

'I would love to take your photo,' said Jake rather seriously.

Katie watched them both as they chatted. Hang on a minute, she thought, something is going on here. I'll grill Sally about it later.

Jake then turned to Katie and said, 'I guess we should get started.'

Over the next hour or so Katie watched Jake work. He started at the back of the shop taking pictures of the courtyard outside. He took shots inside as well. He had a load of kit with him. There were flash heads for the lighting set ups and reflectors. He took pictures of pretty much every area of the shop. Katie also watched how he took every opportunity to glance at Sally. It was a Monday so things were quiet but there were still the regulars. They were happily sitting with drinks and cakes, watching the added amusement of the photoshoot. She was grateful to them as Jake had said he wanted to show happy customers in his shots, enjoying the books and bakes shop experience. Sally was at the counter serving them. Katie also noticed how pretty Sally looked today with her glossy blond hair circling her face and her big blue eyes twinkling as she chatted with the customers who were amused by the photography and interested in the upcoming article as Sally explained what this was all about. She watched the interaction between Sally and Jake. Was there something going on there? Katie had assumed Sally was too dedicated to Sam and Jenny to get involved with anyone. Maybe she was wrong and there has been someone since Jim died. Katie smiled to herself as she remembered Jenny's comment about how nice it would be if her mum had someone to hug her. Katie found herself mulling over what Joe had said this morning again. Surely what he had said meant he loved her. Perhaps it was time for her to come clean with him about how she felt and see where that took them. Her musing was interrupted as Jake called to her.

184

'Okay I am ready for you now. I think I would like to take a shot of you by the cakes but preferably without the coffee machine in the background. If you move to the end of the counter and lean against it, I should be able to get the shot I am looking for.'

Katie did as she was asked, and Jake started photographing her. He got quite bossy as he issued demands about how she should stand and how she should hold her head. The customers enjoyed the show until Jake finished with Katie. He started to pack up and casually turned to Sally and said, 'Maybe if you get a chance, we could have a catch-up drink sometime?'

'I suppose we could. Leave me your card and I can get in touch, if an occasion arises,' Sally replied rather unenthusiastically.

Jake rustled in his pocket and handed a business card to Sally.

'Right, I'll be off then,' said Jake, plainly disappointed by Sally's business-like response to his suggestion that they have a drink.

'Bye Katie. Thanks, you were great. Hopefully see you soon Sally,' he said as he left the shop.

Did Sally have history with Jake? She had never seen her behave like that. There was more to this. Katie was intrigued and, as Sally came back to the counter, Katie pounced on her immediately.

'What was all that about?'

Sally looked like a naughty schoolgirl caught smoking.

'Nothing,' said Sally. Katie raised an eyebrow.

'Really, it's nothing. Okay, I met Jake about a year after Jim died. He was kind and supportive but then things developed, and he wanted more.'

'Gosh, Sally. He seems really nice. Is he still a prospect for you?' asked Katie.

'He is nice,' said Sally. 'But as they say, it's complicated. I liked him but felt it was too soon to start another relationship. I felt guilty as if I was being disloyal to Jim. Anyway, that was about three years ago now. I have to admit that I have wondered how things would have turned out if I had made a different decision. It probably wouldn't have worked as we are quite different. I wasn't ready to get involved with someone else. I needed to make Sam and Jenny my priority which they still are,' explained Sally.

'You can take your mind off thinking about it by serving that group of people who have just walked in. It looks like a coach trip has landed and we need to make the most of it.'

'On it,' said Sally saluting.

Chapter Twenty-Two

Today was the day the feature about Broxburgh would be published in the Sunday Press and the article about The Books and Bakes Shop would appear. Katie didn't know what the article would say, and she wondered which of the photos Jake had taken would be published. After Jake had bumped into Sally again, Katie got the impression he was trying to rekindle things between them. He was a nice guy. Sally hadn't spoken to Katie about it but she thought Sally wasn't as keen on Jake as he was on her. It was early days, but things did not look too favourable for Jake. She hoped Sally would let him down gently. Assuming the article was favourable, they were going out for a drink tonight with Sally. Jake was joining them. Sally was such an independent woman. Joe had been a bit prickly thinking Jake was after Sally which was obviously true. She could understand that. He was being protective of his sister. She turned towards Joe who was lying next to her and she listened to him snoring as he slept. A wave of love came over her and it almost felt like pain in her tummy. They spent pretty much every night together now. It was only if Sally needed help with Sam and Jenny that he went "home". Often Katie would go with him and stay over at Sally's.

She got up. She couldn't wait to log on and see if the article was featured in the online version of the paper. She went over to her favourite spot, by the window and opened up her laptop. She felt Joe come up behind her and he gently massaged her shoulders and kissed her on the top of her head.

'I'll make some tea,' he said, 'while you pull up the paper.

'Thanks, Joe,' she replied.

Katie felt anxious but excited as she clicked on the link to the paper. As the pages appeared on the screen, Joe returned with tea. He pulled up a chair next to her as she selected the Culture section of the paper; there it was. The headline "Broxburgh, Superb Short Break Destination". Katie opened up the article about The Books and Bakes Shop. She gasped with excitement as she saw the interior shot Jake had taken.

'Joe look,' she said. 'This is fab!'

'I'll quickly get dressed and pop out and get the printed version,' said Joe. 'I reckon it will look even better than that in print.'

'Thanks,' said Katie. 'I'll read the article while you're out and see what they say about me!'

She started reading straightaway. The article talked about Broxburgh generally and the local hotels and restaurants. She read on as it described places of historical interest and local beauty spots. And then there it was, a description of The Books and Bakes Shop. She was just starting to read what the feature said when she heard the click of the door downstairs. Joe was back. She could hear him leap up the stairs as he burst into the room.

'Katie,' he shouted. 'Look at the picture of you. You look amazing.'

'Hey slow down,' said Katie. 'I haven't scrolled down that far yet; I was just about to read the review of my shop.'

'Come over here and take a look,' said Joe as he spread out the paper showing the article on the sofa.

'Wow' said Katie. 'I see what you mean. This is quite a feature.'

She greedily read the text. It described her shop in glowing terms. It talked about the decor and how the two different areas complimented the books on the surrounding shelves. Praise was given to the "experience" of being in the shop. The best bit, according to the article, was the experience of browsing the books and sampling one of the delicious cakes. Katie hadn't' mentioned to Lydia about how she had come up with the concept. She was therefore thrilled to see that the combo of books and eating cakes had worked. Plainly Lydia had picked up on this from her visit. Then she saw the picture with her leaning against the counter.

'My,' said Joe. 'You look more tempting than the cakes!'

'Thank you,' said Katie, turning to kiss him.

Katie carried on reading The article went on to compliment her and saying she obviously had great entrepreneurial sense for one so young. Katie could barely believe what she was reading. This was going to be great publicity. She then looked at the time.

'Crikey,' she exclaimed. 'I had better get a move on and open up. It looks like it may be a busy day. What are you up to today?'

'I'm off to do my coaching with the lads this morning. But I will be back by lunchtime to see how you're getting on.'

'Okay. I'll see you when I see you. Sally has offered to come down later. Jenny wants to come and help as well so you may end up looking after Sam,' said Katie.

'No problem. You know how I enjoy being Uncle Joe.'

He so obviously adored Jenny and Sam. As she showered and got herself dressed and organised, she wondered again if now was the right time to tell Joe how much she wanted children. Perhaps Caroline was right after all and Joe wants the same thing too.

Her thoughts were interrupted as Joe was about to leave. She kissed him goodbye and ran down the stairs eager to open up. As she unlocked the front door, she saw Nick from the deli opposite wave over to her.

'Great article,' he shouted. 'I'm jealous!'

'Thanks,' she replied giving him a thumbs up.

She went to the counter to start up the coffee machine and opened up the patio doors as it was dry and warm outside, and her customers might enjoy sitting in the courtyard patio. As she came back in, she suddenly felt anxious. She had a sense of fear. She realised she was nervous of everything being so good. Being with Joe was wonderful. Okay they hadn't really sat and talked about how they felt but it was only a few months into their relationship and so early days. The Books and Bakes Shop was doing well before the article. She was breaking even which was great as she had not been open that long. Now with this article she could get really busy and start making a reasonable profit. She just couldn't help feeling that her luck might run out and she couldn't bear it. She shrugged her shoulders and pushed the sense of doom from her thoughts as she could already see customers coming into the shop for a look around. It was going to be a busy day she thought. She smiled and went forward to greet her customers.

As predicted, she was rushed off her feet. A lot of the locals called in initially just to have a nose around but generally ended up buying a coffee and some cake. The visitors to Broxburgh were more lucrative as they were keen to buy a book as well as part of the "experience".

Joe was as always as good as his word and came back about midday. She was up to her eyes in serving and making drinks. He looked a bit helpless as he stood by the counter.

'Crikey Katie,' he said. 'I didn't expect there would be quite this reaction.'

'I know it's great, isn't it?' replied Katie.

'I'm really sorry,' said Joe looking apologetic but I've been asked to do an urgent job at one of the holiday properties this afternoon. It's good money and I don't want to turn it down. I didn't realise you would be so busy.'

'Don't be silly, Joe. I wasn't expecting you to start clearing tables. Sally's coming in a bit, so you go off and do what you have to do.'

With that she kissed him quickly and turned back to sorting out orders.

She was very relieved to see Sally walk through the door with Jenny at about two o'clock.

'Crumbs,' Sally exclaimed. 'Looks like you have been up against it!'

'You could say that. I haven't stopped all morning. I knew the feature would generate interest but not this much.'

'How exciting. I'll get stuck in. You take a break.'

'Thanks, Sally. I could do with one.'

'I'll start loading the dishwasher,' said Jenny grinning. She loved helping out and it was a pleasure to have her around.

Katie made herself a cup of tea and took it up to the flat. She flopped on the sofa grateful for the break. The response to the article had been brilliant. She knew it would not always be this busy, but it certainly had generated what she hoped would be a momentum. She would need that drink tonight.

She was suddenly disturbed by Jenny prodding her.

'Are you okay, Katie?' she asked. 'Mum sent me up as we wondered where you were.'

'Oh crumbs,' replied Katie. 'I'll come down. I must have nodded off.'

The day was over. Sally and Jenny had left shortly after they had woken her up. Katie couldn't believe that she had taken nearly £300 pounds, the best day so far. The drinks were on her this evening she thought.

She finished cashing up and went upstairs. Joe was already there slumped on the sofa. He grabbed Katie's hand as she walked past and pulled her on top of him.

'So, am I hooked up with a celebrity now?' he said as he kissed her.

'Yup, guess so, "Hello" will be doing a feature on us next. Now let me go as I need to get ready. We are meeting Sally and Jake at the pub at seven.'

'I'll never let you go,' he whispered as Katie tried to get up. Katie looked into Joe's eyes. He looked back with an intensity she had not seen before. Was this it, the moment when he said he loved her and she told him she felt the same? She could feel the blood rushing to her head as she was about to reply. Then suddenly she heard his phone ring.

'Damn,' said Joe. 'Who the hell's that?' He looked at his phone. 'It's Sally,' he said. 'Guess I had better answer it.'

Katie listened as Joe answered the phone and spoke to Sally. She smiled to herself as she heard Sally's slightly bossy tone reminding her brother that they were due to meet at seven. She also heard the irritation in Joe's voice when he told her they would not be late. She was envious of the sibling banter. If she was right about what Joe had said then, one day, she might be part of that family and that would mean becoming Sally's sister-in-law. Stop it. What he had said in the shower this morning was not a proposal. She knew she loved Joe and wanted to spend the rest of her life with him, but it was still too soon to be making those sorts of decisions. Her thoughts were abruptly broken as Joe came off the phone.

'She can be a bossy so and so sometimes,' said Joe.

'No comment,' said Katie 'so we best get cracking before we are in more trouble.'

'Okay boss,' said Joe tapping her lightly on her bum.

With that she headed off for a shower and to prepare for the evening.

Katie was at the bar in the White Hart. She had said the drinks were on her so here she was getting the round in; beer for the boys and gin and tonics for her and Sally. That said Katie wasn't sure she really fancied a drink. That wasn't like her, but her tummy felt a bit unsettled. It was probably just the result of such a busy day and the excitement of it all. She also saw Joe staring at Jake talking to Sally. Honestly, he needed to stop being so grumpy about Jake. He seemed like a really nice chap and was plainly into Sally, but Sally plainly wasn't into him. Katie put the drinks down on the table and snuggled in next to Joe. She put a reassuring hand on his leg and whispered in his ear.

'She will be fine. Trust me, Jake is not on the agenda. Just chill and drink your beer and help me celebrate my day.'

'You're right, I'm sorry,' he replied and kissed her on the lips and turned to chat to Jake. Katie looked around her. She had a sudden flashback to the time all those years ago when she had first laid eyes on Joe when he had walked into that pub. She trembled with the memory of it. Funny how life swings around. Here she was with Joe and Sally pretty much like it was back then. Then her tummy turned over again and she had that gloomy feeling again, like this was all too good to last. Perhaps she would stick to plain tonic for the rest of the evening. If she got the rounds in, no one would notice she was missing gin in her tonic.

Jake ended the evening by suggesting they grab some chips on the way home. He seemed resigned to being just a "friend" to Sally.

So, they made their way out for fish and chips on an evening still warm enough to sit on a bench by the sea. A great way to finish a successful day.

Chapter Twenty-Three

On a sunny morning in early August, Katie was setting up ready to meet her first customers of the day. She had certainly had plenty of visitors since the article had been published.

Joe was away for a few days. He had volunteered to teach at a residential football coaching course. She expected to be busy today which should distract her from missing him too much.

Her Saturday regulars started to filter in. She chatted to them as she served their drinks and encouraged them to choose from Sally's fresh batch of bakes. The morning whizzed past and suddenly it was early afternoon and Sally breezed in.

'Hello,' she said, 'how's it been today? You look busy.'

'I am and so glad to see you,' said Katie with relief in her voice.

'You go and take a pew,' said Sally. 'I'll make you a cuppa.'

'Thanks,' replied Katie 'but before you do, there is something I want to run past you.'

'That sounds ominous,' said Sally.

'Oh, it's nothing sinister,' said Katie. 'I just wanted to run by you some ideas about getting more help.'

'I agree, we certainly need some. Ever since that article the momentum really seems to have taken off and it doesn't look like letting up any time soon. What did you have in mind?'

'Possibly someone quite junior. What I think we need, is someone to help serving and clearing up. We want someone with a sunny personality who gets on with our regulars.'

'I'll have a think and ask around a bit. Sounds like a great weekend job.'

'That's what I thought,' said Katie.

Katie turned around to make the next order of coffee, so she did not see the next customer come in. All she heard was Sally coming up next to her and whispering,

'I'm just going to tidy the books at the front. Some bloke has just come in who doesn't look like our usual touristy visitor.'

'Right you are,' said Katie as she carried on frothing up the milk for the lattes that had been ordered.

Sally came back. 'All okay, I think. He's just a bit smarmy for my liking.'

Katie turned around to place the lattes on the counter ready for serving. Then she saw the man Sally had been talking about. If she had not already put the mugs down, she would have dropped them.

'What the hell is he doing here?' she exclaimed.

'You know him?' asked Sally.

'Oh yes,' replied Katie. 'I know him alright. That's Gary, my ex. And one thing is for sure, your instincts were right, Sally. He's up to no good.'

Katie was in shock. She thought she had said goodbye to her old life. She felt anxious and disappointed in herself that Gary still had the ability to undermine her confidence and make her feel inadequate just at the sight of him. She sighed and drew in a deep breath. She had achieved so much in the last few months. She wasn't going to let her scummy ex-boyfriend ruin things for her.

'Well, well,' announced Gary, 'fancy seeing you here.'

Katie looked at him in disbelief. How corny was that? She steeled herself against him.

'Gary,' she said smoothly. 'What a surprise. Are you and your family visiting for the weekend?'

'No, I am here all on my own,' he replied. 'The family is in London. Traveling with babies is such a pain with all the baggage which seems to come with them.'

Gary hadn't changed. He was just as selfish as she remembered. The thought of how much of her life she had wasted on him depressed her. It was funny how she saw things so differently once she was distanced from her former relationship with him. She found herself feeling quite sorry for Tara, having to cope with twin babies with probably limited support from Gary. That said, the familiar pang of jealousy shot through her, twins, how lovely.

Gary interrupted her thoughts.

'I have to say, this place certainly looks as smart as it was presented in that article, I saw in the paper a few weeks ago. You must be making a packet out of all this. I heard a rumour that you had inherited something, but I didn't really give it a thought. I never would have thought you had it in you, Freckleface, to make a go of something like this,' said Gary.

She hated that nickname he had for her. It really got to her. Years ago, when they were first together, she had thought it was a term of endearment. Now she understood it wasn't. He mocked her by using it.

'I don't understand why that is any of your business.' Katie heard Sally say sharply. Katie chuckled to herself, good old Sally; she gets it and is ready to tackle him head on. Then the penny dropped. Gary was true to type. Gary was here for money. It was always about money with Gary. He must have got it into his head that she had acquired money to which he had some misplaced claim. He must have seen the article which presented her as a successful businesswoman. And lo and behold here he was, all bright and breezy as if the acrimony between the two of them had never happened. She didn't know how things were going to play out, but as the saying went "forewarned is forearmed". So, she broke into a broad smile and said, 'can I get you anything?'

'A cappuccino would be lovely, thank you, and I might try one of those yummy looking cakes,' said Gary.

'Go and find a seat and I'll bring them over,' said Katie.

Katie watched Gary as he glanced around the shop, taking stock. If he thought he could bully her into giving him some money, he was mistaken. She was a different girl these days, not that submissive one he used to know.

Katie took his coffee and cake over to him. She could feel Sally frowning behind her but what could she do? She couldn't ask him to leave or perhaps she should. She put the coffee on the table and turned to go back to the counter. Gary grabbed her hand and said, 'why don't you sit with me for a bit?'

Katie snatched her hand away and looked at him. He had that childish grin on his face which used to make her go all soft. It didn't now but somehow, she felt she couldn't be bothered to be mean to him, so she said, 'Okay. Just for a bit, but I am busy'.

'I can see that' he said, 'but you've got someone helping you. So, what's the problem?'

Katie sat down opposite him. He looked pretty much the same. He still had that false suntanned tinted face and short light blond hair. He was handsome in a traditional kind of way with piercing blue eyes, so different to Joe. She felt guilty sitting with Gary, as though she was being disloyal to Joe in some way. That was silly as she wasn't doing anything wrong, but she was glad she had her back to Sally, because she could feel her eyes glaring at her. That made her blush which annoyed her as Gary plainly misinterpreted it as he said, 'am I making you feel uncomfortable?'

She tackled him head on.

'No of course not, Gary. Why would you? Look, tell me why you are really here. I just don't believe it is some random chance that you chose Broxburgh for a little bit of "me time".'

'Ouch,' replied Gary, 'you've changed. That's not the reaction I would have expected from the Katie I used to know. I like it,' he said.

Katie watched him as he leaned back on the chair and ran his eyes over her as if he was sizing her up. She didn't like the way it made her feel. He unnerved her.

'Look Gary, I need to get on so if you have something to say then just say it.'

'Oh, I won't bother you if you are working, but I am around for a few days, so perhaps I could pop back when you are free, and we could have a drink together and a chat for old times' sake.' He got up and left without giving her a chance to respond or offering to pay for the coffee and cake.

Sally had served the customers and Katie could see from her face that she was in for a grilling as she walked back to the counter.

'Don't even begin to say what I think you are going to say,' said Katie. 'I really don't need to be told. Gary was always pretty easy to read, but I was just too pathetic to see it. He saw the article in the paper and thinks that somehow because of our previous relationship he has some entitlement to a slice of my success.'

'I hope you're not going to fall for it,' said Sally.

'No of course not. But I do want to get rid of him. Knowing he's nearby makes me anxious and I hate the way he is still able to make me feel like that.'

'Be careful, Katie. I only managed to gain a swift view of him, but it wasn't good. He's a snake waiting in the grass.'

'It will be okay, I'm sure' said Katie slightly unconvincingly.

She was rescued from more grilling from Sally, as more visitors came in and needed attention.

Chapter Twenty-Four

Katie was in her flat. She had just come off the phone after speaking to Joe. She really missed him, and he missed her too, but the course was going well, and he would be back in a few days. She hadn't mentioned anything about Gary turning up. There wasn't really anything to say. She was hoping she had seen the last of him after he had left the shop, so rudely, expecting her to bear the cost of the coffee. She knew she had asked him if he had wanted anything, but it had annoyed her that he had not at least offered to pay. There, he was getting to her again. She shouldn't let his visit wind her up. But it was hard not to. If her instincts were right, he would be back. He was after something.

Her phone rang. She suddenly panicked that it might be Gary, but then remembered he did not have her mobile number. It was Caroline. She breathed a sigh of relief and answered the phone.

'Hi Caro,' said Katie.

'Hi. You okay? You sound a bit weird,' said Caroline.

'I'm okay, I think. I'm just a bit thrown as Gary turned up today.'

'Blimey, that's big enough news to make me go into labour,' said Caroline.

'Please don't,' said Katie laughing, 'but yes, you know me and you're right, he has shaken me up.'

'How's Joe dealing with it? He can be a bit clingy, can't he? In a good way, mind,' she said hastily.

'I haven't told him. He's away this week. We've been in touch obviously, but I've not said anything about Gary turning up. There didn't seem much point.'

'Whoah, steady on, Katie,' said Caroline. 'From what I remember Gary could not be trusted. Although

200

you never saw that when you were in a relationship with him.'

'I know. But I feel different now. At first, as soon as I saw him, he made me feel like I used to. You know, not worth very much and like I should be grateful for his attention. But then he got on my nerves expecting me to drop everything and sit and chat with him as if nothing had happened between us.'

'Well, he did always like to be the centre of attention.'

'Anyway, I realised I didn't care what he thought of me anymore. He picked up on that as he looked at me differently, sort of surprised. He's up to something. I'm sure of it.'

'Watch out,' said Caroline. 'He'll be after money. I've said it before, he was always after a quick buck.'

'You know, Caro, you're probably right. He seemed impressed with my shop and made some snippy remark about me making a "packet" out of it all.'

'There you go, so predictable.'

'Well, I've got the measure of him now, so I won't let him bully me.'

'Good for you.'

'Enough of me,' said Katie 'How are you?'

'Good, near our time now. The consultant says everything is ready for delivery. I just want it over and can't really get my head around it. It doesn't seem very real.'

'Oh Caro, I am so jealous but also so delighted for you.'

'I know, Katie. Make sure you call me if you get a wobbly moment with Gary and tell Joe he's turned up the next time you speak to him. I know there's nothing in it, but you don't want him to misinterpret anything. Joe can be a little jealous about other men around you sometimes.' said Caroline.

'Yeah, I know but I'm sure all will be fine. Take care of yourself, Caro.'

'Bye.'

It was late and Katie was tired, so she switched the lights off and headed off to bed. She was woken up by a thudding sound. Roused from sleep she didn't immediately work out what it was. Then as the thudding started again, she realised someone was knocking on the door. Perhaps Joe was back early? But he wouldn't knock as he had keys. She crept out of bed and went over to the window at the front. She knelt down and looked out just above the windowsill. She could just about see someone on the pavement below. Then she worked out who it was as the figure reeled back and nearly fell into the road. It was Gary, looking a bit unstable. She guessed he had had one too many beers. She ducked down to hide just in case he could see movement at the window. She waited. The knocking stopped and when she peeped another look there was no sign of Gary. She got up and went back to bed. She was shaken up by it all but closed her eyes and tried to get back to sleep. What on earth was Gary playing at? It looked like it might not be so easy to send him packing as she thought. Eventually after thinking of Joe and some deep breathing she went back to sleep.

The following day she was on edge. She stayed at the back of the shop. Eventually she was busy with customers, so she didn't notice when Gary came in. She was just wiping a table when she turned around and bumped into him.

'Gary,' she shrieked. 'What the hell are you doing here?'

'Ah, pleased to see me then,' he said grinning at her. That made her cross.

'How dare you creep up on me like that. Particularly when I am working.'

'Don't be cross, Freckleface'

Grrr, that nickname again. That only made her even more mad.

'Don't call me that, Gary. My name is Katie.'

'My, you are prickly. You never used to be like that.'

'Gary, what do you expect?' said Katie. 'We split up over two years ago when you went off with Tara. I've moved on with my life and made a new one for myself here. You never tried to get in touch before so why you have decided to pay me a visit now?'

Before he could answer, Katie was distracted by more customers.

'Look Gary, you're getting in my way and I need to serve these customers. So, I would appreciate it if you would leave now unless you want to purchase something.'

She turned her back on Gary and moved towards the front of the shop to welcome the customers. More customers followed so she was kept busy and didn't notice Gary leaving with a scowl on his face.

At the end of day as she was tidying up, she wondered if Gary had got the message that there was no point in trying to see herm, whatever his motive was. She hoped so. She would be speaking with Joe later. Perhaps she should mention Gary to him.

In the end she didn't. Joe had been so full of the course and how well it was going that she just felt there was no need to mention it to him. She was sure she could sort things out and send Gary on his way if he turned up again. She could then tell Joe all about it once he was back.

Sally was in the following day.

'So,' she said. 'Have we seen the last of the dastardly Gary or is he still lurking about nearby?'

'To be honest, Sally, I don't know. I told him not to pester me yesterday as I was busy with customers, but I can't be certain he got the message.'

'Well, he struck me as someone who was here with a purpose so you might not be so lucky. What do you think he is after?'

'Certainly not a reconciliation, I think he has some idea in his head that he is entitled to a slice of my inheritance.'

'Why on earth would he think that?'

'I'm not sure but I know him and see his character flaws more clearly now. He's not a bad man. Okay he was a bit controlling but to an extent I let him, and I think that comes from his low self-esteem. He has to show off to sort of prove himself somehow. It's a bit pathetic really.'

'If he turns up again today, I'll send him away with a flea in his ear,' said Sally.

'Thanks, Sally, but on this one I think I am ready to fight my own battle.'

'Okay but let me know if you change your mind and need a bit of back up.'

The day passed. Customers came and went, and Sally finished her shift.

'Bye, Katie' she said. 'I'm back in on Friday. Joe's course finishes then, doesn't it? So, he should be back then.'

'Yes, that's right' replied Katie. 'I can't wait.'

'See you then.'

Katie said goodbye to the last customer before she was about to lock up and tidy up at the end of the day. Then she heard someone come in through the door.

'So sorry but we are closed now,' she shouted.

'It's only me.' It was Gary. In her heart she had known he would come back, but his surprise entrance unnerved her. He unsettled her and somehow made her feel as though something was about to go wrong, but she couldn't exactly work out what. She took a deep breath and gave herself a talking to. He was nothing to do with her anymore. He had made the decision to go off with Tara. She was no longer under his influence and did not owe him anything. She turned around to face him.

'Hello,' she said cheerily. 'What do you want?'

'Well, that's to the point,' said Gary. 'Aren't you pleased to see me?'

Katie was astounded. Was he really that delusional? Did he genuinely think that after all that had happened, she was still interested in him? She looked at him. He looked all puffed up and pleased with himself. Time to burst the balloon.

'The truthful answer Gary is, no, I am not pleased to see you. So, I'll ask again why have you suddenly turned up in Broxburgh after we split up nearly two years ago, when you left me for Tara? You must be after something?'

'Now, now Katie,' he said, 'no need to be so nasty'.

'I'm not, I am just asking a simple question. What do you want?'

'Okay,' said Gary. 'Look, why don't we sit down and have a chat?'

Katie didn't want him in her shop or to be on her own with him. She felt uncomfortable as if he would get the upper hand of the situation somehow. She needed to get him out of the shop and into a public space. She had to get her act together and stand up to Gary who was, Katie now realised, weak, materialistic and opportunistic. The brave new businesswoman she had become, could take him on.

'Look Gary I have had a long day. I am not sure we have a lot to talk about, but I am more than ready for a glass of wine. There is a nice bar just down the road which looks out over the high street. Why don't you join me for a drink and then we can say our goodbyes?'

'Yeah, I fancy a beer, so I'll take you up on your offer.'

Katie rolled her eyes. So, she would be paying then. Fortunately, Katie had left her handbag behind the counter. She didn't want to risk leaving Gary on his own to snoop about even if it was only for a few minutes while she went upstairs.

Katie checked the doors at the back were locked and then turned to Gary and said 'Come on then. Let's go.'

The bar was only a short distance away so there was not much time to fill with conversation while they walked there. The tables at the front were all full. They found one slightly set back from the window in the middle of the bar which still had a view through to the high street.

Gary sat down. Katie was not surprised.

'So, Gary what would you like?' asked Katie.

'I dunno, a bottle of decent beer? A Peroni or something like that?'

No "please" or "thank you". Ah well, she just had to concentrate on getting rid of him. Katie went up to the bar and ordered Gary's beer. She had lied to Gary. She was not desperate for a glass of wine. She did not fancy one at all. She had that unsettled feeling in her stomach again. She had woken up with it this morning as well. It was probably the anxiety around Gary which was causing it. She ordered a mineral water and asked for it in a gin glass with a slice of lemon, so she could fob Gary off by pretending it was a gin and tonic. They could sort out the bill out later.

She returned to the table and set the drinks down. There was no point in small talk and the best thing to do would be to take Gary head on.

'So, Gary, further to what I asked earlier, why are you here?'

'Hey, that's no way to be,' he said. 'We had a lot of fun together so why shouldn't old friends share a drink together.'

'That's because we are not "old friends" as you put it. We were boyfriend and girlfriend for nearly seven years. I assumed we would stay together and have a family, but you never seemed keen on the idea. Not until you met Tara and she fell pregnant. Then, suddenly, I was off the agenda.'

'That's not quite how I remember it. You used to be such fun and then you went off the boil a bit.'

'I wanted a baby, Gary. I wanted us to move on in our lives, not carry on with the party lifestyle. Yeah, I admit it was fun at first, but life changes and I wanted something different. I foolishly thought that would be with you. You're a dad now. You can't go back to your partying days. Just grow up, Gary.'

Katie watched Gary as his glossy smile faded and his face took on a serious expression.

'I guess you're right. Okay, I admit I have been a bit overwhelmed by the twins thing. When I saw you in that article in the paper, I remembered what a good time I had before I got tied down. I was envious of your achievement and felt I was entitled to a slice of your success, given I had contributed to it,' said Gary.

It was as she thought. Gary has come to Broxburgh to try and get some money out of her. That was not going to happen. Since he had turned up, she had had a chance to look at him for what he was. She was no longer intimidated by him.

'Hang on a minute, how on earth do you think you have "contributed" to The Books and Bakes Shop?' asked Katie.

'Oh, come on, Katie. I pretty much supported you financially when we lived together,' he said rather pompously.

His smug expression incensed her. How dare he?

'That's not how it was Gary. Okay, I didn't earn as much as you when we first met, but I paid my way. You seemed to like to show off and pay for our nights out. Even when you were able to buy a flat and I moved in, I still paid rent. If anything, it is me who contributed to your "success" as those payments went towards the mortgage. I trusted you and, stupidly, I didn't get that formalized which meant you were able to wriggle out of giving me anything when we split up,' said Katie vehemently.

'Blimey Katie, you've changed. You're not the meek little freckleface I remember.'

Katie was furious at his attitude. The mention of "freckleface" again was almost enough to make her lean across the table and slap him but she didn't want to give him the satisfaction of knowing he was getting to her.

'You are so right, Gary. I have changed. I have made a success of The Books and Bakes Shop. I have worked damned hard, and I am not going to be bullied by you into giving you any money.'

'I have to say,' said Gary. 'I quite like this new feisty Katie in front of me.'

Katie was exasperated. She just wanted to leave. Then she thought she saw someone staring at her through the window at the front of the bar. It looked like Joe and she was about to get up to wave him in. Suddenly Gary leaned forward to kiss her. She wasn't quick enough to avoid him. She looked back towards the window. Whoever it was had gone. It couldn't have been Joe anyway. He wasn't due back until tomorrow.

'How dare you,' said Katie, outraged. 'Try that again and I will get the bar staff to call the police and get them to arrest you for assault.'

Gary looked startled. She seemed to have seriously rattled him this time.

'Hey Katie, I'm sorry. I don't know what came over me.'

'Look, Gary,' said Katie. 'That's enough. You know you can't get any money out of me. It was pathetic to try. And, as you have noticed, the "freckle faced" girl you used to know has changed. So, it's over. Let's call it a night. I'm going home. You can pay for the drink. I never want to see you again.'

Gary scowled. Katie knew he wouldn't want to accede defeat, but she could see a look of acceptance in his eyes and he reluctantly nodded. He got up and went to the bar to settle the bill. She was amazed. Perhaps the message had got through and he realised he wasn't going to get anywhere.

Gary followed her out of the bar. Katie turned around and faced him.

'I meant what I said, Gary. You won't get a penny out of me and have no right to claim anything. So, go back to London and face up to your responsibilities.'

Gary shoved his hands in his pockets and glared at her.

'I don't agree with you, but I'll say goodbye,' he said petulantly and slumped off.

Katie sighed and walked back to her flat. She knew Gary couldn't completely back down, but she was confident that having faced up to his bullying that she would not hear from him again. She would fill Joe in about Gary's visit when he was back and that would be that. He would be back tomorrow anyway. She checked her phone. There was no message or missed call from Joe. She hoped everything was okay. Back at the flat, she made some peppermint tea and curled up beneath the duvet. She was proud of her behaviour standing up to Gary and was so looking forward to seeing Joe tomorrow.

Chapter Twenty-Five

Katie woke up excited. Joe would be back today. She checked her phone to see if he had messaged her. He hadn't. Never mind, she was sure he would be in touch soon to let her know what time he would be back.

She opened up the shop. As it was Monday, she had a few regulars during the morning, but was not rushed off her feet. By lunchtime she still hadn't heard from Joe. She started to worry. She was being silly. She would call him. She grabbed her phone and dialled his number, but it went through to voicemail. She left a message.

'*Hi Joe, just leaving a message to see how you are getting on and when you will be back. I miss you. Call me. Bye.*'

The afternoon was busy enough to distract Katie from her thoughts. If he had been in accident, surely, she would have heard? Sally would have let her know. At the end of the day, she checked her phone. Still no message from Joe. She was seriously worried now. She called Sally.

Her phone went through to voicemail as well. She must be busy with Sam and Jenny.

She went up to her flat. She was tired. She seemed to be a lot more tired these days. She slumped on the sofa and opened up her laptop. She would do some stock taking. Then her phone rang at last 'Joe?' she answered. But wasn't, it was her mum.

'Hi Mum,' she answered, not able to hide the disappointment in her voice.

'Oh dear,' she said 'you sound a bit down in the dumps. What's up?'

'I'm okay. Just tired, that's all. I haven't been feeling too great over the last few days.'

'Maybe all the excitement and hard work over the last few months is catching up with you. If you need a break and some rest, you are always welcome to come and stay here for a few days.'

'Thanks, I'll be okay. A few early nights should see me right. Are you alright?'

'Yes, I am fine, I just thought I would say hello.'

'That's nice but no offence, that's unlike you, are you sure everything is okay?'

'Yes, I am, more than okay actually. I wanted to tell you first and I would have preferred to have done it in person.'

'What? Spit it out, Mum it can't be that bad.'

'It's not. It's great. John has asked me to marry him, and I have said yes.'

'Oh, that's great news,' said Katie. 'Really it is. He is a lovely man and makes you happy so I couldn't be happier for you both. Do you have a date in mind?'

'John wants to marry as soon as possible, but I want to wait a few months or so. I want it planned properly.'

'Well, keep me advised of your plans and let me know if there is anything I can do to help. Make sure you send my congratulations to John.'

'I will, but enough of me,' said Susan. 'How's Joe?'

'Okay, I think,' said Katie with a sinking feeling in her stomach. 'He was away for the weekend and was due back today, but I haven't heard from him which is unusual. I expect he has just got caught up with stuff and will turn up later.'

'That doesn't sound like him,' Susan said. 'I hope everything is okay. Look, I'll leave you to it and remember I am always around if you need anything, even if it is just a chat.'

'I know, Mum and thanks. Congrats again.'

She hung up. Still no message from Joe. She was really worried now. She tried his phone again. It rang for a bit then went to voicemail. She didn't want to leave another message. Perhaps he would just turn up. Sally was due in tomorrow with a batch of bakes so if she hadn't heard anything by then she could grill Sally. She shrugged off her feeling of unease and took a long shower and headed to bed. She kept her phone nearby waiting for a message from Joe and lay awake listening for the door in case he came in. He didn't, and the fatigue she was feeling overwhelmed her as she drifted into a troubled sleep.

She woke the following morning feeling not feeling too great again. She immediately checked her phone. Still no message. She dragged herself out of bed knowing that she had slept badly but needed to get on with the day ahead. She was now panicking that something had happened to Joe.

Sally was due to deliver early. Katie started preparing the coffee machine and setting out the display plates for the cakes. There was a knock on the door. That must be Sally, so she eagerly went to let her in. Sally pushed past her with her boxes of cakes in her arms. Katie couldn't see her face but could feel that Sally was very angry about something.

'Whatever's the matter?' asked Katie.

Sally dumped the boxes on the counter and turned to Katie. She looked cross.

'I am really trying to believe you wouldn't allow yourself to be manipulated by that smarmy ex of yours,' she said.

'What on earth are you talking about?' asked Katie. She was stunned at Sally's attack. Something was very wrong here.

'You and Gary? I can't believe you would dump Joe like that and run back to Gary after all you said about him.'

'Sally, I really don't know what you are talking about. I got rid of Gary and sent him packing. What do you think? That I want him back after all I feel for Joe?'

'Yeah, well nobody actually knows what you really feel about Joe. He saw you with Gary, at the bar, on Thursday night.'

Now Katie realised what must have happened. The man she thought had been Joe looking through the window must have been him after all.

'When did Joe get back?' asked Katie.

'Late Thursday afternoon,' said Sally. 'The course finished earlier than expected, so he came back earlier than planned. Joe said he went looking for you and found you kissing "some bloke" in a bar. I mentioned to Joe about Gary turning up to see you as I assumed you would have told him. It seems you didn't. I don't know why not. Anyway, Joe has concluded it must have been Gary you were kissing.'

'But that's just not true. Yes, it was Gary, but it was me getting rid of him. He turned up here Thursday evening and wanted to settle in here for a chat. I felt vulnerable and wanted to get him out into a public place, so I suggested a drink. As it turned out I didn't have one, but I managed to make Gary see there was not a pot of gold at the end of my rainbow for him. He realised what an idiot he had been and agreed to leave me alone. Suddenly Katie understood what must have happened. 'Oh no,' exclaimed Katie as she covered her face with her hands.

'What?' asked Sally.

'Gary decided to lean over and kiss me goodbye, and I wasn't quick enough to swerve out of his way. I saw someone looking through the window at the front and thought it was Joe. I knew it couldn't be as he was away but now it seems it was him. He can't be daft enough to think I was seeing Gary behind his back,' said Katie.

'That's exactly what he thinks,' said Sally.

'That's crazy Sally. I need to see him and explain.'

'Well good luck with that. You know how stubborn he can be. He has dug his metaphorical heels in and won't be budged.'

'You have to help me, Sally. He has got it so wrong. I must speak to him. Can I come round tonight? You mustn't tell him, or he will find an excuse not to be there.'

Sally looked hard at Katie. 'Okay. I believe you, Katie. I know how you feel about Joe. It's so obvious when I see you together and I met Gary and could see what a prat he was as soon as I laid eyes on him. But you know Joe. He hurts easily and remember, you left him once before.'

'Look I am sorry Katie, but I have to go. I have a shift starting at nine-thirty. Come round about six-thirty. Joe should be in from work by then. I'll tell him I need him home to look after Sam and Jenny. That always works.'

'Thank you so much. I am sure once I have had a chance to explain, we can work it out.'

Katie noticed Sally didn't look convinced. As Sally left Katie set herself to work to distract her thoughts from the panic that was slowly starting to rise up from her stomach. Joe couldn't really think that all the time they had been together and had become so close that she was still holding a torch for Gary. Yes, Sally was right he did hurt easily. He was also prone to jealousy. Look how he had been over Peter Blankfield. But he must know he was the one for her.

The day seemed interminably long. She tried hard to be cheery with the customers and visitors, but her heart wasn't in it. She couldn't wait to see and speak to Joe.

She left the shop at about six o'clock. She was still feeling a bit off colour. It was about a thirty-minute walk to

Sally's house. She walked briskly thinking the exercise would help her emotional turmoil.

Katie started running. She couldn't get to Sally's quickly enough. This was so stupid. She was sure Joe would understand once she had explained, there was no way he could seriously believe she had kissed Gary.

She arrived. She suddenly felt nervous. She knocked on the door. Jenny answered.

'Hi Katie' she said as she launched forward and wrapped her arms around her in a hug. 'What are you doing here?'

'I've come to see Uncle Joe. Is he here?'

'Yes, he is. He's a bit grumpy though. He is not saying much and is just slouched in front of the telly.'

'Maybe I can cheer him up,' said Katie.

'I hope so. He is in the lounge so help yourself.'

Katie walked down the small hallway and went into the lounge. Joe was lying on the sofa watching football. Katie stood silently observing him. She could see that he was facing the television but felt that he wasn't really watching the football. That wasn't like him.

'Hey,' she said, 'what's going on?'

Joe jumped up off the sofa and faced Katie.

'What are you doing here? I told Sally I didn't want to see you.'

'Jenny let me in,' said Katie slowly. 'Joe, what's going on?'

'What's going on? That's rich from you. I can't believe you would let me down like you have. You gave me all that bullshit about bad Gary and all the time you were seeing him behind my back.'

'What are you talking about?' said Katie.

'I saw you, Katie, in that bar kissing him. I am away for a couple of nights and you cash in to make the most of your opportunities. What was I, a bit of rough on the side? Once you had made your success you just went back to your old life? You must think I am very stupid.'

There was so much she wanted to say but Joe seemed so closed and convinced of his position.

'Joe, Joe, listen to me. Yes, I met with Gary, but he turned up unexpectedly over the weekend. It wasn't intentional because you were away. He turned up because he had seen my article. He thought that somehow, he was entitled to a slice of my success. He threw me and made me feel vulnerable. It was like he pushed me back into that controlling space which I now understand I used to be in with him.'

'Katie, I just don't buy it. You hurt me so bad all those years ago and I'm not going to let you do that to me again. It's over. I don't want to see you anymore.'

'Joe don't be daft. We have so much together. Do the last few months mean nothing to you?'

'Yes, they do. But I don't think that they meant the same to you.'

'Joe don't do this,' begged Katie.

'It's for the best. I always felt there was something you weren't telling me. I never worked out what that outburst was when Caroline was here after the opening. You never talked about that so now I can see it was because despite what you said you still hankered after Gary. Once again, I wasn't good enough, just a carpenter in Suffolk.'

'Oh, Joe that's so not true. You can't believe that after all we have been to each other over the last few months. You have to believe me. Gary really did turn up out of the blue. There is no way I had, or want to have, anything to do with him. I want you, Joe,' pleaded Katie.

Katie looked at Joe's face. It was tense with anger and what pained her the most was the look of hurt in his eyes. This was not happening. It was like things were happening

216

outside of herself. She didn't know what else to do to make him see she was telling the truth and he had got things so wrong. She could hear him talking loudly but firmly at her. She refused to register the words. He was telling her he didn't want to be with her anymore. She wanted to put her fingers in her ears to block out what he was saying, but she just stood there trying to take it all in.

'I can't be messed around again, Katie. I can see now what I thought you felt for me was not true so as far as I am concerned it's over. I've thought about this and I am certain it is the best for both of us so please leave now.'

Katie felt rooted to the spot for an instant but then realised what he was saying. She wanted to run to him and spread out her arms around him and beg him to see sense. But she couldn't. His expression and body language made it clear. So, she turned round to hide the tears which were starting to flow and ran out of the lounge into the hallway and opened the front door, slamming it behind her.

She ran back down towards the town and her flat. Tears were pouring down her face. How had she managed to mess things up so spectacularly? She should have listened to Caroline and opened up to Joe about wanting a baby so much and why she had been so jealous of Caroline. Joe had completely misinterpreted what had happened. She should have told him about Gary as soon as he had turned up. She had underestimated the fragility of Joe's male ego. She thought he had been proud of what she had achieved. She hadn't done it to make him feel inadequate.

She was back at the front of her shop. She hastily unlocked and opened the door and then fell back against it. It was all so unreal. There she had been full of love for Joe and loving her Books and Bakes Shop. In a flash it had all tumbled down around her. She couldn't bear it. She dragged

217

herself upstairs and crawled fully clothed into bed. She was exhausted and so drifted into a miserable sleep.

She had slept deeply despite her distress. As soon as she woke up, she remembered what had happened and had that big thump of a sinking feeling in her stomach. She felt a bit nauseous, so she heaved herself out of bed and to the bathroom.

She looked at herself in the mirror. What a mess. Her eyes were still red and swollen from crying. She had sort of convinced herself that Joe would calm down and come to his senses and realise she was telling the truth. That's what she was telling herself, but her heart wasn't feeling it. But she had a shop to open up. Goodness knows what her regulars would think of her face. She would have to come up with a good explanation as to why she looked so pale and dejected.

She showered and managed a cup of tea and a bit of toast. With a heavy heart she went down to open up the shop. Somehow the sparkle had gone out of it. She suddenly felt very alone. She realised that since she had come to Broxburgh she had pretty much made her life around Joe. Okay, she had made acquaintances from her customers, but her only real friend was Sally. That friendship was bound to suffer if she was no longer with Joe. And then there were Sam and Jenny. She had become so fond of them both. She had felt she was starting to become part of that family. The realisation that she would lose all that hit her like a physical blow.

Her thoughts were temporarily distracted as the first customers of the day started to drift in. One of her regulars, Marjorie breezed in and said, 'my usual please dear.'

Then she looked at Katie and said, 'oh my dear you look dreadful. Whatever's the matter?'

'Oh, nothing really,' Katie lied. 'I seem to have developed an allergic reaction to something overnight which has made my eyes swell up. I am sure it will pass.'

'Should you be working?' asked Marjorie.

'I'll be fine,' replied Katie. 'My colleague, Sally is due in at lunchtime, so I can take a break then.'

'Well, if you say so dear. I'll just have my coffee then.'

Much to Katie's relief, she was busy all morning. It was August and peak time for visitors to Broxburgh. The season finished off at the end of the month with the carnival. Adrenaline kept her going and although she was miserable inside, she kept smiling for the customers and hoped the swelling in her eyes was going down.

She saw Sally coming in through the door. Thank goodness. She might have some news about Joe.

'Crikey, Katie,' she said, 'you look awful.'

'Thanks, Sally, that's just what I wanted to hear. Though I'm not surprised after crying myself to sleep. I'm still in shock that Joe seems to believe that I have been hankering for Gary all this time. He couldn't be more wrong,' said Katie.

'Oh, so you couldn't convince him then. I haven't seen him. He had gone to bed sulking by the time I got in after work. I hope you get this sorted out Katie, as our house is not a pleasant place to be at the moment,' said Sally.

'I'm so sorry Sally. I don't know how to get through to him.'

'What did he say exactly?' asked Sally.

'Well, it is all a bit of a blur as I just couldn't believe what I was hearing. He has split up with me. He said he believes I don't think he is good enough for me. He is convinced that I have been keeping something from him and after seeing me with Gary the other night he has put "two and two together and thinks it is him. Oh Sally, I just don't know what to do. I can't bear it.'

Katie could feel she was about to burst into tears again and didn't want to in front of any customers, so she dashed off up the stairs to her flat to compose herself.

She just wanted to curl up and disappear. Sally hadn't said anything encouraging. Katie felt in the pit of her stomach that Joe was going to stick to his guns. He had fixated on what he had thought he had seen, and she was not going to persuade him otherwise. Katie felt unutterably exhausted. It must be the trauma of dealing with Joe's rejection. She heard Sally shout up the stairs.

'I'm fine down here for a couple of hours so take a break.'

'Thanks Sally. I will,' Katie shouted back.

Katie went into her flat and laid herself out on the sofa. It was only lunchtime but as exhausted as she was, she felt she couldn't nap. She needed to speak to someone. She tried calling her mum. She didn't answer. She had said anytime but she couldn't expect her to drop everything when she was at work. Who else would be around to listen? Caroline? Katie dialled her number.

'Mmm... unusual time to call, what's up?'

That was enough for Katie as she promptly just burst into tears.

'Oh no Katie, what on earth has happened?'

'Joe has dumped me.'

'What? No way, why?'

Katie outlined the whole sorry tale about how Joe had seen her with Gary and as a result made all sorts of wrong assumptions.

'I just don't know what to do, Caro. He wouldn't listen to me. He was so angry and adamant he wanted nothing more to do with me. I just can't bear it.'

'Perhaps he will calm down and see sense,' said Caroline hopefully.

'I don't know, he seemed so convinced he was right. I know he can be stubborn, but he has to see he is wrong.'

'I'm sure he will. Try and calm down for now and give it a few days. He may come around with a bit of time.'

'Maybe,' said Katie 'but I'm not holding out much hope. Sorry it is all about me again. How are you?'

'I'm fine, a bit heavy, but not long to go now. Give me a call soon and let me know it there is any change. Katie, will you be okay?' asked Caroline in a serious tone.

'I'm sure I'll survive. Thanks, Caroline you take care,' replied Katie.

Katie felt slightly better after speaking to Caroline. She always had that effect on her, and she was right. She would be okay eventually but once again she had to be resilient. She would take one day at a time. Maybe Joe would come around. In the meantime, she still had her Books and Bakes Shop and should get back down there. Work always helped her deal with hurt. What would her Uncle Simon, who had started all this off, have said? Something like *"pull yourself together, it's Joe's fault if he couldn't trust you and in the long run, you'll be better off being on your own than with a possessive jealous partner"*. Katie sighed. Joe wasn't possessive though. Yes, he could be a bit jealous, and this tendency had taken him too far this time. But really, he was warm, gentle, kind and funny. She loved him and she had blown it. Damn Gary for messing up her life for a second time.

Chapter Twenty-Six

The days passed. Katie just went through the motions of day-to-day life. It was like she was living in a cloud of fog. Fortunately, as it was August, she was very busy which stopped her from dwelling too much about what had happened. But dwell she did, going over and over again about what Joe had said and tormenting herself by trying to think of ways to make him see how wrong he was. Perhaps she had got it wrong. She loved him but maybe after the initial lust of getting together after all those years the glamour had worn off for him and he had used seeing Gary as an excuse to get out of the relationship. She went round and round in circles in her head. There was no point in speculating on what may or may not be the case. She would never know if Joe would not speak to her.

Things between her and Sally were inevitably strained. Sally was trying hard to be the friend Katie needed, but she was in a tricky position. She said she had tried to get through Joe's "thick stubborn head", but he had truly dug his heels in. It was if he had convinced himself without even thinking that he may have misinterpreted what he saw. His mantra was, 'I know what I saw.' Sally thought that given the way he was behaving, there was little prospect of him changing his mind any time soon.

Sally also said Sam and Jenny were asking why Katie didn't come and visit them anymore. Had they done something wrong to upset her?

Katie wasn't surprised to hear that Maggie was veering to Joe's side. Katie felt awful that this affected all the family. It was impossible to keep things just between her and Joe. What a mess.

It was a Tuesday evening. Two weeks since Joe had told Katie he did not want to be with her anymore. She was now starting to adjust to the misery of that. She had worked hard during the week. Sally had been a bit absent. Katie understood that. She felt that all the emotional trauma was making her ill. She thought she would not sleep but she seemed to be exhausted, and each night fell into a troubled sleep.

She sat at her familiar table by the window. Well, her relationship with Joe had gone horribly wrong, but there was still her Books and Bakes Shop which was turning out to be a real success. She was obviously destined to be on her own. Thank goodness for Uncle Simon who had given her such an opportunity.

Her phone rang. It was her mum. Katie's heart sank; she was going have to explain to her that it had all gone wrong with Joe. She had put off telling her. She didn't want to burst her bubble about getting engaged to John. She had thought that if she hung on for a few days, things might have sorted themselves out by the time she spoke to her, but obviously not. It was stupid but she felt bad about that, given that her mum would be full of news about her wedding to John.

'Hi Mum,' said Katie, 'what news?'

'Oh, sweetheart I am so excited. John and I are making such plans.'

'That's great,' said Katie bravely.

'What's up?' asked Susan. 'Has something happened to Joe? You were worried the last time we spoke.'

'Oh Mum,' said Katie breaking down. 'Joe has finished with me and I am in bits.'

'I thought something was up when we last spoke.'

Katie went through the whole miserable story once again.

'Oh, Katie, love I am so sorry. I just don't know what to say.'

'There's nothing to say. I just can't make Joe see the truth. Actually, I just feel so exhausted I want to curl up under my duvet and never come out.'

'Mmm... that bad?'

'I'm just being dramatic, I'll be fine.'

'I know you will eventually, but you may need a bit of support in between. I'll call you tomorrow.'

'Okay, thanks, Mum.'

Katie was in the shop. It was Wednesday which was usually a relatively quiet day for customers. Most of the visitors came on Thursdays and at the weekends. She turned around from the counter to welcome the next visitor. She was gob smacked to see her mum walk through the door. She ran over to greet her. She wrapped Katie up in a big hug.

'Oh Mum,' exclaimed Katie 'it's so good to see you, you didn't say you were coming.'

'I know but you sounded so down on the phone I thought taking a couple of days off work for a break by the sea to be with my daughter was a good idea.'

Katie was delighted to feel the warmth of the embrace from her.

'Katie love, you don't look so good. I know the split up with Joe has taken its toll but there is something else. Have you been eating?'

'Not much,' said Katie. 'I don't feel like eating and actually the whole thing with Joe has made me feel a bit nauseous most of the time.'

'Pop upstairs and put your feet up. I can take care of things here.'

'Oh Mum,' said Katie. 'Thank you.'

Katie went upstairs with relief. She was so tired. She curled up on her bed and fell into a deep sleep, knowing her mum had taken control downstairs. The next thing she knew,

224

she had woken up and her mum was sitting on the end of her bed with a cup of peppermint tea.

'I thought something herbal and mild might hit the spot for you. Sweetheart, we need to have a conversation,' said Susan.

'If it's about me and Joe getting back together you can save your breath.'

'No, it's not about that but it is linked. You have told me about feeling off kilter and you look, and are, tired as well as feeling nauseous. Katie, is there any possibility you might be pregnant?'

Katie sat up slowly and took the mug of tea from her. She sipped the tea before replying.

'It had crossed my mind. But I have pushed the thought away. It's not just because I have ended up in such a mess with Joe, but also because I didn't want to even think that after all this time so desperately wanting a baby that it might finally happen to me and then be devastated if I turned out not to be.'

'Well putting your head in the sand won't solve anything,' said Susan. 'I'm minded to pop to the chemist and get a test for you now, but it's past six o'clock and they probably will be shut.'

'Gosh, is it that time? I must have slept all afternoon,' said Katie.

'Yes, you did,' said Susan, 'but stop trying to change the subject.'

'I'm not, Mum, you're right. I need to find out one way or another so, let's do it tomorrow. What do you fancy doing for supper? I don't really feel like going out.'

'Don't worry, it's all sorted. Before I woke you up, I popped out and got some eggs and some bread and soup. Hopefully that will be enough to tempt you.'

'Thank you. That's sounds perfect.'

'You freshen up and sit yourself on the sofa. I'll heat up the soup and do some scrambled eggs.'

'Sorry I have been so wrapped up in myself, I haven't asked if you want to stay.'

'Don't fret. No offence but I didn't fancy kipping on the sofa, so I have booked into the Greendale Hotel. I checked in before I came here so we are all sorted.'

Katie sat herself down on the sofa and switched on the television. She could hear noises of her mum clanking about in the kitchenette making supper for them. She couldn't stop thinking about being pregnant now. What if she was? Would she tell Joe? How would he react? Surely, he wouldn't reject his own baby? So many questions whirled round in her head, but she couldn't keep down the rising excitement she felt that after all these years of longing, she finally might be pregnant.

Susan came over and gently stroked her head.

'Stop thinking,' she said, 'I can hear you whirring from the kitchen. Why don't you make yourself useful and set the table? We can eat supper and enjoy the view of the high street.'

Katie managed to eat more than she thought she would. Nothing like bread and tomato soup when you are feeling under the weather. They sat at the table staring out of the window. Her mum didn't press her to talk about Joe and she was grateful to her for understanding that, if she did, it would make her even more miserable. She needed a break from dwelling on things, so she had asked her to talk about her wedding plans with John.

Susan explained that they wanted something small and simple which would make it more special and different to their respective first weddings. They had not decided on a venue yet but wanted to get married sooner rather than later. She now agreed with John, there didn't seem much point in hanging about at their age. Katie listened patiently. She so wanted to be part of her happiness, but it was a struggle.

By about eight o'clock, Susan declared.

'I'm tired, sweetheart so I am going to head back to my hotel and leave you to get some more rest. I am not going back home until tomorrow afternoon so I will be here first thing to give you time to find out once and for all if there is another reason making you so tired.'

'Thanks for everything,' replied Katie. 'I'll come down with you so I can lock up.'

At the door Kate gave her a big hug.

'Sleep well,' she said. 'See you tomorrow.'

Katie made herself more peppermint tea and tucked herself in under her duvet. She seriously started to think maybe she was pregnant. It was not just that she felt under the weather, but here she was in bed at nine o'clock with a peppermint tea. The normal Katie would have been drowning her sorrows in a glass of sauvignon blanc. But she didn't fancy any. Those questions started whirring round in her head again. So much of her wanted to be pregnant, but the circumstances couldn't have been worse. She felt silly now thinking about her foolish daydreams of being a happy family with Joe and the rest of his family. She was isolated and alone. Her mum was getting married and wouldn't want her single-mum daughter hanging around. Tears threatened to fall, but she pulled herself together. She would do the test tomorrow. In the meantime, she turned off the light and tried to sleep, just in case it was for two, if only.

Susan was true to her word and knocked at the door at eight-thirty. Katie was up. She had after all slept well. Today was the first day since her split with Joe that she felt some anticipation about the day ahead. She had decided to wait until the evening to do the test. She knew her mum wanted to be there, but Katie felt it was something she

227

needed to do on her own; persuading her mum of that might be more of a problem.

'Morning Mum, lovely to see you. How was your night?'

'Good thanks. I slept well. I will let you know into a secret,' she said, a bit giggly. 'John is fabulous in so many ways but my, he snores. It was good to have a night without that. Something to think about when we are married. How did you sleep?'

'Like you, I slept unexpectedly well,' replied Katie.

'So, shall I pop to the chemist?' asked Susan hopefully.

'We need to have a chat about that,' said Katie.

'Oh, have things changed since last night?'

'No not at all. The thing is, I am all over the place with the break from Joe. I have foolishly got involved with his family and so it gets even more complicated. Sally is due in today with fresh cakes. I don't want her to pick up on anything because if I am pregnant, I need to deal with that and Joe without interference. So, I really need to be on my own to find out. I know it's not what you want, but this how I need to do this.'

'I can't deny I am disappointed. I want to support you and, if I am honest, to be with you when or if you find out you are pregnant. I would love a little one in our lives.'

'I am sorry, Mum. As Sally is due in sometime today and until I know what's what, I don't want any hint of what's going on to reach Joe. If I am pregnant, I will have to think carefully about what I do.'

Katie saw the look of alarm on her mum's face.

'Don't look like that,' said Katie. 'You must know that whatever the circumstances, I would never get rid of a baby. It's just about how I would deal with Joe and all the other members of his family who I had become so close to. I admit I'm a bit scared but need to cope with this at least initially on my own.'

228

'Okay, I'm not happy about it, but you are your own girl and always have been. Let's get on with sorting out your shop today. John is coming to pick me up later. He was very clear that he wanted to say hello to you in person. So, if nothing else please say hello to him later.'

'Of course, Mum. Thank you for understanding. I will be thrilled to see John. I really am so pleased you are marrying him. But, if there is a baby, at the moment that is something I need to get my head round and I don't need any other distractions.'

'Well okay. So, while I am here, I can do some cleaning and make sure you have something else to eat.'

'Thanks. Any chance you could throw Sally off the scent too when she turns up?'

'I'll try. Now let's clean down those tables and open up.'

So, they did and worked through the day. Sally came and delivered the cakes. She was lovely, friendly Sally as usual but didn't stay around too long. She was not scheduled to work in the shop today and didn't offer to help. Katie kidded herself that was because her mum was there but really the situation was hard for her and so Katie had not just lost a valuable friend, but also a key support to her business.

It was quiet in the shop in the afternoon when John turned up about four-thirty. Her mum looked tired, and Katie was overwhelmed with love and gratitude for her. John looked so pleased to see her and she watched enviously as he picked her up in a huge hug.

Once he had put her back on the floor, he turned around to speak to her.

'Hello, Katie' he said. 'Good to see you. Would we be able to have a little chat?'

Katie was both surprised and alarmed. She suddenly thought John was going to tell her something bad about her mum. John obviously saw the concerned look on her face and said, 'Don't worry, Katie it's nothing bad. I just want permission to marry your mum.'

'Oh, if that's all then, yes let's chat!' said Katie.

Susan said, 'I'll make a cuppa. Why don't you both sit down so you can have a talk?'

Katie found them a table at the back of the shop.

'Don't be concerned Katie, I have just come to collect your mum. She is worried about you which is why she came up to see you. I just wanted to say that I know you don't need a stepdad but as far as I am concerned you are part of Susan and so will be part of my life too. I don't ever want you to think that you are not welcome either to visit or stay. I love your mum very much and can't wait for her to be my wife, but you must know that by doing that, it does not exclude you. Sorry, that was quite a speech.'

'Not at all,' said Katie and to her dismay felt tears in her eyes. 'Thanks John. I know you love her and will take good care of her. As you say, I don't need a stepdad but it's good to know you've got my back as well.'

Susan brought over their drinks. Katie said 'I know you need to get back, as you have your own job to go to tomorrow. You've been a fabulous help. I'll be fine. You know how resilient I can be. If I have any news, I will text you later.'

'Okay love but text me anyway.'

Katie left John to finish his drink and busied herself at the counter. She gave her mum and John big hugs as they left. She grabbed her coat. There was still time to get to the chemist before it closed.

Chapter Twenty-Seven

It was about seven o'clock. She was in her flat. She had spent an hour or so building up courage since she came back from the chemist. She had just done the test and was waiting to see if that blue line appeared. She closed her eyes. She could hardly bear it. Part of her wanted it to be negative because being pregnant now would be so difficult on her own. But most of her desperately wanted to open her eyes and see the blue line. She did. The blue line was there. She was pregnant.

This was a moment of quiet for Katie. She had waited so long for a baby and now it was happening. To her surprise, all those difficult questions she expected, failed to materialize in her head. A sense of calm crept over her. She was going to be a mum and it felt wonderful.

She wandered over to the window and stared out at the familiar view over the high street. She should let her mum know but she didn't really want to talk about it. This was her time to clear her head from the misery of Joe and try and fill it with the joy of finally being pregnant.

She was going to have a baby!

She sent a text to her mum. '*Positive. Thrilled. Want to be alone tonight. Speak soon. I am fine.*'

And she was. Katie knew all the difficulties she may have to face by being a mum on her own, but she was prepared to face all of those to have her baby. She could feel a sense of excitement about it all. She sat again in her favourite spot by the window as she indulged herself with a vision of what a baby in her arms would feel like. She grabbed a cushion from the sofa and cuddled it. Then she imagined what it would look like, Joe? Damn, her misery about his treatment of her overwhelmed her again. Yes, she was pregnant, but she was so angry with Joe. She had done nothing wrong, and she was so disappointed that he obviously didn't trust her. She knew she would have to tell him he was going to be a dad. Then she thought maybe he would think the baby wasn't his. Damn again, she was overcome with emotions. She tried to kid herself it must be her hormones, but tears pushed through, a mixture of thrill and misery. She so wanted to speak to Joe and be with him to share her news.

How was she going to play this? She absolutely felt it was her call about the baby. He or she was hers. She didn't want Sally to know as she would understandably feel obliged to tell Joe and she needed to do that on her own terms. But then again, she would need Sally to take on more responsibility with the shop. Thoughts were whirring around in circles in her head.

'Best get some rest, little one,' she said, talking to her tummy and gently stoking it. 'If it's just going to be you and me, we need to keep our strength up.'

The following morning Sally was due in. Before all this upset had happened, Sally had been given notice of reduced hours at the supermarket, so Katie had offered her longer hours at the shop. The original plan had been for her to spend more time off with Joe, as Katie was always working in the shop. But now it might work well, if Katie needed to take more time off because of the baby.

She heard the door open and Sally came in. Things were less difficult between them now. They had both adjusted to the change with Joe and were getting on okay despite the obvious elephant in the room, the split up. She had to be careful Katie thought to herself. She didn't want Sally guessing as she would definitely let the cat out of the bag not only to Joe but to the rest of her family. She needed to deal with this in her own way and in her own time.

'Hi, Sally,' said Katie breezily. 'Good to see you.'

'Hey, Katie. How are you? You look a bit less dark under the eyes than you have done recently.'

'Thanks,' said Katie. 'I'm fine.'

'Okay. I believe you but thousands wouldn't. Look, I know this situation is rubbish. It's tough for me because I have a stubborn miserable brother at home who won't listen to reason and you're my friend. Anyway, this is business and I am thrilled at the chance to work more here. So, shall we stick with that for now?'

'Fine by me and thank you, Sally. So, shall we start talking about a rota?'

'Yup. Absolutely. Funnily enough I have created a spreadsheet to populate when I can work if that is okay with you?'

'Yes. Thank you. Since things have changed, I want to spend more time with my mum. She needs some help with organising her wedding.'

'Okay' said Sally. 'I can take as many hours as you can give, frankly. The supermarket has made cuts because of the new Tesco opening up in Southfield. Ironically for me, your split with Joe means I have him around again to help with Sam and Jenny. So, let me know what you need. Sorry, that was a bit insensitive,' said Sally apologetically.

'Well, Sally,' said Katie. 'I think, I need a bit of a break so let's look at your schedule and see what we can work out.'

So, they sat down and looked through Sally's spreadsheet whilst serving the steady stream of customers. They had a plan. Sally had also found a couple of potential young part-timers who might be able to help as well.

'Katie,' said Sally in a serious tone. 'I know the thing with Joe is hard for you and that is an understatement, but is this planning to have me help more because you are thinking of running away again? If you are, I would wait a bit. I know my brother and he is being a bit of a stubborn idiot at the moment, but I so hope he will come around and see there is nothing in his misguided perception. But he is my brother and I need to support him too.'

'I know and I am not planning a midnight flight but, if I am honest, I may decide to leave and take a holiday or something at some point. I am finding being so close to Joe, but not being with him, intolerable and I miss you and your family, particularly Sam and Jenny. So, I may have to cut my losses and take a break for a while. It won't be the same as the way I left before. I will let you know, and Joe, if he would ever listen to me again.'

Katie heard her phone ping. Her first thought still was, is that Joe? It wasn't. It was a text from Andy.

'*Caroline had our lovely Lily at three am this morning.*'

'*Amazing news*' replied Katie. '*Congrats, send both my love.*'

Katie felt overwhelmed with emotion. She needed some fresh air and to get out of the shop and away from Sally before she broke down. If she did, she would probably end up telling Sally she was pregnant, and she couldn't let that happen. Not yet.

'Sally, I am going to pop out for a bit, if that's okay,' said Katie.

'Yeah fine,' said Sally. 'According to my rota, I am here until three o'clock this afternoon so, take your time.'

'Thanks, Sally,' said Katie. She picked up her phone and bag and headed for the door.

It was a lovely day and she made her way towards the sea. It seemed a while since she had done this walk. When she had first arrived in Broxburgh, she had walked along this path determined to make a go of things here and a life for herself. The shop was a success so far, but she had spectacularly messed up the rest of her life and now she was thinking of leaving.

She wasn't going to let herself cry. She knew if she started, she would never stop. She just had to get on with things and put her baby first. That brought a smile to her face. Then she heard someone calling her name. Damn, she wasn't in the mood for being sociable.

It was Peter Blankfield. He bounded up. 'Hello, Katie,' he said, 'you look well.'

'Do I?' asked Katie, thinking she couldn't possibly. She must look red-eyed and drawn, but maybe not. She hadn't looked in a mirror properly for a while so perhaps she was starting to bloom as a "mum to be".

'How are you?' asked Peter.

'I'm doing okay,' said Kate guardedly.

'You don't sound too sure. Look, I don't want to pry, but because of my friendship with your uncle and the involvement as a result in your life, I feel I have a paternal interest. I heard a rumour which troubled me. You know how small this town is. I heard a certain carpenter is going around with a miserable look on his face because you and he are no longer an item. I do so hope that isn't the case,' he said.

Katie could feel her lower lip tremble. She did not want to cry out here in a public place. It was bad enough that people were talking about her. She drew a deep breath and replied. 'That's right. Joe and I split up.'

'Oh, Katie, I am sorry to hear that. I had hoped it was all a misunderstanding. Is there anything I can do?'

'I don't think so but thanks for the offer. I'm okay. It's just a bit difficult being near to Joe but not with him and now I know I am part of the town's gossip circle,' said Katie.

'Oh no, you're not that,' said Peter hastily. 'I didn't mean to suggest that. It's just you have become very popular since you arrived and made such a success of The Books and Bakes Shop. People care about you.'

235

'That's lovely to hear, but I think I need to get away from Broxburgh for a bit, until I become old news at least.'

'That's your call, but I do so hope it is not permanent. Make sure you say goodbye if you do decide to leave. Maybe I could buy you a drink?'

Katie laughed.

'What's so funny about that?' asked Peter looking amused.

'It's not funny,' said Katie. 'It's the reason Joe and I have this misunderstanding. He saw me having a drink with my ex-boyfriend. There was absolutely nothing in it. Just a parting of ways, but he saw it differently. He misinterpreted what happened. If I've got any chance of sorting things out with Joe, it's not going to help being seen again by having a drink with another man.'

'Joe's a fool but you know that. Take care of yourself Katie.'

'Thanks, Peter. I will. I am just a bit all over the place at the moment, but I will sort it out.'

Peter moved towards her and embraced her. Katie disappointingly felt herself stupidly looking around just in case Joe saw her. This paranoia was rubbish. Joe had dumped her without truly listening to her. She was pregnant and that was such an overwhelming thrill, she had to make her baby a priority. Joe had made his decision and that was that.

She released herself from Peter's embrace. 'Thank you, Peter, I know we will be friends and I will keep in touch.'

She turned around and started to walk back to the shop. The walk and the chat with Peter had done her good. Her focus had moved away from her misery about Joe and moved to the joy and protectiveness she felt about her baby. She would head back home to her mum and John for a bit. It was the right thing to do. She knew they would look out for her and she could decide what to do about telling Joe and his family about the baby. But all that could be in her own time and on her own terms.

Then she thought of Caroline. Once again, she seemed to be caught up in her own woes, she had forgotten about the people close to her. She popped into the card shop to find something to send to her and Andy.

She allowed herself to go into the "Joules" for juniors' shop to look for something to send Caroline for Lily, lovely name. Visits to these shops used to be painful, but for a moment she was distracted from her misery about Joe as she gazed at the lovely clothes for little people. She found the baby section and ran her hands over the tiny little baby grows. She found one with little teddy bears on, perfect for Lily.

She made her way back to the shop. Sally greeted her.

'Hi,' she said. 'You look better for your walk.'

'Yes, it was good. That sea air always works. I bumped into Peter Blankfield and had a good chat with him.'

'I bet you did, the old rogue,' said Sally.

'Hey Sally, it's not like that. I know he has a twinkle in his eye, but he has always looked out for me.'

'I know that, Sally, and I always told Joe that. I'm only teasing you and trying to bring a smile back to your face.'

She had forgotten to disguise her purchase and Sally pounced on her, pointing at the Joules shopping bag.

'What are you up to, something you need to share?' asked Sally jokingly. Katie suddenly panicked. This couldn't mean Sally had worked out she was pregnant surely. As casually as she possibly could, she said, 'Andy texted me earlier while we were chatting about your rota. Caroline had a baby girl, so I just had to buy her something.'

'Oh, that is good news. I only met her at your party but do send my good wishes,' said Sally.

To Katie's relief, Sally seemed satisfied with her answer. She watched as Sally went back to work.

She could see that Sally was in control. Katie stood at the front of the shop and watched her. She was serving coffees to one of the tables and chatting to the customers. Katie could hear her encouraging them to treat themselves to a cake and make sure they browse the books before they left. Sally was so warm and welcoming; the customers couldn't resist, and she saw them get up and go to the shelves to look. They would buy something before they left. The Books and Bakes shop would be in safe hands with Sally.

She walked towards the back of the shop and put her parcel at the bottom of the stairs, ready to take up to her flat. Things were quietening down in the shop. It would be a good time to talk to Sally. Katie looked round. There were no customers now and as it was the end of the day, she decided to shut a bit early so she could have proper discussion with Sally. They sat down with two mugs of tea.

'Sorry if I was a bit snappy with you earlier,' said Katie. 'I know it's hard for you being stuck in the middle between me and Joe which is why I have a proposition for you.'

'Oh, that sounds intriguing.'

'You don't need telling how hard this is for me. I love your brother and I thought he loved me. I had some rosy dream of being part of his future and so part of your family. I am furious with Gary for turning up like did and furious with Joe for not trusting me. But it's happened and it looks like I am not going to be able to change Joe's mind anytime soon, if at all. So, I have decided I need to get away for a while. I am not sure how long for, but I am going to hide out at my mum's for a bit.'

'I thought this might be on the cards,' said Sally, 'which is why I mentioned it earlier.'

'I don't plan to stay away forever; I just need to get away and get my head around what's happened. But I need you, Sally, to look after things in my absence. You have taken on more hours since your shifts were cut at the supermarket so I was hoping you could do more and manage the shop while I am away. I will still be able to keep an eye on stock and do any ordering. I can easily come back for a day now and then. What do you think?'

'Oh, Katie, of course I will help. I love working here and chatting to the customers. I am just so sorry that you feel you have to go away. I wish I could knock some sense into that stupid brother of mine, but he has really locked himself down.'

'I know and it's not your fault. I think my leaving for a bit should help you as well. I will come back because I love Broxburgh and have made my life here and I am proud of the success we have made of this shop.'

'We?' asked Sally raising an eyebrow.

'Yes of course. Without your cakes and input this shop would never have got off the ground, so thank you.'

'Yeah, it's quite an achievement, isn't it? Look, Katie, I will have to tell Joe that you are going away. I'll need to explain the extra hours I am doing here.'

'I know Sally,' said Katie. 'Frankly, given the way he seems to feel about me now, he will probably be relieved.'

'Oh, I don't know. Maybe you going away for a while might make him reflect on things and realise how silly he is being. Anyway, in the meantime you can leave your shop in safe hands with me.'

'Thanks, Sally. That's a big relief. I'll call my mum tonight and sort things out.'

Sally got up to leave.

'I'll see you tomorrow.'

'Okay and thanks again, Sally.'

Chapter Twenty-Eight

Back in her flat Katie was curled up on the sofa with a big mug of peppermint tea. She called her mum.

'Hi sweetheart,' Susan answered, 'everything okay?'

'Yes, I am much better and pulling myself together a bit. I have been thinking. I need some time to get used to the idea that I am finally going to be a mum. I also need to work out how I am going to manage Joe. I know he has the right to know about the baby, but I am still too raw to deal with him right now.'

'I can understand that. So, what do you want to do? Do you want to come and stay with me and John for a bit?'

'Yes, I would, if that's okay with you. Tell John I am not moving in. I love my shop and my life in Broxburgh. I just need to adjust to it without Joe being by my side.'

'What are you going to do about the shop?' asked Susan.

'I've asked Sally to manage it for me. She's up for that. If it works out, then I have a plan for coping once the baby's born.'

'So, when are you thinking of coming?'

'At the end of next week if that's okay. It's coming to the end of the season here and there is Broxburgh carnival next weekend. I will stay for that and then come to you.'

'Well John and I will come and collect you. Would Sunday be okay?' asked Susan.

'Perfect. Thanks, Mum and I am sorry to be a burden, particularly now when you should be concentrating on your new life with John.'

'Don't be silly, Katie. Of course you're not a burden. It's such wonderful news about you being pregnant. I know it is exciting but also a difficult time for you and you have things to work out. John is, as you know, a kind and lovely man and understands you need some support right now. So, it's not a problem. I have to say I am furious with Joe and John is quite angry about it too. So, I hope we don't run into him when we come up as John may show his feelings.'

'That would be interesting!' said Katie, managing to laugh. 'Come whatever time suits you on Sunday. Text me when you are on your way and I'll make sure I'm ready.'

'Okay sweetheart, see you then and call me in the meantime, if you need to.'

Katie hung up and started to cry. She wasn't sure if it was the effect of her hormones being all over the place or just everything. She decided just to give into the tears and after a good wail she got up off the sofa and went to shower before going to bed.

She woke after a long sleep. The baby certainly made her tired which meant she slept well. But as she woke up, she felt that thud in her stomach which came every morning as the slow realisation swept over her that Joe was not there beside her. She pushed back the tears which wanted to start again. She didn't want to begin another day crying. She started to think that being miserable would have an impact on her baby. A bit daft, maybe but the thought reminded her that what she was feeling was not the most important thing. Her baby came first.

She opened up the shop and then thought about who she should tell that she was going away for a while. She had made a lot of connections in the relatively short time she had been here. She didn't want to lose any of them. It was a small community in Broxburgh. Most people had known that she and Joe had been a couple and she suspected, if Peter Blankfield was anything to go by, most people would know by now that he had dumped her. She would make a list. She started by chatting to some of her regulars and began to explain that she was going away for a break.

One of her favourites, Marjorie, the same Marjorie who had seen her with her blotched face from crying the other day, said, 'I hope it's not because that silly boy you were with has got cold feet. You shouldn't be driven out because of that.'

'It is partly that if I'm honest,' said Katie. 'I am the subject of town gossip at the moment and that will die down if I make some distance for a bit. I am always looking over my shoulder to check Joe's not around. I know it's cowardly, but that's the way I feel. There is some other stuff going on as well. A stay with my mum should allow me to get my head around things.'

'If you say so, dear, but in my experience running away from problems rarely solves them.'

'I'm not running away,' said Katie a bit defensively. 'It's just a bit of a break.'

'Mmm...' muttered Marjorie, plainly not convinced. 'Just take care of yourself. I'm an old bird and have got an idea about the "other stuff". I hope it all goes well for you, but don't underestimate the impact that may have on Joe. Does he know?'

Katie was surprised. How had Marjorie worked out that she was pregnant? She needed to be careful about how she responded. She couldn't risk any hint of her being pregnant going out to the gossip community in Broxburgh. The sooner she left the better.

'You're right, Marjorie, there is a lot going on,' replied Katie. 'My mum is getting married again nearly fifteen years after my dad died. I want to support her with that. I think that commitment thing by Joe is part of the "other stuff".'

'If you say so, dear,' said Marjorie with a knowing smile.

Katie wasn't sure how far she had managed to deflect Marjorie's intuition. But it was the best she could do. It was only eleven o'clock, but she was exhausted already. She hoped Sally might come in early but then again, she had to be really careful because Sally was very good at picking up on things. If dear old Marjorie had cottoned on to the idea, she might be pregnant, Sally would pick it up in a moment. It would be okay. It was Wednesday. Katie was sure she could cover up her condition to Sunday. On cue Sally came in through the door.

'Hello, only me,' announced Sally.

Marjorie winked at Katie and pressed her finger against her lips a in gesture confirming she would not give anything away.

'Crumbs, you look tired, Katie, are you okay? Sorry, silly question, of course you're not. I can manage here if you need to rest or do something else.'

'Thanks, Sally,' replied Katie. 'Actually, I made a list of people I wanted to explain to that I am going away for a bit. It is always better to do that in person if possible.'

'Mmm... I guess so,' said Sally.

'What does that mean?' asked Katie a little defensively.

'Well, as I told you, I had to explain to Joe why I am taking on so many extra hours and that, as a result, I am thinking of giving up my job at the supermarket. You know I need him to help with Sam and Jenny. So, I said you were going away for a bit. I was surprised by his reaction. He got quite agitated and started muttering about leopards and spots not changing. I think he was referring to when you left before without saying anything. He does seem to have got a bit of a bee in his bonnet about it.'

Katie suddenly felt angry. What was she meant to do? He didn't want to set eyes on her anymore, let alone speak to her. She hated this. She was sure deep down he still cared for her. It was like he was punishing them both and his stubborn pride wouldn't let him back down. She didn't want to show her feelings to Sally. So, she smiled bravely and said, 'well I am truly sorry, but if he won't speak to me there's not much I can do. Thanks for looking after things here for a while. I'll just pop upstairs and get my list.'

Katie spent the rest of the day calling on neighbours and other acquaintances she had come to know over the past few months. She knew it was a small world in Broxburgh but had not quite appreciated the extent of the jungle drums. She was the talk of the town. They had all heard of her split up with Joe and seemed genuinely upset for her. This just made her more certain to leave. It would only take one of these people to get a sniff she was pregnant and the news would fly round the town. Joe and his family would find out and she just wasn't ready to face them all about it yet. She would have to at some point but when she was confident about what was best for her and the baby. She got a thrill every time she said the "baby" word to herself. It had finally sunk in what was happening and the feeling of excitement overwhelmed her.

As she made her way back to the shop, she started to wonder a bit about the baby. Would it be a boy or a girl? Would they be able to manage living above the shop in the flat? How would Joe react when she finally got to tell him? There was no point in tormenting herself about that now. She would start packing tonight as it was Saturday tomorrow and her mum and John would be here on Sunday to collect her.

She desperately wanted to speak to Caroline to share her news but had decided to leave her in peace. She would be up to her eyes adjusting to her new life with Lily in it. She decided just to send her a quick text just so she knew she was thinking about her.

'*Hi. Caro, so thrilled for you. I am going back to mum's for a bit so may meet Lily soon. Xxx*'

Katie didn't expect Caroline to reply so she was surprised that her phone rang about an hour later. As always, she had that jolt of expectation that it might be Joe, but it wasn't. It was Caroline's number.

Katie answered. 'Hi Caro, I didn't expect to hear from you so soon. How's it going?'

'Exhausting, amazing, bewildering, all at the same time,' said Caroline, 'but crikey, Katie, I had no idea how incredible such a tiny little thing could be. She is absolutely gorgeous. Sorry, Katie, that was a bit insensitive. I don't want to rub salt in your wound.'

'You're so not believe me. I am really pleased for you and I can't wait to meet her,' said Katie.

'So, what's going on?' asked Caroline. 'Why are you running back to your mum again?'

'I'm not running,' said Katie, a little affronted.

'Sounds like it to me or is something else going on here?'

Katie smiled to herself. That was so Caroline, always sniffing things out.

'Well, you're right, things have got complicated. Caro, I'm pregnant,' Katie blurted out.

'What!' exclaimed Caroline. 'How did that happen?'

'Oh, you know, the usual way,' replied Katie, unable to stifle a laugh.

'Oh crikey, Katie, that's wonderful. What does Joe say?'

Katie paused.

'So, you haven't told him yet', said Caroline. 'I'm not sure that's your best move. He has the right to know and it might just be the thing to knock some sense into him.'

'I know he has the right to know. It's just about timing for me. I just can't cope with the brouhaha the news would cause, not just with him but Sally and his mum and dad. I can't deal with that right now. I need to get my head round what's happening and then sort things out on my terms. My priorities have changed, and the baby comes first' said Katie emphatically.

'I certainly agree with that,' said Caroline.

Katie could hear Lily crying in the background.

'So sorry, Katie, I'm going to have to go. Someone's woken up hungry!'

'Go to her, Caroline. I'll let you know when I'm at mum's and sort out a visit. Love to you all.'

'Thanks, Katie. Take care' said Caroline as she hung up.

Chapter Twenty-Nine

It was carnival week in Broxburgh and the town was busy with visitors and locals making the most of the candy floss stalls and fun fair. It was early on Saturday morning. Katie had had a troubled night and so had decided to go out for a walk to get the sea air to clear her head. Katie found a bench on the coast path and watched the children on the beach as they ran down towards the sea and ran back squealing with excitement as they escaped away from the waves. She loved this place and knew in her heart she would come back. She just needed some time to adjust.

There would be a big firework display down here tonight for the end of the carnival. It felt like the event would mark the end of another chapter in her life. She felt a strong connection with the town. She had been so happy here. She could not bear the thought that somehow, she would not sort things out and come back here. It was her home now. Damn Joe and his silly envy.

She pushed those thoughts to the back of her head and got up from the bench. She stretched her arms above her head and shouted out to the sea "I will be back better than I was before and with my baby".'

Nobody heard her actual words, but she got a few strange looks. Time to head back.

By the time she got back to the shop, Sally had locked up for the day. Katie was relieved. One less opportunity for Sally to suss out the true reason Katie was going away. She went up to her flat and made some tea. Funnily enough, she fancied a glass of wine which was the first time in a while. But that was definitely off the agenda, so she picked up her mug of tea and went back to sit at her table by the window. God, she couldn't cope with much more of a roller coaster life. It had been turned upside down again and again. It was time to calm down and think of her child.

It was about seven o'clock in the evening. She had spent the whole day going over things. She was leaving Broxburgh tomorrow and she couldn't bear it. It was not just that she was probably hormonal, but she found herself really angry with Joe. How dare he think she was having a thing with Gary. He should have trusted her and not have jumped to wrong conclusions and then refused to dig himself out of a stubborn hole. Sod him, she and the baby would be fine without him.

She got up and went into the kitchen to make some toast and maybe heat up a bit of soup. She rubbed her hand over her tummy in a reassuring way. She sorted out her supper and walked back to the table and stared out of the window looking out over the high street.

It was dark now and she could see the fireworks flaring up above the roofs on the other side of the street. She managed some soup but left most of it. She wanted to feel sorry for herself. She had gone from being brave about Joe and angry with him to being utterly miserable.

She was in the mood for punishing herself now. She went back into the kitchen to wash up her cup and plate.

She felt the urge to go outside and say another farewell to Broxburgh. She wouldn't have a chance tomorrow. She grabbed her cardigan and ran down the stairs, shutting and locking the front door behind her.

She decided to take a different walk to her usual route. She turned left along the high street rather than crossing the road as she usually did to use the cut through to the coastal path. There was a full moon so despite it getting dark she could still see where she was going.

She carried on walking. She could feel her hormones trying to take her over, but underneath all of that was a genuine grief about the loss of Joe. She kept on walking until she found herself outside the hotel where she had spent the night all those months ago with her mum, after Uncle Simon's funeral. She stood in front of it and then turned round.

The carnival evening was in full swing and she could see the firework display ahead of her. She couldn't help herself, but she re-traced the steps she had taken to her shop, when it had been so run down and had made her so sad. She faced the sea and found her feet taking her down towards the shelter where she had that first kiss with Joe. She remembered again that moment in painful detail. Joe: the thought of him overwhelmed her. She ran down to the bench. Tears were streaming down her face. She felt so dreadful it was almost a relief. She was there now, at the exact bench where they had their first kiss. Her feelings overwhelmed her again. Dear god she loved him and just couldn't bear it that he no longer wanted her. With tears continuing to stream down her face, she stumbled back up towards the road and her flat. Her feet gathered pace. How could he? How could he reject her and not trust her? She knew she was being irrational but wanted to wallow in her misery, so she imagined herself and Joe as a happy family with their child. They should be here next year watching the fireworks together. She turned around and started running back down towards the sea. The area at the front was busy with revellers out to see the fireworks. There was a pub on the corner which was full and she could see people spilling out on to the pavement with drinks in their hands.

As tears poured down her face, she didn't notice the discarded ice cream on the pavement. She slipped and fell over onto her side. She felt a shot of pain in her ankle as she struggled to get up. She collapsed back down. The shock of the fall and the pain made her cry out. Then things appeared to happen in slow motion. She heard someone shout, 'Hey don't move, just stay where you are.' She thought she recognised the voice, but in her shocked state she couldn't make it out. She felt someone lean over her. He smelled familiar. There was the voice again. 'You took quite a fall. Where does it hurt?'

Katie couldn't see though the blur of her tears, but as she moved again to try and get up, she felt a twinge in her stomach. A bolt of fear raced through her. Her baby, what if something had happened to her baby. Her hand instinctively went to her stomach. She could hear herself starting to gabble.

'Oh no, oh no, my baby. Please someone help my baby.'

She heard someone talking to her.

'Katie, Katie it's me, Joe,' he said softly. 'Calm down. Where does it hurt? An ambulance is on its way. I've been told not to move you, but I want to try and make you more comfortable' he said as he took off his jacket and used it to cover her. She smelt his familiar scent. He turned around and sat on the pavement. She could feel him gently lift her head and rest it on his lap.

Katie was blabbing, 'Joe, the baby, what about my baby?'

'I don't know what you are talking about. You're not making any sense,' he said.

Katie felt herself relax under the calming care of Joe. She looked up at him and could see him staring at her with concern in his eyes. What she had to do became clear. She had to tell him.

'Joe,' she said softly. 'I'm pregnant.' She watched for his reaction.

Immediately she could see the impact as he tried to take in what she had said. At first his face went blank and for a moment Katie thought he might not believe her. Then he leaned down and he looked at her and his eyes bore into hers. She saw his expression soften.

'Katie, Katie, my love, why didn't you tell me?' asked Joe.

'How could I? You had made it clear you wanted nothing to do with me. I am so angry with you for not trusting me and jumping to all sorts of wrong conclusions.'

'Tell me Katie. I am so, so sorry, but I'm listening now,' said Joe pleadingly.

'Bully for you, Joe,' said Katie as she shouted her anger through her pain. 'Where have you been in the last few weeks? Nursing your misplaced wounds and punishing me for nothing.'

As she spoke Katie felt a spasm of pain shoot through her ankle.

'Aarrghh,' she screamed.

She felt Joe's arms tense round her and hug her.

'Oh my god, Katie what's happening? You're scaring me now.'

'I'm scaring you!' screamed Katie. 'You have no idea how I feel. I have always been desperate to have a baby, that's why I stayed with Gary for so long because I thought he wanted that too. As it turned out he did, but not with me. How do you think that made me feel? I was too scared to tell you how I felt because I thought it would send you running. That outburst when I found out Caroline was pregnant wasn't about wanting to be with Gary, it was about being so jealous that Caroline was pregnant, and I wasn't. How messed up am I? But you've dumped me, so you don't have to bother anymore.'

'Oh Katie, I have got things so wrong. How stupid is this? I have completely messed things up. After I saw you with Gary, I used it as an excuse to break up with you because I convinced myself you were going to leave me again, like you did all those years ago. I kept dwelling on that while I was away on that course. You are so amazing, Katie. You have made such a success of your bookshop. I just felt you were too good for me and wouldn't stay around in sleepy old Broxburgh just to be with me, a simple carpenter.'

'But Joe, I love you, how could you not know that?'

'Because you never actually told me,' he said almost silently.

'Joe, I am so sorry. I was silly and stupid. I thought after everything if I told you that I loved you and how desperately I wanted a baby you would get cold feet and finish things between us. I thought that pressure of commitment would turn you away. As it turned out you binned me anyway so, now I can put my heart on my sleeve. Crikey, what timing, I'm cold and in pain and desperately worried about our baby.'

'Katie, Katie I am so sorry. I love you and now am completely overwhelmed that there is another one of us on the way. I love you so much. I always have. How could you doubt that? There has only ever been you. You stole my heart all those years ago and I got it back when you came back into my life. Listen, I can hear the siren. The ambulance is almost here. You and our baby will be fine. I won't let anything happen to you both.'

With those words he leaned down and kissed her full on the lips. Katie lent into that kiss and this time took control as she opened her mouth and drew him. He pulled away as she heard the siren of the ambulance. She was no longer scared. She and her baby were safe with Joe. She felt his arms tighten around her as they waited for the paramedics to arrive.

Epilogue

Katie was in the kitchen. She was exhausted. With Sally away for a few days, she had had to do more hours in the shop. They had a great young assistant now, Georgie. She worked four days a week. She was lively and kind. She was great with both the regulars and the visitors. But she still needed Sally as someone more senior around to keep an eye on things.

She decided to sit and have a cup of tea before the rush began. Today was a celebration day. Her mum and John would be here. She smiled to herself. How well that had all worked out for her mum. Katie still thought of her dad. However, John had slowly and unobtrusively stepped up into a supportive role for her. She had grown truly fond of him over the last year and what a year it had been. She and Joe had got married after they had sorted things out following her fall. It had only turned out to be a bad sprain. Then her lovely baby boy arrived. She had named him after her dad. She couldn't help the big smile that broke out over her face when she thought of Harry. He still is a true joy to her and worth the wait. He was her baby, so obviously she thought he was gorgeous. He was the spit of Joe and it made her heart sing sometimes when he looked at her with his big brown eyes. He was upstairs sleeping at the moment. She would go and check on him in a bit. She had the baby monitor on and could hear him softly breathing. He needed his sleep as it was his big day, his first birthday.

She looked around her. Everything was ready. Balloons were up and a caterpillar birthday cake was on the side. It was probably too old for him, but Katie liked it. Laid out on the kitchen table was a selection of buffet snacks supplied from the local deli. She would get John to fire up the barbecue as well.

She heard a knock at the door. Peace over, she got up to open the front door. Jenny burst in.

'Katie, do you like my dress?' she asked enthusiastically.

'Let me have a look, love,' said Katie. 'Oh, my, it is pretty' said Katie as she appraised Jenny's dress. It was a deep turquoise with pretty, embroidered pink flowers around the neck. Jenny was growing into such a lovely girl. She remained very special to Katie.

'I couldn't wait to show you. The others are coming in a minute, but Granny let me go ahead.'

'Well then, we had best get ready for the party.'

'Is Harry awake? I can go and get him if you want?'

'No, sweetheart, leave him to rest as long as we can. It will stop him getting too tired and grumpy later and spoiling the party.'

'But it's his party so he can do what he likes.'

'True, but it's a celebration party for my mum too. Remember, she just got married so this is a welcome back for her and John too.'

'Oh yes of course. They will be thrilled to come back to a party. Uncle Joe is picking them up from the station.'

The doorbell rang. Jenny dashed off to open it. It was Joe's parents. Maggie strode in first and came into the kitchen with his dad in tow loaded up with presents.

'My,' said Maggie. 'This all looks lovely. Now where is the birthday boy?'

On cue a cry screamed though the baby monitor into the kitchen.

'He's certainly awake now. Why don't you pop up with Jenny and bring him down? The others will be here soon so hopefully he will have stopped crying by then.'

Maggie and Jenny went upstairs to collect Harry. Katie looked sympathetically at Reg who looked uncomfortable, burdened with all the presents. He seemed stranded and not sure what to do.

'Take them through to the lounge,' said Katie, 'we can open them with Harry later.'

'Right you are,' he said.

The doorbell rang again. This time as she opened it Sam burst in and wrapped his arms around her waist with a big hug.

'Lovely to see you too, Sam,' she said. 'You as well,' said Katie as Sally came in with her usual stride. 'I am so glad you are back from your holiday. How was it?'

'Rather good, if you want to know' said Sally enigmatically.

'That sounds interesting,' said Katie. 'Keep those details for when we are on our own.'

'I will, and they are worth waiting for,' replied Sally smiling sheepishly.

It was just the immediate family for Harry's party this year. He was still so young. But Katie looked forward to the time when she would be entertaining lots of friends on his next birthdays.

Another ring at the door. It must be her mum and John back from their honeymoon. They had been keen to marry as soon as possible but, in the end, they waited until Katie had Harry and she and Joe were "settled". As her mum had said she wanted to do I "properly". So, they hadn't minded that she and Joe had stolen their wedding date. Katie chuckled to herself. She and Joe could hardly have done it "properly" with her being five months' pregnant.

And then in the doorway was the last guest for the party, Joe: crumbs, he still took her breath away when she saw him. He stepped towards her and said 'Hello lovely. Are we all here?'

'Yes,' said Katie as she turned to see Jenny bring Harry towards them in her arms.

They watched Jenny as she took Harry through to join his first birthday with all his close family.

Joe kissed Katie and said, 'it would be great if he had another brother or sister to play with, wouldn't it?'

'It would, wouldn't it?' replied Katie, as she gazed at him knowingly.

'Really?' said Joe in stifled delight.

'Yes, really, but let's keep it our secret for now. We can tell Harry later. It will be a lovely birthday present for him, even though he won't understand it like the rest of his presents!'

'Won't it just,' said Joe as he bent down to kiss her full on the lips. 'I love you Mrs Katie Lewis Parker.'

'I love you too, my lovely Joe.'

About the Author

I am a hopeless romantic and devotee to a happy ever after.

I fell in love with romance on a teenage trip to Florence, when I spent an unexpected magical evening of ice cream and sweet kisses with a gorgeous young footballer from AC Milan. This inspired me to dream of romance and so I started writing love stories in my head.

I was side-tracked by a career as a lawyer, defending allegedly negligent solicitors. From time to time, I leave them to look after themselves, so I can devote myself to writing my stories.

The Books and Bakes Shop is my debut novel and the first in the Broxburgh Series.

I live in rural Hertfordshire with my husband, David, and over-indulged tabby cat, Freddie.

I write in a summerhouse looking out over fields. When I am not writing or advising lawyers, you can find me reading, baking and growing organic vegetables.

For more information visit me:

Website www.elainewalsh.co.uk
Twitter @WalshAuthor
Facebook.com/WalshWriter

Printed in Great Britain
by Amazon

69729778R00156